Praise for *Carnival at Bray*

"*The Carnival at Bray* is a phenomenal book of first love, loss, family, and discovery. I highly recommend to any lover of YA novels."
— *Irish American News*

"Foley's prose is lovely, definitely a step up from your average YA fare. But even more important is her deftness with her characters and story."
— *Literary Chicago*

"The story, writing and talent of Jessie Ann Foley are strong."
— Louise Brueggemann, Children's Services Supervisor, Naperville Public Library, Book Prize Judge

"*Carnival* is a complex, eloquent, and deep look at one teen's journey. Highly Recommended!"
— *Wandering Educator*

"A story that sticks with you long after the last page is turned, with raw, funny characters and brilliantly colorful scenes. It made me want to pack up and have my own adventure, something as gritty, true, and defining as Foley's *Carnival*."
— Kristen Simmons, *Article 5*

"Audiences [will] enjoy the adventure that is *The Carnival at Bray*."
— *Chicago Literati*

"A unique and wonderful picture of adolescence from a fresh new voice."
— Emil Ostrovski, *The Paradox of Vertical Flight*, Book Prize Judge

THE CARNIVAL AT BRAY

A NOVEL

WITHDRAWN

BY JESSIE ANN FOLEY

ISBN: 9780989515597

Library of Congress Control Number: 2014937608

Printed in the United States of America

Book Design by Amanda Schwarz,
Fisheye Graphic Services, Chicago

First Edition
10 9 8 7 6 5 4 3 2

Elephant Rock Books
Ashford, Connecticut

For Denis, the measure of my dreams

If you're lucky, at the right time you come across music that is not only "great," or interesting, or "incredible," or fun, but actually sustaining. Your emotions shoot out to crazy extremes; you feel both ennobled and unworthy, saved and damned. You hear that this is what life is all about, that this is what it is for.

— Greil Marcus, *Ranters & Crowd Pleasers: Punk in Pop Music, 1977–92*

September 1993

The carnival at Bray stood braced against the rain on the rocky coastline of the Irish Sea, the pink and green lights of the old-fashioned Ferris wheel winking and dissolving in the reflection of the waves. Maggie had already ridden the Takeoff, which made her feel like a pebble being skipped across a lake; the Crazy Frog, which whiplashed her back and forth so hard that she dinged her head off the safety bar and emerged with a painful purple egg already rising from her temple; and finally, Space Odyssey, which spun around so fast that gravity suctioned her and Ronnie to the cushioned wall like splattered bugs. Halfway through the ride, a girl who was pinioned across from them barfed, but the suction was so strong that the puke no sooner arced from her mouth than it was sucked back with a wet *splat* all over her own face. The ride ended abruptly, sending everyone thudding to the ground, and the sisters fled the sour smell of peanuty vomit on wobbly legs.

"Where to next?" Ronnie was counting the remaining tokens in her palm. "I still have enough for three more rides."

"Aren't you getting *cold*?" Maggie looked at her little sister, whose pale, wet hair was plastered to her head and whose hand-me-down windbreaker hung to her knees as warm and waterproof as a plastic grocery bag.

"Yeah, but Mom said she wasn't going to pick us up until

the carnival closes." Ronnie squinted across the dark road at the row of pubs and moss-streaked hotels where their mother had fled with Colm. "Do you think they'll get back sooner?"

"And interrupt *honeymoon time*?" Maggie laughed. "Be serious."

"What does that even *mean*?"

"I'll tell you when you're my age."

"But that's what you said about 'douche,' and 'condom,' and the first line of that Liz Phair song," Ronnie complained.

"Well," Maggie said, putting an arm around her sister's thin shoulders and drawing her under the leaky umbrella, "honeymoon time is kind of like all three of those combined. When *you're* sixteen and I'm twenty-one, we'll talk *all* about it. Now—where should we cash in the rest of those tokens?"

"Bumper cars!" Ronnie shrieked, breaking free from the protection of the umbrella and racing ahead to the arena, where empty cars pointed every which way like in one of those apocalyptic movies where a whole city evacuates to escape an infectious disease.

"Don't you want to go on the Ferris wheel?" Maggie called after her. She reached up and touched the lump at her temple. It was hot and throbbing, and dotted in the center with a small smear of blood.

"C'mon! Let's do the bumper cars! Please? Please? Please? *Please*?" Ronnie hopped up and down beneath her sodden windbreaker.

"*Fine*," Maggie sighed, holding out her hand to the rain to clean the blood from her fingers.

Ronnie flashed a winning smile, infectious and gap toothed, and they lined up behind the small herd of other little kids who stood waiting to turn in their tokens. Maggie was taller than all of them by at least a head. Earlier, they'd passed a group of Irish teenagers, kids of about Maggie's age—maybe even her future classmates at Saint Brigid's. The boys were dressed in tracksuits and gym shoe brands she'd never heard of, and the girls wore tights under their skirts and heavy gold necklaces. Not one of them had even glanced in her direction. Maggie was quickly learning that being Irish-American, as she was, was quite different than actually being Irish. Now, she stood behind Ronnie and watched the group as they walked toward the road. Their clothes, their slang, the way they wore their hair: all of it was foreign and unfamiliar; all of it was new, intimidating, and strange. *I'm never going to fit in here,* she thought.

The announcement that, after four months of dating, their mother was marrying a man five years her junior and they were all moving to his hometown in Ireland so he could help run his brother's construction business wasn't really all that surprising. Since the day ten years earlier when Maggie's father had walked out on them for a woman known in their home only as Bitch, her mom had developed a tendency to fall madly in love with whatever loser she was currently dating. It had always been easy for Laura Lynch to meet men—she was still young, had high, round breasts and green eyes fringed in long, mascara-tarred lashes, and she spoke in a gentle, low voice that men leaned in to hear. Each of her romances was a whirlwind, and each ended in total disaster. In the aftermath, Laura would lubricate her despair with great quantities of red wine and the occasional sleeping pill. Over the years, whenever this happened, Maggie had learned to quietly pack a bag for herself and Ronnie, drag it up the stairs, and knock on the door to their grandma's apartment on the second floor of the two-flat.

"Mom's having one of her moments," she'd explain.

"How bad this time?" Nanny Ei, dressed in pleated jeans and a seasonal turtleneck, would step out in the hallway and the three of them would listen to the noises drifting up the stairs from the first floor. Sometimes there was sobbing. Other times there was drunken snoring. For the really bad times, there was Bob Dylan's

The Freewheelin' blasting from the tape player, and for the really *really* bad times, there was Joni Mitchell's *Blue* album, with Laura howling along in an off-key soprano.

"Okay, girls," Nanny Ei would sigh, herding them into her cozy apartment of faded beige carpets, fried breakfast smells, and cable TV. "I'll make some pork and beans."

When she met Colm in April, Laura was coming off a *Blue*-level breakup with Ned, the gambling addict who had spent most of his days walking around the apartment shouting bets into the cordless phone and crop-dusting the air with silent, sulfurous farts. Colm possessed all of the qualities that Ned—and, for that matter, all of Laura's previous boyfriends—lacked. He had a job, for one thing, and teeth that appeared to be brushed regularly, for another. Not only that, he seemed to be as crazy about Laura as she was about him. In August, they were married at the Cook County Courthouse. In September, they moved to Colm's clean little house in Bray, a damp, briny town a half hour outside Dublin.

Ronnie chose a shiny yellow bumper car, while Maggie picked pale blue. The ride operator turned a switch, and the electric current beneath Maggie's car hummed to life. She lurched forward just as a jug-eared boy who could barely see above his dashboard stomped on the gas and reversed into her at full speed. His laughter trilled into the night while Maggie's head whipped back. White, drifting stars filled her vision. She managed to steer over to the rubber edge of the ring and park while Ronnie and the other kids flew past, yelling, laughing, crashing.

By the time the ride operator switched off the power and Maggie wobbled across the track to find her sister, Ronnie had befriended all the other kids from the bumper cars, even the jug-eared boy with the demolition streak. One little girl was unfurling sheets of pink cotton candy and handing them out to the others. She gave Ronnie a long piece, and Ronnie took it and folded it up into squares, like origami, then shoved the entire parcel into her mouth. The other kids laughed, and some of them began folding up their pieces, too. When Ronnie saw Maggie, she waved.

"Hey!" She called, her mouth full, "we're going to go back to Space Odyssey! Come on!"

But what was the point? Maggie thought. What if the teenagers, the girls in the dark lipstick and jean skirts, saw her walk by with this group of ten-year-olds?

She waved her sister away. "Nah," she lied, "I'm just gonna go meet some people at the Ferris wheel. I'll see you when Mom gets here." Ronnie looked at her across the wet pavement and the ringing lights of the booths—Dart-a-Card, Smash-a-Can, Roll-a-Coin—as if she was trying to figure something out. Finally she shrugged, and ran to catch up with the other kids.

The drizzle had quickened into a heavy rain, and the clouds over the sea rolled by, their dark shapes blackening the whole sky. Maggie stood alone beneath the Ferris wheel, its great twinkling arms reaching up in spindly supplication to the low sky. Fat raindrops poked holes into the choppy gray surface of the sea. When they'd first arrived in Bray, Colm told them that it was just like Chicago: if you want to know what direction you're going, just remember that the water is always to the east. But on the Northwest Side of Chicago, you had to ride the eastbound bus for over fifty blocks before you began to smell the water; here, the sea was pervasive. On sunny days it glinted from the crests of hills or between the walls of buildings, and at night, while Maggie lay in bed, its restless sighing shaped a feeling in her chest that she couldn't quite name. Even her clothes and hair began to take on its fishy, expansive smell, but eventually, and sooner than she expected, she stopped noticing, the way a woman stops noticing the scent of her own perfume.

"Last ride! Last ride!" a man called, the tip of his cigarette glowing in the cozy shelter of his ticket booth. Maggie felt in her pocket and produced a few coins that flashed in her palm like silver fish. The man took her money and dumped it in a drawer.

"Sit wherever you like," he said, jabbing a thumb at the empty Ferris wheel.

She sat in the nearest carriage and pulled down the safety bar. The ride jolted, and she was lifted into the dark, misty sky. Colm had told them, if you want to be a true Irishwoman, you've got to become an expert on water. Salty water and clear water, thick rain and misty rain, downpours and trickles, thundery rain and soft rain. He had explained the difference between a sea and an ocean, but now she could not remember and her head hurt too much to think very hard. She reached up and ran her fingers over the lump. It started just under her wet hairline and stood out from her scalp at least half an inch. Back home, she thought, the bell would just be ringing on the last period of her first day of her sophomore year.

The ride climbed and climbed, arcing away from the center of the wheel, until Maggie was higher than the steeple of Saint Paul's Church, and the group of teenagers walking down the shore, huddled together against the rain, were as small as board-game pieces. Across the asphalt strip from the carnival, at a pub called Quayside, she could see into a bright square of window. Even as far away as she was, she could tell that the two dark heads leaning together were Colm and her mother, sitting at a table with drinks between them, oblivious to the rest of the world, completely and totally and nauseatingly in love. One by one, she watched the lights of the carnival booths winking out, and still the ride climbed higher. She looked east, out to where there was nothing but waves and darkness. Breathing in the dampness, Maggie wondered what would happen if she tumbled out of her seat, splashing into the lapping nothingness, and how long it would take before someone noticed she was gone.

The weekend before they moved to Ireland, Ronnie, who had a green belt in tae kwon do, was chosen to perform at an exhibition with her dojo in Milwaukee. The whole family was set to go, until Maggie came down with the summer flu.

"Vicks VapoRub and a dehumidifier," fussed Nanny Ei, "and you'll be right as rain in the morning."

"Saltines and a can of Coke," Laura advised.

"No, no. For a flu, what you need to do is boil an onion in milk, add honey, and drink it down in one go," Colm said.

Maggie burrowed into the velvet nest of her grandma's couch, half-listening in her feverish state to the discussion about what to do with her. When the conversation had reached an impasse, her uncle Kevin, who was twenty-six and still lived at home with Nanny Ei, emerged from the cave of patchouli and Newport smoke that served as his bedroom. Sandwiched under his armpit was a copy of *Ranters & Crowd Pleasers: Punk in Pop Music, 1977–92*, a book that lately he'd been quoting from at family dinners.

Maybe it was because there was only ten years between them, or maybe it was simply because of the way he was, but Maggie had never viewed her uncle Kevin as an authority figure— more like an adored older brother. Uncle Kevin was the youngest of Nanny Ei's three children, and though it would be unfair to call him spoiled—Nanny Ei's household had been one of tough, blue-collar love, the kind where Christmas stockings were stuffed with practical gifts like socks, toothbrushes, and hard, bitter navel oranges—he was certainly the most doted upon. This was partially due to the heart condition he'd been born with, the two open-heart surgeries before the age of two, the long white scars across his chest, the warning from his doctors that he was never to play contact sports of any kind. Which was just fine by Kevin: he never had any interest in sports. He'd begun playing the guitar at age six, formed his first band by age twelve, and lately had finally begun to find some local radio play with his band, Selfish Fetus, and to book shows at venues that people had actually heard of—the Empty Bottle, the Hideout—and which people actually began to attend. To those around him, he emanated the nervous energy of someone who is close enough to touch a dream they've been chasing all their life.

"Let the poor kid stay home if she's sick," he said. "I got no plans this weekend. I can watch her."

Colm and Laura glanced at one another and burst out laughing.

"Absolutely not," Laura said. "I love you, Kev. But there is no friggin' way I'm letting you watch my kid all weekend."

Kevin threw himself on the couch next to Maggie and lit a cigarette.

"So let me get this straight," he said, exhaling. "You'd trust me with Maggie's spiritual upbringing—her very Catholic *soul*, but you won't trust me to give her some Nyquil and make sure she's in bed at a decent hour?"

"Christ on a *crutch*, Kevin," Laura glared at him. "If I had known how much you were going to throw it in my face, I would never have made you her godfather."

"Well, you did, sis. And what God has joined, no man shall put asunder." He put an arm around Maggie and floated a halo of smoke in Laura's direction.

"Well, the only *reason* I did was because Dave was stationed in the Philippines. You were ten years old—I figured, how much harm could it do? How was I supposed to know that you'd grow up to be a man with about as much sense of responsibility as your average poodle?"

"Aw, now, love. You're not being fair," Colm said. "Even a poodle can be house trained." He was referring to an incident earlier that summer when Kevin had come home drunk and peed in a corner of the living room.

"Well, why don't we ask my goddaughter what *she* wants?" Kevin said, ignoring Colm's bait. He turned to Maggie, who was emptying her nostrils into a tissue. "Mags, would *you* like me to watch you this weekend?"

Of course she did, and everyone in the family knew it. But all the reasons why Maggie loved Kevin—his long, unwashed hair, his incessant guitar playing, his curse-riddled rants about the corporate takeover of radio stations, his dog-eared copy of *Ranters & Crowd Pleasers*—were all the reasons her mother deemed him an unfit caretaker, godfather, and brother.

"May I interject?"

Nanny Ei, dressed in a pair of khaki shorts and an Andre Dawson jersey that was at least two sizes too large on her little-old-lady frame, came in from the kitchen carrying a plate of sliced pears.

"It *is* only one night, Laura." She put the plate on the coffee table next to a pile of Maggie's balled-up tissues. "And everybody deserves a second chance. Sometimes even a third and a fourth. Now eat those, young lady. They got Vitamin C."

That settled it. The rest of the family left for Milwaukee while Maggie and Kevin stayed back and watched a marathon of *This Old House*. Halfway through the fourth episode, Kevin reached across the couch and poked Maggie's socked toe.

"You're not really sick, right?"

"Of course I am!" Maggie sat up in her cocoon of blankets. "I've had a fever for, like, three days!"

"Bullshit. You just didn't want to go to your sister's karate thing. And I respect that."

"Uncle Kev, I swear to God, I really am sick. If I wasn't, I would tell you." She bit into a droopy piece of pear while Kevin reached over with the back of his hand and felt her forehead.

"Feels just fine to *me*."

Maggie batted his hand away.

"Nanny checked me like an *hour* ago. I was almost 102 degrees!" Maggie lifted her own palm to her forehead. But Kevin was right. It was as if he had channeled some strange godfatherly powers: she could feel the fever draining out of her.

Kevin stood up and stretched.

"Well, okay, Mags. If you say you're sick, you're sick. It's just too bad though, because if you *were* faking it, I was going to bring you out to see a show with me tonight—a *big, huge, epic, life-altering show*. But it looks like you need your rest." He deposited his empty beer can in the kitchen trash. "I'm going to hit the shower. If you make a miraculous recovery by the time I get out, let me know."

An hour later, Maggie, her face slick with Nanny Ei's rose-scented makeup, was strapped into the passenger seat of Uncle Kevin's silver Chevy Nova. He'd bought it a few months earlier at a stolen car auction in Galewood for $800, and had just enough money left over to order a vanity plate. He dubbed the car AG BULLT— "AG being the periodic element for silver," he explained to her as the engine roared to life. "Remember that next year in chemistry class." As they peeled out onto Milwaukee Avenue, he shoved Soundgarden's *Badmotorfinger* into the tape deck and began to lecture her, mainly about music, but also about religion, economic trends, and the situation in Kosovo. Maggie tried to absorb it all as her skinny butt floated off the seat every time he turned, pressing her chest against a duct-taped seatbelt that she prayed would hold.

They stopped in front of a decrepit apartment building and

Kevin trumpeted AG BULLT's horn until three of his friends emerged, all dressed in slight variations of a faded black uniform. Maggie recognized Rockhead, Taco, and Jeremy from their late-night forages through Nanny Ei's refrigerator. Taco, the fat one, threw open the passenger side door.

"Get in the back, kid," he said. "I need the leg room."

Maggie looked at Kevin, who was switching out *Badmotorfinger* for Jimi Hendrix's *Are You Experienced?*

"Go on, Mags," he said, turning the music to its loudest possible volume. "I can't have Taco's fat knees jabbing into the back of my seat. It interferes with my concentration."

She climbed into the back, sandwiched between Jeremy and Rockhead, who passed a joint back and forth over her head as they drove east through the summer night. All the windows were rolled down and the speakers hissed and crackled, threatening at any second to blow out completely. A cyclone of ash gusted around the car, settling in Maggie's hair and in the lap of her black jeans. The music and the wind made it too loud for talking, so she just sat and looked out the window at the city rushing by while Jeremy and Rockhead smoked their weed, until they reached Clark Street and the traffic came to an abrupt standstill.

"What a shitshow," Rockhead said, leaning out the window and flicking away the cashed end of the joint. A line of concert-goers in T-shirts and torn jeans and see-through tops snaked from the entrance of the Metro all the way down Clark for nearly half a mile.

"Where the fuck are we gonna park?" Taco asked. "I *told* you we should've taken the bus. I can't walk that far!" He turned in his seat to look at Maggie. "Football injury."

"Don't believe him, Maggie," Jeremy confided. "He's always making excuses to cover for his morbid obesity."

"Excuse me, asshole, but most of this is muscle mass." Taco reached into the backseat and presented them with a flexed, beefy forearm. "Touch my arm, Maggie! Pure solid muscle."

"Do *not* touch his arm," Kevin instructed from the front seat as he scanned the street for a parking spot.

"The problem with you, Jeremy," Taco continued, withdrawing his arm, "is that you don't know shit about physiology. It's not weight that matters, but *body fat percentage.*"

Before Jeremy could respond, Kevin slammed on the brakes, yanked AG BULLT into reverse, and swung the car into an open spot directly in front of a fire hydrant.

"Dude, you can't park there," said Jeremy. "They'll tow your ass."

Kevin thrust the parking brake into place.

"One has a moral responsibility to disobey unjust laws," he declared, turning off the ignition.

"*What?*"

"That's Martin Luther King, ignoramuses. 'Letter From Birmingham Jail.' "

"Can someone please explain to me what's *unjust* about *not* parking in front of a fucking fire hydrant?" Taco sighed. "If this shit gets towed, I am *not* paying for you to get it untowed."

Kevin got out of the car and winked at Maggie.

"Let's go," he said.

The huge, epic, life-altering show was none other than the Smashing Pumpkins, playing at their favorite hometown venue, just weeks after the release of *Siamese Dream.* After being patted down by security, Maggie reminded herself not to freak out at these facts, at least not visibly, as she followed Kevin and his friends up the curving linoleum staircase that was crammed from rail to rail with sweaty fans.

"So, do we have good seats?" she asked, scrutinizing the ticket stub that she already knew would be a keepsake for the rest of her life.

"*Seats?*" Taco laughed. "What do you think this is—the goddamn opera?"

"Leave the girl alone, jagoff," Jeremy defended her, slipping a hand around her waist. "She's only, what, like eighteen?"

"Sixteen," Maggie blushed, feeling the clammy pressure of Jeremy's fingers on the curve of her waist.

"Yeah—as in too young for you," said Rockhead.

"Damn if she don't look full-grown to me."

Kevin, who was just ahead of them on the stairs, turned and looked down.

"Get your hand off my niece," he said, "or I will cut your fucking dick off." Jeremy's hand slithered away, and Taco and Rockhead, cowed, averted their eyes and rummaged their pockets for beer money.

At the top of the stairs, the crowd piled toward the stage, slurping beer from plastic cups and holding their cigarettes aloft while the sound check filled the auditorium with screeches and drum trills. And then all the lights went out. When they came on again, in a blinding burst of white, the opening chords of "Rocket" began like an explosion in the middle of Maggie's chest. She squeezed her eyes shut, trying to contain it.

"Hey! Mags!" Kevin was kneeling down in front of her in the hazy flashing light. "Get up here!" She climbed onto her uncle's shoulders and he stood up, squeezing her legs to his chest. Only one hour earlier, she had been sitting on Nanny Ei's couch, her life dribbling unremarkably along, Vicks VapoRub slathered across her wheezy chest and a mug of boiled milk and onions untouched beside her. The explosion of music that had started in her chest was now expanding outward and outward, encompassing the entire room, the entire city, the entire world.

"How's the view?" Kevin shouted, lurching closer to the stage while she clutched at his soaking hair to balance herself. Everything around her was shiny with the patina of smoke and sweat, and a hundred feet in front of her were the Smashing Pumpkins.

The show was chaos—moshing, shattered bottles, and music so loud that it didn't even feel like music but just a thumping in her chest, a wailing guitar, and Billy Corgan, who screamed until his throat sounded blood-gargled. After an hour, Maggie lost Uncle Kevin and stumbled through the crowd, fighting the urge not to panic, and then she found him in a corner making out with a blond woman whose shirt was all cut up so that Maggie could see not just the woman's cleavage but the cleavage *under* her boobs—she had not known this was possible. He pulled away from the woman, wrapped Maggie in a sweaty hug, and took her up to the bar and bought her a pop. She drank it, fighting the feeling of exhaustion and fever that had descended on her brain and sinuses, and when it was over and the lights were turned on to reveal a shiny-eyed crowd wafting animal smells and trembling down from whatever high they'd been on, the music had latched hold of her. She felt half-crazed, elated, having forever transcended the world of high school, where she was noteworthy only for her ability to diagram sentences faster and more accurately than anyone else in Mr. Blackwell's English class. One thing was for sure: she would never diagram another sentence, at least not willingly, for as long as she lived.

Kevin put one arm around Maggie and the other around the blond woman and, together with Taco and Rockhead and Jeremy, they tumbled out into the city and found AG BULLT, adorned with two parking tickets that Uncle Kevin tore from the windshield and dropped down the sewer, and they piled into the car where Maggie was placed on the blonde's warm, pulsing lap, and they went to someone's fourth-floor apartment of milk crate bookshelves and more music. Maggie pretended to fall asleep so that Kevin would carry her off to bed, which he did, except she suspected the bed was actually a dog bed—at least it smelled like one—and then she really did fall asleep. She woke up once in the middle of the night, feverish, and saw the shadows of two people moving up and down—Uncle Kevin and the blonde—and the blonde was moving on top of him and he was holding her breasts in each of his hands like Christmas ornaments. Maggie knew what they were doing but it didn't look so frightening or clinical as when she learned about it during those awful movies in health class. And it didn't look as disgusting as the porno she'd seen at Katie Grant's house, which was all spread legs and shaved bodies and smirking plastic faces. This looked—nice, or something. Real. She didn't know. She fell back asleep.

In the very early morning, Uncle Kevin shook her gently awake.

"You want some breakfast?" His breath was thick and beery.

She nodded sleepily, and he helped her up from the dog bed. He leaned over and kissed the blonde on the forehead, who stirred a little beneath the thin white sheet, her clothes in a pile on the floor, the soft outline of her breasts moving up and down with her breathing. They tiptoed out of the apartment, climbed back into AG BULLT, and drove to the Golden Nugget at Diversey and Clark. Kevin picked a vinyl booth by the window, and as they ate their breakfast, the sky beside them was a pink-dyed Easter egg turning an August blue above the flat rooftops of record stores and hookah shops.

"So, who was that blond girl?" Maggie asked, cutting into her French toast.

"Sonia? Ah, she's nobody. A friend."

"Is Jeremy going to get you a bootleg tape of the show?"

"Now why would I want one of those?" He plucked a bit of mushroom from his hobo skillet and wiped it on the edge of his plate.

"I don't know. He said he gets bootlegs of all the shows he goes to."

"Jeremy's a moron. Bootlegs totally defeat the purpose of going to a show. They take away from the preciousness of the lived experience. It happened. You were there for it. And now it's *your* responsibility to remember it, not to try and re-create it all the time by listening to some shittily recorded attempt at preservation." He pointed his fork at her. "Everything that ever happens to you only happens once, so you better never stop paying attention. Now eat your breakfast, kid."

He went back to picking at his skillet while Maggie nibbled her French toast and tried not to intrude on his mood, tried to hold in the magic of just being around him. She was glad to be Kevin's niece. It meant that he would never go sneaking off into some morning without even saying good-bye to her.

When they got home, Laura, Colm, and Nanny Ei were pacing the front stoop. There had been a fire in the laundry room at the Days Inn Milwaukee and they'd been evacuated. By the time they'd gotten the all-clear signal it was too late to go back to bed, so they'd driven home in the middle of the night and arrived at dawn to an empty apartment. Colm stood behind the two hysterical women with his arms crossed while Laura followed Maggie and Kevin into the house, picked up a sombrero-shaped ashtray, and chucked it at Kevin's head. He ducked, and it shattered against the front room wall.

"Where the hell have you been? Are you *drunk?*" she demanded, grabbing Maggie's arm.

"Not at the moment," Kevin responded.

"You should never have left her alone with him," Colm said. He was looking at Kevin the way you'd look at an infected wound.

Kevin opened his mouth to speak, but nothing came out. A look came over his face: the same hunted look he wore whenever his family got on his case about what a disappointment he was. He picked up the pieces of the sombrero ashtray, placed them on the coffee table, and walked into his room, closing the door quietly behind him.

"Are you *okay*?" Laura demanded.

Maggie nodded. She was more than okay. Not only was she no longer sick, she felt as if she'd just awoken from the long, safe torpor of her childhood. The night had blasted her free of that shell, and she had emerged new and raw and ready. She felt the ticket stub folded carefully in her pocket. How many kids in Bray would be able to say they'd stood just feet from Billy Corgan, that they'd been at the Metro for the *Siamese Dream* record release show, that they'd seen Lake Shore Drive on a Sunday morning through the prism of a concert comedown, the runners looking so silly with their skinny legs and their neon shorts, chugging along the footpath with their calorie counters and Gatorade?

"We had fun, ma," said Maggie. "Nothing happened."

"I'll *bet* it didn't," fumed Laura. "Get upstairs, you."

The night before they moved, Laura's boss at Oinker's, the neighborhood tavern where she bartended nights, threw the family a going-away party. He ordered trays of roast potatoes and fried chicken from Papa Chris's and let everybody drink all they wanted for ten bucks a wristband. All of Colm's construction buddies came, and so did Laura's friends from the neighborhood. Nanny Ei even got a few of the livelier members of the Altar and Rosary Society to stop by for Bailey's and coffees. Maggie and Ronnie spent the night wandering around the bar and giggling at the idiotic behavior of the adults who had either forgotten or simply didn't care that they were in the presence of children. It was only when the Irish construction guys started singing sad songs that Maggie got sad, too. Gingerly, as if she was touching a scab, she let herself wonder why Kevin hadn't come. She couldn't believe he wouldn't even want to say good-bye to his niece, his goddaughter, his Maggie. She knew he was flaky, and that he didn't show up at Christmas sometimes, or at Thanksgiving dinner. But this?

And then, at the end of the night, when her eyelids began to feel like paperweights and Ronnie was already snoring away in the corner of a booth, she was jolted awake by someone forcing open the back door, and the bartender, Mikey, forcing it shut again, and Colm and Laura yelling in that shrieky way of the very drunk.

"*Never* forgive 'im," her mother slurred, waving her cigarette wildly. "Don't mess with mama bear." Colm nodded. He gripped her thin waist; his right hand snaking down the long pocket of her tight black jeans to squeeze her butt.

"It's only right," he muttered.

Through the window, illuminated like an angel in the glow of an Old Style sign, Maggie saw her uncle, his hair long and wild, his guitar strapped to his back as essential a part of him as a turtle's shell. He pounded on the window like he wanted to break it until he found Maggie's eyes. He pressed his face against the glass, his breath fogging the window. His mouth shaped one word—he was either saying "bye" or "why," she couldn't tell—and then, lifting his hand in a gesture of farewell, he turned on the heels of his black boots and walked away. Maggie, gulping back tears, shoved her way past all the drunk people, fists clenched, in the direction of her mother, who was slumped with Colm near the video poker machine.

"I'm not going!" she screamed, grabbing her mother by the shoulder. But Laura didn't even turn around. She hiccupped, once, and watery vomit splashed onto the floor between her legs. Maggie let go of her mother's shoulder then, her rage replaced not exactly with pity, but with such a tired disgust with her whole pathetic family that she gave up.

Kevin never came home at all that night, and the next afternoon, Nanny Ei drove them to O'Hare.

On a damp Saturday afternoon in late October, Maggie sprawled on her bed, leafing through an issue of *Spin*. To her mother's absolute shock, Kevin had made good on his promise to send a care package to his goddaughter, and it had arrived earlier in the week, a large manila envelope stuffed with Twizzler's licorice, a tape of Selfish Fetus's new single, "Nightstick," and all the September music magazines. "I can't believe it," Laura had said in wonder. "He never keeps any of his promises."

"Maybe not to *you*," Maggie responded, snatching the package from her mother's hands. As she marched off to her room, the sudden anger that had flared up inside of her was now replaced just as quickly with a sour feeling of guilt—these days, she seldom felt the same emotion for more than ten minutes at a time. She closed the door and settled onto her bed with the candy and the magazine, happy, at least, for the privacy of her bedroom. One of the nice parts about moving to Ireland was that Maggie had her own room for the first time since Ronnie was born. And although she sometimes missed the simple reassurance of her little sister's breathing in the night, Maggie could now listen to "Nightstick" without being asked what the lyrics meant, or cry when she felt sad without being asked what was wrong, or change her clothes without having to hide in the closet so that Ronnie wouldn't stare at her breasts and ask her how old she was when she grew them ("I don't know, it's not like they inflated one night while I was sleeping"), and what they felt like ("skin"), and whether she needed help with all those bra hooks ("No, weirdo!") .

The house was quiet—Laura had gone into town, where she'd picked up part-time work as a cashier at Dunne's, Ronnie was over at a new friend's house, and Colm was outside cutting the front grass. If she listened very carefully, Maggie could hear the waves at the edge of town sucking cold pebbles out to sea and hurling them back again. Just as it occurred to her that this wasn't such a bad way to pass a Saturday, she heard a tentative knock at her door.

"Yeah?"

She put down her magazine and the door opened just enough for Colm, sweaty and reeking of fresh grass, to stick his head in.

"Neighbor's dog had puppies last night," he said. "I thought I'd go up and have a look. Wanna come?"

It might have occurred to Maggie to say no—or even to be insulted for being asked. It was a Saturday evening and she was sixteen—she might have plans! But she didn't, of course, and her new stepfather wasn't the type of person to pretend any different in order to protect her pride.

Socially, there had been possibilities at the beginning of the school year. Maggie had ridden along in the exodus of Saint Brigid's open campus lunch policy, when the girls would eat hurriedly in the canteen and then, for the extra half hour they had free before classes resumed, roll up their skirts to expose their thighs and head out to roam the town in search of Saint Brendan's boys. The Irish girls in her class, Maggie found, weren't a whole lot different from the American girls she knew back home. Around guys, they acted shrill and shrieky, pushing their crushes playfully and unable to hide their wounded hearts when the boys made off-handedly cruel jokes about their heavy legs or too-bright lipstick. Maggie wasn't good at flirting, and as a result, had never been kissed. Being around the shouting boys in their loosened ties both excited and intimidated her. When she joined her classmates on these boy hunts, she became practically mute. She didn't bring anything to the table—didn't make anyone laugh, didn't attract more attention—and so by the time the fall bank holiday arrived, the little buzz she'd garnered by being a Yank had subsided, and she couldn't blame the small pack of girls she'd made inroads with when they stopped inviting her to come along with them. It was almost with a sense of relief that Maggie returned to the canteen for the whole lunch hour with a smattering of other unimportant girls: the fat, the dandruffed, and the shy, working on their French conjugations and trying not to be embarrassed for each other.

The owner of the dog was Mike O'Callaghan, who was the nephew of Dan Sean O'Callaghan, Bray's most famous resident. At ninety-nine, Dan Sean was one of the oldest men in County Wicklow, but according to Colm, that was not what made him so notable. It was the fact that he was still in such good health for his age that he gave the younger members of the town hope that they, too, might grow old with dignity, avoiding the piss-smelling retirement homes or the palliative care center in Dun Laoghaire. Though frail, Dan Sean still lived on his own, free of oxygen tanks or babbling dementia or wheelchairs. He still went on pilgrimages every year to various Catholic holy places: Knock and Croagh Patrick in the Irish Republic, but also as far away as Israel and Medjugorje. On doctor's orders, he'd grudgingly quit smoking at age ninety-five. He'd flatly refused to quit drinking.

Dan Sean's only child, a daughter, had died fifty years earlier of tuberculosis. Five winters after that, his wife went out to the shed to water the cows and was knocked down and trampled to death by their polly bull. For the near half-century that followed, Dan Sean had lived alone at the top of the hill, and now Mike and his wife, who were themselves nearing seventy, lived at the bottom and looked after him.

All of this old-fashioned tragedy—murderous bulls, tubercular infants—was totally alien to Maggie; it did not seem possible that in 1993, she could meet a man whose past read like a Charles Dickens novel; who, as an eighteen-year-old, had ridden down to Cobh to wave his handkerchief at the crowds on the deck of the Titanic as it disappeared to its doom on the high North Atlantic. But, Colm explained, this is why it was essential that after they went to see the puppies in Mike's barn, they climb the hill to pay their respects.

"For such a tiny island, you wouldn't believe the massive changes that have happened here even in these past few decades," Colm told her as they set off through the back field, their boots making farting noises in the mud and stomped grass. "Dan Sean was here for all of it. Any day now, he might pass, and it'll be another light that goes out in our history, one less voice to remember the way things were. Do you know he's never even driven a car? Only a horse and carriage. Jesus, what do you think he'd make of these Chinese taxi drivers with Dublin accents?"

As they crossed the field and found the narrow road that led toward the O'Callaghan farm, Colm and Maggie fell into a comfortable silence, broken only by the intermittent bleating of a neighbor's sheep or the occasional passing of a car. It began to drizzle as they approached Mike's barn, which really wasn't a barn at all, but an A-frame shed, packed with farming equipment and stacks of turf. Inside, the close air was heavy with the smell of new life, unmistakable and not unpleasant, but somehow too intimate for Maggie and her new stepfather, who, feeling it too, moved away from her in the darkness. Raindrops thrummed on the peaked roof and Maggie could hear the rustling of six wriggling puppies, vying for space at their mother's side. They were so small they looked like baby birds, their skin hairless and puckered pink. The mother, a large gray sheepdog, half-lifted her head and watched Maggie and Colm's approach with one eye, then, losing interest, rested her head back on the wooden slats of the barn floor.

"Can we touch them?" Maggie asked. She was whispering, though she didn't know why.

"We could, but let's not," said Colm. "Mike'll be up at Dan Sean's, and he'll know if there are any males in the litter."

"Why do you prefer the males?"

"Better guard dogs. And they don't get pregnant."

As if to apologize to the present company, he squatted down and patted the mother on the head.

"You can't separate them for at least a week anyway," he explained. "They have to be with their mothers until they can see."

Behind the barn was a sloping gravel path that led up to Dan Sean's house, but it was hard to make out as the late afternoon had already dissolved into darkness. There wasn't much twilight here, Maggie had noticed, at least not in the fall. Gray afternoons just darkened into grayer evenings; only the rolling clouds served as a reminder that the world was moving at all. Colm led the way up the muddy path dotted with clucking chickens, slogging through one tractor tire track while Maggie followed the other. A goat watched the pair of them as they ascended, and nattered at them when Maggie tripped over a rock. Mist clung to the air, and the higher they walked, the harder it was to see anything, so that Colm became just a gray shadow, a blockage of displaced air, somewhere off to her left. His disembodied voice explained to her that the house had been built by Dan Sean's grandfather in the early 1840s, an era that brought to mind the eerie green quietness of a famine memorial Maggie had seen in Ohio on a trip with Nanny Ei a few summers earlier, when Ireland was still more of a feeling for her than an actual place.

It was so foggy at the top of the hill that Maggie only knew they had reached it because her calves no longer burned from climbing. She could make out two squares of window hovering in front of them. Somewhere between the windows, a door opened.

"Over this way!" a voice called, and they followed it until the fog fell away and they were standing at the threshold of a warm, dry sitting room. At first, Maggie thought that this man standing in the doorway, with his wispy white hair and short, bowed legs, must be Dan Sean. But when Colm shook the old man's hand, he said, "Mike! What's the craic?" and Maggie realized that Dan Sean's *nephew* looked at least a decade older than Nanny Ei.

A fat brown cat and a filthy dog moved freely about between the sitting room and the dirt yard, tracking mud and chicken feathers on the faded carpet. It needed a good sweeping, but it was cozy, heated by the turf fire that burned in an enormous fireplace. In front of this fire, County Wicklow's oldest resident rocked slowly in his chair. His wrinkles were deep folds, his eyes milky myopic slits behind thick government-issued glasses. But this was counterbalanced by a jaunty three-piece navy suit and a large fur Cossack's hat beneath which his turtle-like face appraised the group with an expressionless but not unalert gaze. There was not an air of death about him, or morbidity, just a quiet staleness, like a plant that needed watering.

"Who's this!" he demanded, gesturing at Maggie with arthritically puffed hands. Colm made the introductions, and Dan Sean stared at Maggie from beneath his Cossack's hat.

"You'll have a drink!" he finally yelled, waving at a rusty potbellied stove and a card table lined with a variety of dark liquids: cordials, whiskey, and brandy. Mike went over and put on the kettle while Dan Sean, gathering the gigantic, matted cat in his arms, swiveled in his chair and proceeded to converse with Colm and Mike in a dialect so thickly accented that Maggie mistook it, at first, for the Irish language. She found a chair near the window and the dirty white dog presented himself at her feet, waving his paws to get her attention. She scratched the oily space behind his ears and looked around at the walls, which were crammed with faded photographs of Dan Sean's pilgrimages. The only other decorations were photos of the Blessed Virgin and the Sacred Heart, velvety and colorful, reminiscent of the Pink Floyd posters in Uncle Kevin's bedroom.

The kettle wailed, and Mike poured two glasses halfway with boiling water, then filled the rest with a dark red liquid from a huge decanter. He stirred the drinks with a calloused fingertip, then handed one to Colm and the other to Maggie.

"Mikey, she's only sixteen," Colm interjected.

"It's only a drop of port!" shouted Dan Sean, so that the mangy cat leaped off his lap and disappeared behind a basket of coal. "To keep off the chill!"

"It will only go to waste now if she doesn't drink it," Mike pointed out. "This isn't America; a girl can have a drop of port to keep off the chill, can't she?"

"Oh, go on then," Colm relented. "Just don't tell your mother."

Maggie held the hot glass in her hands. It smelled like the potpourri Nanny Ei filled her apartment with at Christmastime. It tasted sort of like wine, which she'd had before, stealing sips from her mother's glass during the dark times between boyfriends.

Once all the men were settled with their drinks, Dan Sean took a poker and stirred the fire, so that sparks showered onto the hearth, dangerously close to the oblivious dog's fur, and launched into a long story that Maggie could tell was a sad one. Colm and Mike sat leaned forward, legs spread, elbows resting on knees, and every once in a while they would stop to nod solemnly or light a cigarette. Sometimes, Dan Sean would stop what he was saying and catch Maggie's eye. Maybe it was that small gesture, or maybe it was the port, or the heat of the tiny, smoke-filled room, but as she listened she felt a part of the conversation, a part of these men, and it didn't even matter that she knew nothing of football or farming or the Scanlon woman up the road whose sister in Antrim had a brain aneurysm, God rest her soul.

Later, the phone rang. It was Laura: her shift had ended, and she needed a lift.

"I suppose we'll be going," Colm said, rising to wash his cup in the aluminum sink. "Ready?"

But Maggie, dreamy and dizzy from the liquor, felt welded to her seat. With Nanny Ei an ocean away, she missed being around old people and their directionless conversations, their stale smells. The glass of port warm in her hands, the soft lull of the conversation, the salty bog smell of the fire, held her in her chair. "I'll walk home," she said, "if it's okay with you."

Colm shrugged, a bit surprised.

"Well. I suppose it's only down the hill."

He wiped his cup and placed it on the drying rack, then shook hands with the men and left. As soon as the door closed, the cat leaped onto Maggie's lap, shedding hair all over her jeans.

"You'll have another drink," Dan Sean demanded, pointing at her empty glass with a fingernail that needed cutting. He insisted on pouring Maggie's second drink himself. Slowly, he unfolded himself from his chair, took her glass, and tottered over to the card table. He poured a splash of hot water from the kettle, then filled the rest with the ruby liquid.

"Fuck's sake!" Mike jumped from his seat. "Dan Sean, that's too much!"

"Ah, the glass is fierce narrow," said Dan Sean, sidestepping Mike with impressive agility for a man of his age and handing the drink to Maggie.

"This is why I usually pour the drinks," said Mike, winking at her. Then he leaned over and whispered, "He does that for people he likes—pours 'em strong so it takes 'em longer to drink. Means he likes your company."

Maggie blushed. "But I've barely said anything," she said.

"A man like that, who's been around for nearly a hundred years? He don't need you to say much to know what you're about."

Across the hearth, Dan Sean raised his glass of port, and they drank together.

A half hour later, the phone rang again. Mike's wife wanted him to come home; dinner was on the table.

"Be back in an hour with a plate for you," he promised Dan Sean. "Nice to meet you, Maggie."

He closed the front door softly as he left. Maggie and Dan Sean, and the eighty-three years between them, watched Mike as he crossed the yard and was swallowed by the fog. They sat for a while with their drinks in their hands, watching the fire like old friends. On the mantelpiece was a large framed photo of a young couple sitting in a horse and trap. The man was dressed in wool trousers and a cap, and he was staring down the camera as if to tell the world that he was not the type of man who smiled in pictures. Next to him, leaning on his shoulder, was a woman with dark, wavy hair. She was grinning for all she was worth, as if to make up for her husband's serious expression. Her lips were brightly painted, and one black eyebrow was arched flirtatiously at the camera. *May, 1919*, was penciled in the corner of the frame. Was everybody just more beautiful back then, Maggie wondered, or was it just a trick of old film?

"What was your wife's name?" she asked.

"Hah?" Dan Sean squinted, leaning forward.

"Your wife's name?"

"*Hah?*"

"Your *wife*. Her *name?*" Maggie shouted, not knowing whether Dan Sean couldn't hear her, or just couldn't understand the nasal cadence of her Chicago accent.

He shrugged, shaking his head so forcefully that the Cossack's hat drooped down to a jaunty angle and perched on the rim of his glasses. He didn't seem to take any notice, so Maggie got up to gently reposition it. The potency of the booze kicked in the moment she stood up, and she lurched toward him on sea legs.

Bending down to fix his hat, she could smell embedded smoke, shaving cream, and very faintly, the vinegar dribble of urine. She felt a sudden tenderness for Dan Sean and this tiny house, filled up with a half century of loneliness. She kissed the furry top of his Cossack's hat. It took three careful steps for her to return to her own chair, and when she sat down, she saw that he had fallen asleep.

Maggie sipped her drink with the cat draped across her lap and the dog curled at her feet. The only sounds in the room were the crackling of the fire and Dan Sean's shallow snores. There were no CDs to play, no radio, no television. There was nothing. She was just sitting there in silence, getting drunk. It occurred to her that a person's first drunken experience should be in the basement of a friend's house, in a forest preserve, behind the bleachers of a football field. Certainly not in the company of a sleeping ninety-nine-year-old man. She giggled a little and wondered what Uncle Kevin would make of it. "Hot port?" he would say. "*Very* impressive, Mags. I would have thought you'd be more of a wine cooler type of girl."

Swallowing the last of her drink, she lifted the cat gently to the floor and tiptoed over to the sink. She washed her glass, put on her jacket, and opened the front door slowly so that its creaking hinges wouldn't wake Dan Sean. Stepping out into the fog, she reached back to close it behind her when the old man's eyes snapped open behind his thick glasses.

"Nora," he said. "That was my wife." Then he crossed himself, a gesture that, for him, seemed as autonomic as blinking, and fell immediately back to sleep.

Maggie descended the dark hill on unsteady legs. The fog blotted out the sounds of the town below; no airplanes flew overhead. Animals peeked out of wooden lean-tos and hens pecked along behind chicken wire, watching her with idiot interest. It could be any year, any century. It seemed suddenly possible that a world of horse-drawn traps and the cries of tubercular babies could not be far away, could not, even, have passed on. In the month she had lived in Bray, Maggie had felt pockets of this—this slowing down of time, these reverberations into the past. In America, everything was replaceable; old stuff was thrown away quickly and entirely to make way for the next thing. But in Ireland, the ruined castles that dotted the landscape, the crumbling stone walls that crisscrossed long-held family fields, these all provided the sense that the past drifted, but did not disappear. It was all around you, like mist.

As she neared the bottom of the hill, Maggie began to wish she had gone home with Colm. Night had collapsed on the countryside; the air was pitch black, cold and brackish on her cheeks. She had an awful thought: how close was the water from here? Where do all these green slopes lead? What if in this darkness she walked straight into the ocean, the seaweed filling her shoes, her liquor-heavy limbs immobile and useless? Of course, she thought, stumbling down the path, of *course* this is how it would happen. Just when I'm starting to like it here, I accidentally drown.

It was at this moment—when she was really starting to freak out, when the dulling effects of the alcohol were burned off by fear, when she could no longer feel her toes inside her sodden Converse—that in this empty field, blotted from sound as if in a great, green closet and seemingly out of nowhere, the vision appeared.

"Hi," said the vision.

Maggie hiccupped.

"You lost?" He was about her age, maybe a little older. It was too dark to tell if he was cute or not.

"Um. Maybe? Do you know how close we are to the ocean?"

"You don't live around here, do you?"

"I just moved here. My mom married Colm Byrne. We live near the Strand Road. I'm Maggie."

"Oh! Right. I heard about that. I'm Eoin." He peered down the hill. "You going for a swim?"

"No," she said. "I was coming home from Dan Sean O'Callaghan's, but I lost my way."

He stepped closer and squinted at her. He smelled of laundry detergent, and he was cute. Extremely cute, actually.

"Was Dan Sean the one pouring drinks?"

She nodded and hiccupped again. He smiled a little so she saw a crooked set of teeth that gleamed white in the darkness.

"The man's dangerous with the pours," Eoin said. "You're not the first visitor to get lost on the way home from a night up the hill at Dan Sean's. If you're living up on the Strand, what you need to do is head back where you came and turn right at the water pump. That's Strand Road." He placed a hand on her back, a warm pressure beneath her shoulder blades, and nudged her gently in that direction.

"Thanks," she said, already beginning to walk, concentrating on her sobriety and the water pump. "Thanks, Eoin." Her tongue felt grotesquely thick in her mouth.

The fog thinned at the bottom of the hill, breaking off into ethereal wisps that snaked around her shoulders as she neared home. *Home.* It was the first time she had thought of Colm's house, which stood white and inviting at the end of the gravel road, in that way. She went in through the unlocked back door. The house, as usual, was empty—Colm and Laura had probably made a pit stop at the Quayside, while Ronnie was over at one of her many new friends' houses. But Maggie was grateful, because now her stomach, knowing that she was safe, staged a revolt. She barely made it to the bathroom before spraying the toilet with burgundy red port puke. Afterward, she brushed her teeth, peeled off her smoky clothes, and got into bed. The headache that crippled her felt like a pulse in her temple: "Eoin. Eoin. Eoin." It bothered her, the way he'd touched her without being asked. Is that what boys did in this country—just touched you moments after they met you? She pulled the pillow over her head, embarrassed for herself. Why did she even care? It's not like it had meant anything. It was as meaningless as a handshake or a stranger bumping into you on the bus.

But meaningless as it was, as Maggie lay in bed before drifting into the heavy black block of sleep, the imprint of that hand, the spread fingers on the sodden cotton of her jacket, was all that she could feel.

By November, Maggie had struck up a friendship with Aíne, a bookish girl from her French class who had perfect handwriting, organized notebooks, and an obsession with getting maximum points in her leaving cert and moving to Dublin to study pharmacy at Trinity College. For the time being, though, she was stuck sharing a bedroom with three younger sisters in one of the damp, shabby estate houses that butted up against the carnival grounds. Aíne's mother was a haggard, lumpy woman with rosacea and veiny legs, and her father drove a taxi, selling loose cigarettes from the trunk that he'd bought for cheap on a trip to Romania. It was clear from the start to Maggie that Aíne was ashamed of her blue-collar family, and that she was fiercely determined not to grow up to become like them. She wore her brown hair tied tightly at the nape of her neck in a stern, pretentious bun and her face was forgettably pretty save for the thin white scar that ran from her left nostril to the top of her lip, from a cleft palate surgery she'd had as a baby. Maggie wondered how Aíne felt about the scar, which wasn't detectable from far away but which a boy in kissing distance would be sure to notice. She couldn't ask, but she was sure that Aíne, too, had never been kissed. The thought of this plain, serious girl allowing her mouth to be explored by the worming tongue of a Saint Brendan's boy seemed somehow profane. Theirs wasn't a friendship that involved giggling over boys.

But even if Aíne wasn't exactly a lifelong soul-mate kind of friend, Maggie was glad to have *some*one to escape with when her sister's eleventh birthday rolled around. For the occasion, Ronnie had invited five of her new friends over for a "slumber party," an American phrase that had enchanted her classmates and terrified Colm, who had fled to the Quayside shortly after the first eye-shadowed pre-teen knocked on his door, leaving Laura alone to deal with the pack of national school girls who, by nightfall, were hopped up on chocolate bars and Club Orange and shrieking along to the 4 Non Blondes. Just after they finished their sing-along to "What's Up," a redheaded girl in a hot pink tracksuit, her cheeks awash in glitter, sashayed past them on her way to the bathroom. Laura began rummaging for a wine opener.

"You sure you want to leave me here with all this?" She raised a dark eyebrow at Maggie, cranked open the wine, and filled her glass nearly to the brim while treble-pitched arguments about what to play next drifted from the sitting room. The synthetic crooning of pop radio indicated a decision had been made.

"Can you imagine if Kevin were here, what he'd say about this dance party?" Laura said.

"Oh, he wouldn't say anything," Maggie laughed. "He would've left for the bar with Colm the minute this thing started."

Laura paused, took a sip of wine. "No," she said finally. "Kevin and Colm wouldn't be going anywhere together. There's no love lost between those two." She peered into her glass, avoiding Maggie's eyes: a classic Laura Lynch evasion tactic.

"Care to explain?"

Her mom shrugged, lit a cigarette, and shook out the match. The smoke curled into the corners of the kitchen ceiling.

"Not particularly." She looked at her watch. "You better get a move on, sister. This Aíne character sounds like the punctual sort."

As she crossed the footpath over the river Dargle, Maggie found her bearings by scanning the sky for the Ferris wheel. It hovered above the pubs and hotels and the sea to the east, and to the west, on the other side of Main Street, stood the stony hulking tower of Saint Paul's Church. Maggie knew that if she stayed between these two landmarks, she was on the right track to HMV. She had always been terrible with directions: earlier that summer, when she'd taken the wrong train home from the dentist and ended up marooned out in Oak Park, she had to call Kevin to come pick her up. He didn't make fun of her cluelessness, as Maggie had expected. Instead, as he pulled up to the el station, he declared, "Give a man a fish and he'll eat for a day. Teach a man to fish and he'll eat for a lifetime." They got a bagful of cheeseburgers at White Castle and spent the rest of the night driving around the city so he could teach her the grid system. AG BULLT rumbled up and down the length and breadth of Chicago as Kevin pointed at street signs and barked out their coordinates: "Western Avenue, 2400 West! Kedzie Avenue, 3200 West! Belmont Avenue, 3200 North!" Up and down and up and down they went as the Clash blasted from the beleaguered speakers and the cheeseburgers dwindled.

"When a city has a grid system and you take the time to learn it, it's impossible to get lost," he explained. "But Ireland is old and mountainous, and it's probably going to be a bitch to find your way around there. Before you go, I'll give you the compass I have left over from my Cub Scout days. For a Magellan like you, it might be your only hope. Now: Division Avenue is located at what-hundred north?"

"1200!" Maggie shouted. "Wait a second—did you just say you were a *Boy Scout*?"

"No, I said I was a *Cub* Scout," he said, tossing a cheeseburger wrapper out the window. "I quit before attaining the level of actual Boy Scout. And you can laugh all you want, but there's only one person in this car who knows Morse code, and it certainly ain't you."

Maggie reached into her jacket pocket now and held the scratched little brass compass. It was nearly twenty years old, and when Kevin had fished it out of the recesses of his closet, they'd discovered that it no longer worked. But she'd brought it with her to Ireland anyway. She didn't know why. She guessed maybe because it was one of the only gifts Kevin had ever given her, and just having it in her pocket, holding its cool, round weight in her palm, always made her feel less lost. She was still angry at her mom for locking him out of the going-away party and denying her a chance to say good-bye, but in the course of three months the anger had calcified into a dull, throbbing resentment—a resentment that was only part of a larger anger at her mom's flightiness and immaturity, for the way heartbreak never seemed to teach her anything, for the way her search for romance was always disrupting their lives. For their part, Laura and Kevin, like many brothers and sisters, could forgive each other as quickly and easily as they condemned each other, and both seemed to have forgotten about the incident at Oinker's. He called the house fairly regularly, and Maggie had talked to him about once a month since they'd arrived in Bray. The last time they'd spoken, Nirvana had just announced its European tour dates, and Kevin frothed with excitement about the prospect of the band from Seattle tearing their way through the staid cities of Western Europe.

"Maggie," he said, his voice shrill and trembling, "if you ever listen to my advice on *anything*, listen to me about this, okay? You. Must. Go. See. Nirvana. In. Rome. It's a two-hour flight from Dublin, and it's at the Palaghiaccio di Marino, and it's going to be transcendent."

"You know I'm sixteen, right?" Maggie said. "Mom would never in a million years let me go to Italy for a Nirvana show! *Maybe* she'd take me to see them in Dublin. But Rome? No way."

"First of all, what are you talking about?" He was yelling now. "You can't go see Nirvana with your *mother.* Second of all, did you hear what I said? Rome! The Eternal City! Julius Caesar! Crossing the Rubicon! The Coliseum! It's like, the giants of the present colliding with the giants of the past. It's like two thousand years of civilization coming full circle. Can you imagine Kurt Cobain's voice drifting across the fucking Tiber? Echoing off the goddam piazzas?" On the other end of the phone, she could hear him plucking compulsively at the strings of his guitar. "Don't you understand, Maggie? This would be like *President fucking CLINTON* playing the fucking *sax*ophone at the—"

His calling card ran out of minutes and the call clicked off. Maggie looked out the kitchen window at Ronnie, who was running in jagged circles around the yard with a school friend, trying unsuccessfully to fly a blue kite. She placed the phone gently back in its receiver and stepped away from it as if it was leaking toxins. It wasn't so much the lecture she had just received—Kevin had been lecturing her all her life about politics, literature, art, and music— but the way he had delivered it. He had not sounded just passionate, but actually unhinged, strung out, crazy. She looked forward more than ever to Christmas, a month away, when he and Nanny Ei were coming. It was so hard to gauge a voice over a phone line.

Aíne, ever punctual, was checking her watch in front of the HMV when Maggie approached. She was dressed in the same nondescript gray coat she always wore, but had slicked on a sad bit of lip gloss. This dollop of pink made Maggie hopeful—maybe her friend *did* care about what boys thought—and as they wandered among the aisles of the store, flipping through stacks of CDs, she considered telling Aíne about the night she'd met Eoin. But, ultimately, what was there to tell? That she met a guy and he gave her directions? That for a brief moment he had touched her back, and all week Maggie had been thinking of that touch? Pathetic. If she told Aíne that this minor incident actually counted as news, as progress, in her romantic life, it would only reveal her inexperience.

In the dance music aisle, they stopped in front of a large cardboard cutout of Kylie Minogue in turquoise hot pants and pigtails.

"Seriously, the pop music over here is even worse than the crap back home," Maggie observed. She felt, then, under the corporate lights of HMV, a subtle change in atmosphere. Somewhere nearby, a crotch was being readjusted, eyes were appraising, testosterone was surging. She turned around just as the store clerk approached. His glasses made him appear older, scholarly; but a glaze of small, bursting pimples scattered across his forehead indicated that he was about their own age.

"You need some help?" he asked, his eyes hidden behind the thick window of his glasses.

"We're fine," said Maggie, glancing at him briefly. "Just looking around."

"You girls go to Saint Brigid's?" The boy ran his fingers nervously along Kylie Minogue's cardboard arm. He was looking intently at Aíne, whose pale skin was now burning red.

"Yes," Aíne said, crossing her arms and smiling shyly, the delicate white line of her palate scar folding neatly in half. "We're in our junior cert year."

"I thought so!" the boy said brightly. "I've seen you during open lunch." He moved forward a bit, stepping almost between the two girls. It was clear that, like a basketball player rolling a pick, he was trying to block Maggie out. She took the hint and wandered away, fleeing to a listening booth where she nestled into a giant pair of headphones and PJ Harvey's *Rid of Me*. As she stole glances at the two of them over the racks of CDs, she wondered about Eoin. Had he really been as handsome as she remembered? Or had he been transformed in her memory by the gauze of the nighttime and her loneliness, the glasses of port and the heat that burned from his palm to her back?

"Did you *see* that?" Aíne demanded, lifting a headphone from Maggie's ear. "How he just came up to me like that?"

Maggie turned down the music and smiled. In the short span of their friendship, she'd never seen Aíne so excited about something that didn't involve her grade on a math quiz.

"He's got a friend—another lad who works here. They want to meet us at the carnival after they finish work."

"What friend?"

"I don't *know*. Some fella that works here."

Maggie looked at Aíne's flushed, hopeful face. In her ear, PJ Harvey panted, *did you ever wish me dead? Oh lover boy, oh fever head?*

"But what do they want to *do* with us?"

Aíne took out her pink lip gloss and began smearing on a fresh layer.

"What do you mean, *do with us?* He was *decent*. He goes to Saint Brendan's. It can't hurt, can it?"

Maggie was unconvinced, but the alternative was going home to help supervise a mob of sugar-crazed eleven-year-old girls, so an hour later she stood with Aíne under the dark metal hulk of the Ferris wheel, squinting through the darkness at the approaching boys.

The carnival, which had been depressing enough at the end of the summer, was now flat-out ghostly. Most of the larger rides were covered in heavy white tarp that flapped in the salty wind like some frightening art installation. Walking through it felt like walking through a collapsible city of billowing white buildings. Corrugated doors covered the gaming booths, some of which were scrawled with orange graffiti. To the east, the sea was calm and abiding, rippling, watching.

Aíne's boy was named Paddy. He was stork-like and jittery, pulling at his pockets and walking in quick, jerky steps. He had a plated, ceratopsian nose, which, along with the thick glasses, made him look like he was wearing a Groucho Marx mask. The light wash of his jeans was outdated and his shoelaces were untied.

"Ever seen the view from Bray Head?" he asked, the long, wispy hairs on his upper lip stirring in the wind.

"Would you believe I've lived my whole life looking at that thing but never actually climbed it?" Aíne said. "I hear it's lovely, though." Her voice was giggly and effusive; she was nearly unrecognizable from the serious girl who wore her uniform skirt unfashionably long and always did the extra practice sentences in the back of their French textbook. Maggie had witnessed this strange occurrence in her mother many times over the years: the transformative power of attraction.

While the two new lovebirds walked ahead toward the hill, Paul, who had been recruited as Maggie's date, sidled up alongside her. He was short and wiry, with jutting brows that overhung his dark eyes like invasive ivy. He reeked of Lynx Dark Temptation cologne.

"So, how do you like Saint Brigid's?" he began. "I heard the nuns there are bitches."

"It's okay," Maggie shrugged. "Pretty much the same as back home, I guess." He looked over at her, his thick eyebrows hitching up as he tried to place her accent.

"Boston?"

"No, Chicago."

"Oh, right. The windy city."

"Yeah."

Although he seemed perfectly polite, his hooded eyes and ropy neck muscles hinted at a future of bar brawls and card-game fistfights. Maggie wouldn't go so far as to describe him as attractive, but he wasn't heinously ugly, either, and as they walked through the hulking tarp figures that flapped in the sea wind, she wondered if maybe, when the night ended, she should kiss him. She felt none of the jittery happiness that trembled from Aíne ten feet ahead of her like a heat mirage on an asphalt road, but she was halfway through sixteen, and wasn't there something to be said, at this point, for just getting it over with?

"You always remember your first kiss," her mom had advised before the freshman year homecoming dance as Maggie sat on the toilet waiting for her curlers to set and Nanny Ei painted her eyelids a frosty silver.

"Yeah, you do always remember it," Nanny Ei acknowledged, "but it usually doesn't mean anything."

Now, Paul walked close enough to her that Maggie could smell his cherry gum, a cloying smell that told her he'd been promised a girl who would make out with him. Was this the kind of night that Maggie wanted to remember forever: the November wind, the neon aisles of the HMV, the chipper where she and Aíne had shared a greasy plate of fries to pass the time before the boys got off work? It had been a pointless, meandering night, Maggie thought, like so many other teenage nights where you sit around, so bored that it actually hurts, waiting and waiting for something to happen. Most of these nights, nothing ever did.

There was a path that sloped upward from the sand, twisting like a castle turret, so that if you made it all the way up, past an abandoned rusty set of railroad tracks, you would reach the top of Bray Head. From there, the two boys explained, you could look down to see the white-covered tops of the carnival rides, the roofs of the town, and even, on a clear night like this, the lights of Dublin over the hills.

Maggie shivered in her jacket. It wasn't that she *minded* Paul at her side, necessarily. It was just that, given the choice between climbing the hill with him or going home to read a music magazine, she'd already be halfway up the Strand Road. But Aíne, who'd been swept up in Paddy and the newfound confidence that comes from a boy's attentions, was already on the onward march, and Maggie had no choice but to follow.

They climbed upwards, pushing away wet branches and snapping twigs. Maggie kept slipping, her Converse useless in the slick mud, until finally Paul took her hand. It was cold and not very comforting. She made up her mind that she would not kiss him.

As they continued their climb, breathing hard, their halting conversation petered into silence. Finally the trees fell away, the sky broke open, and they were standing on a grass bowl jutting out into the world, moonlit water stretching dizzyingly below, and stars, so many stars, crowding the sky.

It was the most romantic place possible for a first kiss. Such a place did not exist in Chicago. In Chicago, a boy might touch you for the first time under the blue line tracks, or in some hidden corner of a floodlit city park. Such water, such sky, was not possible back home. *If I can't feel any romance in this place*, Maggie thought, *then I might as well just accept my future as a lonely old cat lady*. Paul's mouth was eager but not hideous in the starlight, and he put two firm hands on her waist, leaned in, and jammed a cold, limp tongue into her mouth. She didn't know what else to do, so she opened her mouth a little wider, trying to clear a breathing passage, closed her eyes tightly and concentrated on not drooling. His tongue began waving back and forth as if a tiny drunk man was weaving his way down the hallways of her throat. Then he began moving it in circles. Clockwise. Counterclockwise. Maggie opened an eye and saw, over Paul's ear, the moon and the water spread out behind him. When would it be over? He finished with a flourish, rearing his tongue back and striking forward, like a cobra. Then he pulled away with a sharp suck. Maggie wiped her mouth. Across the moon-bleached grass, Aíne and Paddy sat at the edge of the cliff, legs dangling over the crags below. He had his arm resting on the small of her back and as she turned to receive his kiss, her features softened by the stars and the water and the wind blowing her plain brown hair, Maggie saw her for a moment the way Paddy must have seen her at the HMV. When they finally kissed, Aíne's eyes fluttered shut and her fingers spread open in the grass.

"Should we go back and leave them to it?" asked Paul suddenly. His eyebrows sagged with disappointment—it was clear he hadn't enjoyed their kiss any more than Maggie had. They made their way back down the hill, and she slipped a few times on the descent, but Paul only called, "You okay?" from a safe distance behind her.

"Where do you live?" he asked when they'd reached the edge of the carnival.

"I'm up the Strand Road about a mile," Maggie pointed.

"Oh," he said, relieved. "I'm straight in the other direction." He pulled her into a stiff hug, then, and they parted ways. As she threaded her way through the maze of white tarp toward Colm's house, a storm wind kicked up. Maggie stopped for a moment to watch the wind froth the glittering expanse of water, to listen to the sand make whispering sounds as it billowed across the air. And then, with a great *whoomph*, the tarp that covered the Space Odyssey came free, blew right off the hulking machine, and propelled into the air, wavering and blowing over the open water like a low-hanging cloud, until the wind died for a moment and it floated down like a great ash leaf and splashed into the water. Maggie watched it with a sense of elation, glad that the moment belonged to her alone, that she didn't have to discuss it afterwards with Paul, that it didn't have to *mean* anything. The rain began then, a deluge that drowned out every other sound, and Maggie pulled her hood tight around her face. She took one last look at the tarp, which was now far out on the horizon, floating on the water like a great paper crane, and ran the rest of the way home.

She opened the back door quietly, kicked off her sodden shoes, and tiptoed past Ronnie's bedroom, which was teeming with sleeping bags and the glossy heads of snoring eleven-year-olds. The spillover of girls had been given her own bed, and Laura had made up the couch in the sitting room, cozy with blankets and flannel pillows. Maggie brushed her teeth and changed into her pajamas. She did not think she was tired, but fell asleep almost immediately.

She awoke in the darkness. The rain was an insistent splashing against the windows, and the sound of hushed voices drifted from nearby.

"Stealing from my mother again, and it can only mean one thing—"

"Treatment for it—"

"You just don't *get* my brother, baby. The more you tell him he has to change—"

It was her mom and Colm, whispering in their whiskey voices. The little clock over the fireplace read 2:42 a.m.

"Ask yourself whether you want him around the children at Christmastime!"

"But the girls *love* Kevin—"

"—the price of being a fuckin' addict."

Maggie squinted at the square of light leaking in from the kitchen doorway. She felt so drowsy and cozy in her nest of blankets that she couldn't be sure whether or not she was still asleep. What was it with this place, this life, that made you so unsure if what was happening to you was even real? She rolled over, curled back into her nest, and was dropped again into her dreams, where a giant tarp made shapes in the water, undulating and wet as a tongue.

"Pancakes!"

Maggie awoke from the sweaty entanglement of her blankets and sat up. Morning sunlight streamed through the sitting room windows, and Ronnie's friends traipsed past her, still in their pajamas, on the way to the kitchen. She threw off her covers, padded to the bathroom, and looked at herself in the mirror. She prepared herself for the interrogation, sure that her mom would take one look at her face and know that her daughter had been kissed. It was just something that stained you, Maggie thought, a subtle change like the first inkling of real breasts, noticed only and immediately by one's mother.

The kitchen was a flurry of activity: little girls chattering around the table and passing syrup back and forth, Colm hiding behind his newspaper and sipping tea, and Laura running around the kitchen in an apron, frying and mixing and pouring and serving pancakes.

"Morning," she said brightly, the thin red rim beneath her eyes the only sign of a hangover. "You want some pancakes?"

Maggie looked at her mother and blinked.

"Mags! Pancakes! Chocolate chip or plain?"

"Uh—chocolate chip. Thanks, Mom."

Laura slid the pancakes off the griddle and onto Maggie's plate, then went into the cupboard in search of powdered sugar. Maggie brushed a finger across her lips. If something in her face had changed, her mom certainly hadn't noticed. But Maggie didn't blame her. It wasn't kissing that changed you. It was the feeling that changed you. The weak-kneed, stomach-dropping, hand-trembling, heart-fluttering *feeling*. And in kissing Paul, she hadn't felt anything.

Sister Geneve was Maggie's theology and English teacher, a nun of the Order of the Blessed Virgin Mary with Q-tip hair and octagonal glasses. She didn't wear a habit, favoring instead frumpy brown knit sweaters and the same kind of cheap black slacks worn by McDonald's cashiers. When she walked, half-smiling, down the halls of Saint Brigid's with her slow gait and dragging pant hems, even the leaving cert girls who spent their weekends steaming up the backseats of cars found themselves unrolling their skirts and wiping the lipstick off their mouths. Everyone wanted to be better for Sister Geneve.

On the last day of school before Christmas break, instead of discussing Plato's "Allegory of the Cave" or reading yet another article about the lives of the saints, Sister Geneve wheeled a television into the classroom and played a video about the birth of Christ. The story of the Nativity was as familiar to Maggie as the rote prayers she recited at the beginning and end of each school day, but this particular version included a prolonged labor scene, with the Virgin Mary heaving and grunting, a terrified Joseph holding her by one splayed leg while the barn animals looked on.

"There's no need for giggling," called Sister Geneve from the back of the classroom. "This should be a reminder to all of you that Jesus was a *real* person, born to a *real* woman, placenta and all. He was a human being, girls. Even as he was divine. This is the mystery of the Holy Spirit." Then, she returned to her needlepoint, as Mary bellowed one last time and squeezed the savior out into the world.

Aíne and Maggie sat next to each other, passing notes about their plans for Christmas break. Aíne was going to spend most of the holiday at her grandmother's house in Kilkenny, and was worried about how she would survive without Paddy for a whole week and a half. The two of them were already saying "I love you," and Aíne had saved up to buy a new bra—a forest-green velvet and lace number from Brown Thomas that had come wrapped in tissue paper and cost almost twenty pounds—because she was planning on taking her shirt off for him on New Year's Eve.

"Then what?" Maggie scribbled, lobbing the paper on her friend's desk.

"Then I might have to go back and buy the matching knickers," Aíne's responded, raising her eyebrows coyly as Maggie unfolded the paper. Maggie rolled her eyes. Aíne's transformation from dorky valedictorian-in-the-making to lingerie sex goddess had taken all of three weeks. But then again, as Maggie had seen with her own mother, falling in love turns people into strangers and fanatics, people with a wild faith in their new beloved that borders on the religious. Paddy might be a pimple-faced HMV cashier to the rest of the world, but Aíne saw the promise behind those clunky glasses, and had already pooled her dreams with his. The top boy in his class at Saint Brendan's, he planned to study political science at UCD, and his eventual goal was nothing less than becoming the first Taoiseach from County Wicklow. Aíne believed that together, she and Paddy would rise above their blue-collar beginnings and become part of Ireland's elite, with a red-brick palace in Sandymount and a cottage in Connemara where their well-heeled children could play in the surf. If it wasn't all so nauseating, Maggie might almost be excited for her.

The angels sang, the three wise men came, and finally, the video ended and the bell rang in two weeks of freedom.

"You know," said Aíne, as they headed down the hallway, "we could probably convince Paul to go out with us on New Year's Eve. I don't think he's got another girlfriend."

"I don't have a nice enough bra," Maggie said, laughing off the question. The truth was, she'd be perfectly happy if she never saw Paul again, and she was quite sure he felt the same way.

A sleety rain had begun to fall, so they said their good-byes quickly. Maggie clicked open her umbrella and headed toward home, picking her way through the slick courtyard of Saint Brigid's. As she crossed through the steel entrance gates, she saw a spectral figure standing across the street, wearing a sodden leather jacket. He was the only person on the street without an umbrella or a hood, and pieces of dark, wet hair stuck to his face while the cold drizzle slipped down his collar. He was smoking a cigarette, cupping it beneath his palm to protect it from the rain, and exhaling in great clouds of smoke and precipitation. Maggie stopped short.

"Uncle Kevin!" she squealed as he flicked his cigarette into the street and pulled her into a bear hug. "I didn't think you were getting in till tonight!"

"Just landed an hour ago," he said, his voice muffled by the wet shoulder of her coat. "Had to come see you before I did anything else."

Her classmates streamed by them, trying not to stare. Maggie knew exactly what they were thinking—that this was her much older American boyfriend, and he was wearing sunglasses in the rain, and he was smoking with brazen disregard for the dour nuns standing guard at the school gates. They never had to know that he was only her young uncle, and with his simple hug, Kevin had provided her with the one thing she'd lacked since she'd transferred to Saint Brigid's: mystique.

"Nice monkey suit," he said, holding Maggie at arm's length to check out her blazer and knee socks. "You look like a member of the Hitler youth."

"Yeah, well you look positively anorexic," she responded. "I practically walked past you, you're so skinny."

"I'm on the rock star's diet. You ever seen a chubby Kurt Cobain? A portly Keith Richards? A plus-sized Lou Reed? I have an image to attend to, Mags. I am hungry, though. Take me somewhere I can get a Guinness and some haggis."

"Haggis is Scottish, idiot."

"Listen to this!" He swung an arm around her shoulder. "Three months in Ireland and she's a goddamn cultural ambassador."

They walked past Martello Terrace, down by the harbor where boats rocked in the shallow tide and seagulls strutted, pecking at fish bones and hamburger wrappers, and past the shuttered carnival. It was a dark afternoon, and the only people around were clumps of school kids, horsing around happily in celebration of the end of the term.

"So this is Ireland," he said, stopping to look across the water at the dark blur of Bray Head.

"Yeah, this is it," said Maggie. "It's beautiful, isn't it?"

"It has a soggy sort of grandeur, yes," he admitted, "though I resent it for stealing you away from us."

They walked down the Strand Road to Harry and Rose's, a chipper that was popular with the older Saint Brigid's girls. Maggie had never been there before, but she wanted to show him off. They ordered snack boxes, and when they sat down to eat, Maggie was able to get a good look at Kevin for the first time in months. He didn't look well. His hair, which had grown longer, was tied into a limp, oily ponytail at the nape of his neck. His skin was pallid and slick, as if it had been boiled raw, and his face was so thin she could see his bouncy Adam's apple and two slices of cheekbone. Even his teeth were mossy looking, like he hadn't brushed them in a while. His eyes, always his most arresting feature, bulged in their sockets, stream-water clear and dangerously blue.

"So, I quit the band," he said, raking a fry through a plastic cup of curry sauce.

Maggie gasped.

"You *quit*? But *why*? You said Selfish Fetus was going to be the next big thing! I thought you had a gig lined up at the Double Door!"

"*Did*. Don't anymore."

"But why?"

"Me and Rockhead had creative differences. Nail. Coffin. Over." He waved a hand dismissively. "It's band shit, Mags. You don't even want to hear it. You and your teenage girlfriends probably have less drama than we did. It's embarrassing. I don't even want to get into it."

"Well, did you guys have a fight or something?"

Kevin wiped his mouth, leaned onto the back legs of his chair.

"Not really. It's more that our aesthetic visions were at odds. Rockhead wanted to begin taking us, musically, in a different direction—sort of pop rock, bouncy guitars, appeal to a broader audience, et cetera, et cetera."

"He wanted you to start playing *pop* music? That's awful!"

"Look," he said, "I'm not going to fault the guy. Rockhead recently knocked up this girl he's been seeing. The kid's gonna be born in a few months, and working at the tree nursery at Menard's ain't gonna cut it anymore. So I *get* it. He wants to stop playing these small gigs, he wants to make some real money off this thing we have going. But the problem is, he's not going to take something that *I* created and neuter it into something that suburban moms can bop along to while they push the fuckin' cart around the grocery store. Music for the faint of heart, the sedated, the *ungulated*. No thank you."

"So what are you going to do?"

Kevin shrugged, lit a cigarette, tossed the ash in the empty curry cup.

"Gonna do what I always do. Start anew. Rebuild from the ground up. Recruit some new musicians and make a new sound. It's 1993, and it's an exciting time for music. Nine Inch Nails were just on *Saturday Night Live*. Nine Inch Nails! I mean, on network television! This is what Rockhead doesn't get: you don't have to shittify your music to make people listen to it. If it's good, people will listen. Period."

"So who have you been playing with, then?"

"Nobody."

As proof, he held up his hands and showed her the tips of his fingers, once white with bubbled-over calluses. They looked now like regular fingers.

"So no more Selfish Fetus at all?"

"No more Selfish Fetus."

Maggie slumped in her chair, so deflated by this news that Kevin leaned across the table and cuffed her gently on the shoulder.

"Mags, listen to me: Have you ever heard of Fecal Matter?"

"Isn't that, like, feces? Like, *poo*?"

Kevin laughed.

"Well yes, it is *poo*. But more significantly, it's the name of Kurt Cobain's first band. But you've never heard of them—and why should you? It was probably a bunch of little sixteen-year-olds—no offense—doing terrible Sex Pistols covers. My point is that every great musician needs to get a dumb band with a dumb name out of their system—I mean, come on! Selfish Fetus? What the fuck?— before they can become the artist they were meant to be."

"But I liked the name Selfish Fetus," Maggie said weakly.

Kevin crumpled up his bag of fries and smiled at her sadly.

"I know you did, honey. But you're blinded by familial loyalty. It's the *world* that needs to love me—and it's got to happen on my own terms."

He counted out the money, slowly, examining the new coins and bills, and got up to pay the cashier. They walked back to the house in the falling light, talking music, with Bray Head at their backs.

With Nanny Ei and Kevin around, Christmas Eve at Colm's house almost felt like home. The women cooked a big dinner, bumping into each other in the tiny kitchen, and the whole house filled with the rich smells of stewed turnips and roasting meat. Colm played a Johnny Cash album on his old record player, and since it was the only kind of music everyone could agree on, they listened to the same songs again and again—"Folsom Prison Blues," "I Walk the Line," "A Boy Named Sue." Maggie watched the interactions between Colm and Kevin carefully, remembering how her mom had said there was "no love lost between those two," but they acted civilly to each other, if a little stiff. They drank bottles of Heineken kept cold outside while Laura and Nanny Ei sipped hot whiskeys. The air thickened with cooking smells, and the television, a staple of the sitting room most evenings, stood mute and forgotten, drowned out by the chatter and the laughter. The Christmas tree was lit, shining with cheap glass ornaments purchased in a hurry from Dunne's.

It was the happiest Maggie had been in months.

After the plates were cleared and the dishes sat drying in the rack, they all piled into Colm's truck and headed down to the Quayside to hear some Irish music. The pub was packed with families, sleepy and content after their Christmas Eve dinners. A small band occupied the corner near the windows, made up of a guitarist, a bodhran player, and an old man with a tin whistle. They took over the last empty table, and Colm went off to order drinks for everybody.

Maggie had been thinking about Eoin so much that when she saw him ducking through the crowd bussing tables, it took her a moment to recognize that it was really him. He wore the same outfit he had on when she met him coming back from Dan

Sean's: tracksuit pants and a faded red Liverpool hoodie, and he was even more handsome than she remembered, with his close-cropped dark hair and pale blue eyes. He moved from table to table, picking up ashtrays and dumping them into a large metal bucket under his arm. He didn't rush, but he didn't stop to talk to anybody, either. He was unobtrusive, subtle, his movements flowing like a dancer's, as if dumping ashtrays was an art form that only he had perfected. Maggie watched him as he wove through the bar, finally making his way over in her direction. He picked up the tin tray in the middle of their table where Nanny Ei had just crushed out one of her Capris, dumped it, and, setting it back on the table, he looked up and met her eyes with a start. He was seeing her for the first time, she could tell. He smiled a little smile that was meant only for her, a smile that said, "I remember you," and then he was gone, carrying his bucket of butts out through the back door and into the alley.

Kevin leaned across to her.

"Who was *that*?"

"Oh, I don't know," Maggie said quickly. "Just some guy I met a while back." She could feel the color flaring in her cheeks and was grateful for the dimness of the bar.

"You want me to get the lowdown on him or what?"

"No! Please don't say anything to him."

"Mags! I'm disappointed in you. Of course I won't say anything to *him*. I'll just sniff around a little, find out if anyone knows his name."

Maggie, unable to control her smile, said, "I *know* his name. It's Eoin."

"Oh. I see. What a name. Like something from a Sir Walter Scott novel."

"A *what*?"

"Does this Eoin have a girlfriend?"

"I don't know!"

"Well, let's find out, shall we?"

Before she could stop him, he was sauntering up to the bar. First, he ordered a drink from the middle-aged lady behind the counter, then, he convinced her to take a shot with him, and soon enough the two of them were leaning elbow to elbow across the bar, talking like old friends. This was the magic of Uncle Kevin: he always knew exactly what to say to make people fall in love with him.

Ten minutes later, he returned to the table.

"That lovely woman I was just chatting with is none other than Rosie Horan, owner and proprietor of the Quayside bar, aunt and caretaker of one Eoin Brennan, aged seventeen, star forward on the Saint Brendan's football team, Liverpool supporter, astrological sign Taurus, marital status, single. I did not ask whether he was circumcised: I leave that, dear niece, for you to find out for yourself."

This was all too much to process at once—months of speculation had now given way to a ticking off of actual facts—she even knew his last name! Maggie immediately began gnawing at her fingernails.

"*Please* don't tell me you told her you were asking for me?" she begged.

"Are you kidding?" Kevin slugged back his pint. "I was a master of subtlety. You can thank me by buying me my next beer."

In fact, the adults drank many more beers as the night spun on. Ronnie, bored, sat at the table and quietly built a structure of bar napkins and straws. Maggie drank her Club Orange and only pretended to look bored. She felt horribly self-conscious about her clothing, her posture, her hair, and her bitten nails, beset with the knowledge that at any moment, Eoin might be looking at her.

Around midnight, Kevin successfully cajoled the guitar player, a sylphish, crop-haired girl with shredded jeans and combat boots, to let him play a song. He slipped the girl's guitar strap around his shoulder, and the effect of this—the hollow wood nestled against his heart—was immediate. He stood up straighter, he grew taller, a pink urgency flickered into his cheeks. He began to sing "Fairytale of New York," one of the few Irish songs he knew, his lips brushing the microphone, his voice strong and gravelly and full of that strange holiday sadness of twinkling lights hanging in freezing windows.

Old couples began to pair off and spin each other around, and the younger ones lined the walls, clapping and stomping their feet and swishing their drinks. In that little pub, on that little stage by the windows, Kevin was a life force, a star. With the aid of an instrument, he could spend fours hours in a new country and fit in better than Maggie could after four months. He sang about drunk tanks and love and Christmas hopes, but in the spaces between the words of the song and in the cold shadows of his closed eyes rested all the things that he allowed to escape from himself only on the stage. Watching him, Maggie thought of their conversation earlier that day—how he had quit the band, quit his music, hadn't picked up a guitar in months. She could see the way he picked gingerly at the strings on his uncalloused fingers. His voice wasn't beautiful, but it had always contained a kind of arresting truth. Now, too, Maggie detected a new quality—a desperation that had not been there before. Looking around the table at her family, she knew that Nanny Ei heard it, too. Her grandmother was leaning forward, holding her cigarette aloft while the ash grew longer and longer, and she was not listening to her son like the rest of them were but watching him, the movements of his long, skeletal fingers, the closed bruises of his eyes.

He finished singing and handed the girl her guitar. The Quayside erupted into applause and whoops, and Kevin smiled and the men seated at the bar called him over, waving their money at him in a clamor of who could be the first to buy him a pint. Maggie got up to use the bathroom. In front of the sink she smoothed her hair and wished she'd worn more makeup than the smudgy concealer she'd dabbed onto the broken-out skin at her jawline. When she crossed the room and returned to her seat, she felt that change in atmosphere, the quickening of her heart that told her Eoin was watching her. At first she thought maybe it was just wishful thinking, but then she caught him, twice, eyeing her as he wiped down tables with a bar rag, or carried towers of empty pint glasses behind the counter to be washed. The first two times, he looked away as soon as she made eye contact, but on the third, as he stood behind the counter dunking glasses in soapy water, when she looked at him, he held her gaze, steady and unashamed, a half smile, a dare, on his face.

Near closing time, Nanny Ei stamped out her final cigarette of the evening and helped a bleary-eyed Ronnie into her coat.

"It's getting late, Mags. Why don't you come home in the taxi with us?"

"I think I'll stay for a bit," Maggie said, still dizzy from Eoin's lingering, inscrutable smile.

"Aren't you tired? Tomorrow's Christmas, remember."

But Christmas was for children, and Maggie wasn't one of those anymore. How could she possibly go home when, all around her, life was *finally* starting to happen?

"Just for a little longer, Nanny," she said. She kissed her grandmother's talcum cheek and watched her lead Ronnie out by the hand. Rosie Horan closed the velvet curtains and a sing-song began among the local men: minor key ballads, mostly, about Ireland's sad past. By now, every adult in the place was drunk, but Laura was loudly so. Maggie wasn't bothered by the men who lurched quietly and watched the singing with glassy-eyed reverence, but her mother, whose low-cut sweater revealed cleavage that was just beginning to crack into faint wrinkles at the surface, and who was slugging down Bulmers glass by watery glass, dribbling condensation onto the lap of her jeans, was another matter.

When a potbellied old farmer began to sing in the Sean nós style, a form of Gaelic singing unaccompanied by instruments, his rich voice lingered over the high notes and the foreign words in a way that was so hauntingly beautiful the whole pub fell into a reverential silence. He finished the last trembling note, and the place shattered with cheers and applause. Then Laura stood up, wobbly and hippy, and cleared her throat.

No. Maggie said silently. *No no no no.*

But before she could run across the room, put a hand over her mother's mouth and drag her out of the bar, Laura was belting out, with tone-deaf joyfulness, the first verse of "Dancing Queen," destroying the magic spell the farmer's traditional singing had cast over the dark pub.

Maggie sat in the booth, horrified, as her mom leaned her head back, waving two pint glasses above her head like a pair of castanets, and bellowed the first verse of the song while the locals rolled their eyes and drifted toward the door.

"You think that's bad?" Eoin was suddenly next to her, drying a glass with a dirty towel. "You should get a load of my old lady sometime."

He smelled like stale smoke and clean laundry, and the Christmas lights hanging from the ceiling glinted off his black-lashed eyes. Maggie could feel her nerves begin to tremble.

"She's not usually like this," she apologized. "She's usually more . . . normal."

"Hey, you don't have to explain it to me." He put his towel down and sat across from her at the empty table. "So, do you know how to find your way home now?"

"Yeah. Thanks." She smiled down at the table. "I wish I was there right now so I wouldn't have to witness this."

"Ah, this is nothin'." He waved a hand. "This bar's seen much worse. Besides, I'm glad you're still here."

Before she could let this comment sink in and begin

dissecting it for meaning, her mom began to strut around in her tight, stained sweater, eyes closed, red mouth wailing the chorus into the Bulmers bottle she was using for a microphone. Colm stood near the door with his arms crossed, his lips tight with disapproval. The rows of older men standing at the bar with Kevin ogled Maggie's mother with the kind of detached fascination they might display watching strippers, wondering what it would be like to screw her while at the same time being thankful that she wasn't *their* wife. They nudged each other as she sashayed around the bar grinding into their backs, stumbling into the counter until finally Kevin got up, yanked her arm, and whispered something fiercely into her ear. Her singing stopped abruptly.

"Get your fuckin' hands off me," Laura screeched, shaking her arm from Kevin's grasp. He said something in a low voice, his forehead creased with fury.

"Like you should talk!" she screamed, and flung the contents of her pint glass in his face. The pub fell into a different kind of silence now. Kevin wiped his eyes slowly with the back of his sleeve.

"Get your drunk ass out of this bar and into the truck," he said, jabbing a finger centimeters from her nose.

"I'd appreciate it if you took your fuckin' finger out of my wife's face." Colm had put down his own drink now and placed himself between Laura and Kevin, inches from Kevin's face. "And watch how you talk to her while you're at it."

"I'll talk to her however I want when she acts like a drunk fuckin' slob," Kevin said. "What are you gonna say about it?"

"You've been warned now," Colm said slowly. "You've been warned."

Kevin stepped away from Colm and turned his back. A sigh was felt in the room, half relief and half disappointment—it didn't look like there would be a fight after all. Kevin stood still, his shoulders tensing. He seemed to be considering something.

Then, suddenly, he extended a long, white arm and swung. He connected with Colm's jaw with a clean smack that sent Colm's head snapping back. He stumbled backward and crashed against the counter, his arm breaking glasses. A thread of blood pooled beneath his nostril. He wiped it away and grinned at Kevin, a grin tinged with relief, because all was out in the open now. They could finally hate each other freely.

The two men squared up.

"Take it outside if you're gonna fight," Rosie Horan yelled, flapping her bar rag at them. But they were already upon each other. Kevin swung again and Colm ducked, barreling into Kevin's chest with his bulldog head, and both men fell to the ground, kicking down stools and sending bottles skittering and shattering across the stone floor. The men at the counter yelled encouragement while the women shrieked at them to stop. Kevin was sallow and skinny to the point of emaciation, and Colm outweighed him by at least fifty pounds of thick muscle. It would have been a quick fight, except for the fact that Kevin was as vicious and tenacious as a rat. They grappled and rolled across the floor until finally, Colm was able to knock Kevin to the ground and straddle him, his big thighs clenching Kevin's ribs, while Kevin's legs thrashed beneath him. Blood poured from his crumpled nose, his knuckles scraped against the rough floor, and still he flailed and swung, clawing long, pink scratches across the pale, hairless meat of Colm's inner forearms.

"Are you finished?" Colm yelled, ducking the weak punches easily and holding Kevin's face down with a splayed hand. "Give up, will you, before I fuckin' kill you!" He lifted his hand away. Kevin was panting and silent. The rest of the bar began to relax. But Maggie knew better. Kevin never would give up, not until he or Colm was dead. She heard a gurgling in his throat, and then he bucked his hips forward and hocked a white wad of spit into Colm's face. It hung from Colm's eyelid and swung there while

Kevin managed to squirm free, get back on swaying feet, and pull Colm into a headlock that sent the two men bursting out the front door of the pub, tangling themselves in Christmas lights that snapped and popped under their feet. They kicked and tripped across the wet road until they were on the sandy ground before the tarp-covered carnival and the Ferris wheel, which sat creaking in the wind in silent judgment, snow dusting its highest carriages. The bar emptied out into the street and Kevin, as if the salty air had awakened him, began to scream a maniac's scream, the kind Maggie had heard in the Selfish Fetus song "Nightstick," a scream that filled the sky and made the crowd glance at each other warily, until it was silenced, finally, by Colm's decisive fist to his face, and Kevin fell, finally defeated, in the sand. In the darkness, his thin body looked like a piece of washed-up kelp.

Maggie ran to him and knelt next to his body. His eyes were puffed into black slits; his nose and lips ran with blood. He reached up a hand, brushed sand into her hair.

" 'M fine," he slurred through thickening lips. A siren blared, and the guards arrived in a whirl of flashing blue light, scattering the crowd back. Dizzy with the lights and the wailing sirens and an all-powerful relief that that he wasn't dead, Maggie hiccupped, and the four Club Oranges she'd drunk throughout the night reappeared in a fizzy torrent of tangerine vomit in the sand.

Eoin retreated to the bar to help his aunt clean up the overturned tables and broken glasses while Maggie walked home with Kevin, who said nothing but leaned into her, breathed noisily from his mouth, and dabbed at his broken nose with a red-soaked sleeve. She was in bed by the time Colm and Laura arrived home, and she fell asleep, at last, lulled into nightmares by the persistent murmur of their arguing through the wall.

She was awoken in the predawn darkness by a shaking of her toe. She nearly screamed out when she saw the hideous clown face hovering at the end of the bed. Her eyes adjusted, and she realized that the clown was Kevin, his pale blue eyes swallowed up in mushroom bruises, his nose cracked at an obscene angle. He had his bags with him.

"Just wanted to say Merry Christmas, Mags," he whispered. "I'm taking off a bit earlier than expected."

Maggie sat up.

"But I thought you were staying until New Years?"

He found her hand and held it. It was freezing and clammy, as if he'd just been in water.

"Plans have changed. I can't be under the same roof as your mother and that dude."

"They didn't kick you out, did they?" She felt hatred and a wild loyalty rise within her.

"Oh no. Not this time. This time, it's my decision. I gotta get back anyway, got some things with this new band I'm starting that I gotta take care of."

"But—what about us? What about spending Christmas with us?" She was aware that she was whining, that her lip was trembling and she was close to tears. But she couldn't help it. She was so sick of everything being decided by the adults in her life, who only acted like adults when they felt like it.

"Next year, honey," he said. "You really think this marriage is gonna last? This time next year, you'll be back home in Chicago, and we'll have Christmas like normal people." He smiled at her then, his teeth a broken row of tombstones, kissed her forehead, and left the room.

The front door opened and closed, and she watched her uncle limp out to the street, a short-brimmed hat his only defense against the wind. He hitched his backpack on his shoulder, turned once to wave at Maggie's window, then disappeared down the hill and was gone.

6

Maggie lay awake for a long time after Kevin left. She thought about him, about the demise of Selfish Fetus, about her messed-up family. But mostly she thought of Eoin. What was the meaning behind the inscrutable way he smiled at her as he cleared ashtrays and wiped down tables? Around eight she heard Ronnie's quiet footsteps, the static click of the television. An hour later, Nanny Ei's lungs hacked into consciousness, a toilet flushed, and then there was the snap of a lighter and the sighing inhalation of the morning cigarette. The murmur of conversation between Ronnie and Nanny Ei, the sizzle of eggs in a pan. Then, on the other side of the wall, the awful creaking of Laura and Colm. If they were loud when they were drinking, they were almost as bad when they were hungover. Maggie could hear her mom loudest of all, the moaning, the panting. She yanked her pillow over ears. *You'd think that after last night, they wouldn't be in the mood.* The headboard banged one final time, so hard that the pile of CDs on Maggie's dresser trembled. *Why can't Mom be discreet about anything?* She wondered. *Why is it that everything she feels, she has to make everybody else feel, too?*

The family ate breakfast quietly, heads bowed, while Nanny Ei forced the conversation along between gaping silences. Maggie could smell the booze coming off her mom's skin, the stale cigarettes off her stepfather. They guzzled tea through cracked lips.

"Sausage, Mags?"

Maggie took the plate, smiling pointedly at her grandmother to indicate that Nanny Ei was the only adult in the room who she did not want to disown. She bit into the meat, the rich, greasy taste filling her mouth and making her want to vomit. Johnny Cash still played on the record player, but in the gray morning light, with a family-wide hangover, the deep bass of his voice felt alien and threatening. Even so, it was better than the sound of rumbling throats and dry mouths chewing and swallowing.

"Well. Should someone go and wake up Kevin?" Nanny Ei said his name carefully, bleaching out any hint of reprimand she might be directing at Colm as she cleared plates.

"Sure, wake him up," he said, his mouth full of eggs. "No hard feelings here."

Laura smiled tightly and reached for his arm.

Maggie bit into her toast. She wanted to savor this moment until the time when the secret no longer belonged to her and Kevin alone. She waited until Nanny Ei was nearly to the hallway before she made the announcement.

"He left."

Everyone looked at her.

"What do you mean left?"

"I mean, he's gone."

Maggie glanced up from her plate at Nanny Ei, whose face had taken on the same perplexed, fearful expression it had at the Quayside, when she'd held a forgotten cigarette between her fingers and watched her son play "Fairytale of New York," those pale fingers coaxing out of a guitar emotions that he himself would never express. It was a look that wondered how a mother could give a child life and still find herself, more and more as the years went by, locked out and estranged from that child's inner life. Since they'd moved to Bray, Maggie had often caught her own mother looking at her in the same way.

"He left for the airport a couple hours ago," she said, leveling her gaze at Colm. A dusting of dried blood clung to his knuckles. "He said he doesn't want to stay here, under this roof, with you people."

Ronnie began pushing the eggs around on her plate with great concentration. Colm, looking supremely weary, pinched the skin at the bridge of his nose and sighed. Laura got up and threw a handful of dirty silverware into the sink.

"That's just fucking great!"

"Laura Lynch!" Nanny Ei said sharply. "For Christ's sake, will you watch your language in front of your children?"

"Well, I'm sorry, Mother, but here's another family holiday he's ruined. He just *had* to make me and Colm look like the bad guys. It's like he's always trying to pit me against my own children! And it works every time! Because of course, whose side is a teenager gonna take? Her mother's, or her twenty-six-year-old rock star uncle's, who sends her care packages every once in a while?" She pointed a dirty spoon at Maggie. "And let me just say that if you are mad at me or Colm—if you blame us for *any* of this—then you're being incredibly unfair."

"*I'm* being unfair?" Maggie could feel the hotness at the back of her eyes. "*You're* the one who—and *Colm's* the one who practically *killed* him—" She stopped and looked up at the timber-slatted ceiling. She would never forgive herself if she started to cry now. It seemed that whenever she was gaining ground in an argument with her mom, she burst into helpless tears.

"He didn't start that! And you know it!" Laura was standing behind Colm now, her hands pressing into his thick shoulders.

"Well, we can all sit here and fight," Nanny Ei interjected, "or somebody can drive out to the airport and see if we can go get him. It's only 11:00, he surely can't have left yet."

"Oh, let him go," Colm said, pushing his plate away. "He doesn't want to be here, that's his business. Why do ye always let him ruin things? That's why he does this shit, because somebody always runs after and tries to fix it. He's twenty-six fuckin' years old! He ain't a fuckin' cripple is he? He ain't a retard, is he? So let him be!"

"Stop yelling!" Ronnie shouted, and then ran off to her room, her blue nightgown trailing behind her.

"Who cares what *you* think?" Maggie slid back from the table and stood facing her stepfather. "You think you're part of our family now? You're just some guy my mom met at a bar."

"Met and married," Colm said. "I think that counts for something."

"You were just the first one to come along who was dumb enough," Maggie snapped.

"Margaret Marie!" Laura lifted the dishrag to her eyes.

"Mom, I didn't mean—" She looked down at the table full of empty plates. She had intended the words to have an effect, but she hadn't exactly meant to make her mother cry.

"Sweetheart, your uncle is a bleeding fuckin' druggie." Colm smiled at Maggie, a mean smirk that showed the top row of his white, square teeth. "Thought you should know that. So at least when you stand here and defend him, you know what you're defending. Or haven't you ever looked at the crook of his elbow? No wonder he's such an admirer of Kurt Cobain. He's just like him, except for the talent part."

Maggie shook her head. Suddenly, it all made sense: the bulging eyes, the boiled-out skin, the emaciated frame. Self-destruction had a look, a smell. He wore his addiction like a loose cape, as close to the surface as blue veins. That's what had scared her so much, under the garish lights of Harry and Rose's, not his quitting the band. She felt both enraged and impotent. She hated that all her good days had to be followed by bad ones, and she was furious, too, because she knew that Colm was right—that loving Kevin meant always having to defend him. She felt a hand, cool and dry, on her bare shoulder.

"You shouldn't have told her that," her mom said quietly.

"I already knew," Maggie said quickly, shaking Laura's hand away. Maggie would be damned if she'd let Colm think that he could tell her something about Kevin that she didn't already know herself. "I'd still pick him over any one of you, any day of the week."

She walked out of the room and into Ronnie's bedroom, where her sister cried softly under her blankets, her Christmas ruined. Maggie sat at the edge of Ronnie's bed, put her hand gently on her sister's thin back.

"I'm sorry you have to be a part of this crappy family, Ron," she whispered. Ronnie curled tighter into her ball beneath the covers and heaved a sob. Maggie got up, grabbed her Discman and her jacket from her own bedroom, and walked past the table of stunned adults, out into the cold morning. She could still hear Johnny Cash singing as she headed up the road.

It was Christmas Day in County Wicklow, the rain blowing in from the sea, and by the time she made it up the back hill to Dan Sean's house, Maggie was soaked, her face ruddy with rain. She knocked once, then let herself in, as was the custom at Dan Sean's. He was sitting in his usual spot, the high-backed velvet chair in front of the enormous fireplace. Mike had strung Christmas lights and tinsel around the ceiling, and it lightened up the drab Oriental carpet, the wallpaper etched in years of dust, the pictures, brown and fading, in their frames.

He smiled at her beneath his Cossack's hat and waved her in. He was dressed for the holiday in a more dapper manner than usual, a bright green scarf knotted at the loose skin of his neck. Maggie went over to him and kissed his cheek, which was soft and hairless as a baby's.

"Happy Christmas, Dan Sean."

He insisted on making the tea himself, and she sat with him in front of the fire for the whole afternoon, the mug cooling in her hands. There were no arguments or whispered conversations, just the crackling of the fire, Dan Sean's whistled breathing, and the rain against the window. It calmed her. In the presence of all his years, it was hard for Maggie to feel that her problems were all that special. As the shadows lengthened outside the windows, she reached into her jacket pocket and held Kevin's compass in her palm, rolled it across her knuckles like an ocean-smoothed stone, and let her anger ebb away into Dan Sean's great ancientness. His head nodded forward on the lump of his scarf, the cat and dog stretched indolently next to each other, the fire flickered, the tinsel sparkled, and it began to finally feel like Christmas.

Mike came in after the sun went down and pointed at the hunched form in the rocking chair.

"He sleeping?"

Maggie nodded.

"We're just going to have a bit of dinner down at the house," he said. "Dan Sean?" He put a hand softly on a corduroy knee, and the old man awoke with a jerk and a snort.

"I was just on my way, anyway," said Maggie.

"I heard about what happened down at the Quayside last night," Mike said. "With your uncle. Nothing like the holidays to bring out the worst in people."

"They've never gotten along," she explained. "It's just family stuff."

Dan Sean stood creakily and ambled off to the bathroom.

"It's good of you to come up here and see him," Mike said. "Poor old fella. Sometimes it's hard, with the family and the kids and all, to get up and see him as much as I'd like. I hate thinking of him up here all alone for hours at a stretch. But he won't move in with us. Everything important that's ever happened to him has happened within these walls. He says he won't leave till he's carried out in a casket like his wife and child before him, the stubborn old codger."

While Dan Sean held onto Mike's arm and retreated slowly down the hill, Maggie walked home in the darkness. The ditches along the side of the road and the shadows of stone fences were all familiar now. She lingered, walking slowly past Rosie Horan's house where, back from the road, the sitting room windows gleamed their bright warmth. Human figures moved about behind the bright squares like moths, and Maggie walked as slowly as she dared, squinting for a sign of a buzzed head and broad shoulders. *Just to see him from far away would be enough*, she thought, *after a Christmas like this one.* But as she passed by, someone reached up and shut the curtains.

When she got home, dinner was almost ready and nobody asked where she had been. Maggie ate a little roast beef and some lumpy potatoes. The food felt heavy in her stomach and made her tired. Ronnie had gotten a puzzle for Christmas, a giant map whose pieces were every country in the world. When dinner was over, the two of them spread it on the carpet in front of the Christmas tree and split up the continents between them. Africa gave them the most problems, and they stayed up later than all the adults, who had gone to bed early to end the dull ache of their hangovers. By the time the clock had moved past midnight on Christmas 1993, they finally clicked the last piece into place: Angola, nestled between Zaire and Namibia and bordering the vast, lapping Atlantic. Then, having succeeded in putting the world back together, they went to bed.

When Maggie was a little girl, she suffered from terrible ear infections. They always got worse in the middle of the night, while her mom was out working at the bar. When she cried out in pain, Nanny Ei would come into her bedroom, lay her on her side, and squirt a medication down her ear canal that fizzed through the clogging pus, making Maggie feel like her ears were melting from the inside out. The pills she was given made her groggy and heavy-headed, and everything—her bedroom carpeting, the streetlights outside, her pink and gold bedspread—took on funhouse colors that made her reach out her limp fingers in weak wonder.

On these fevered nights, while she tossed and turned, Uncle Kevin would come into her room, sit at the edge of her bed, and play softly on his guitar. He was eighteen then and deeply entrenched in his hippie phase. He wore the same tattered pair of gray corduroys every day and had a ponytail of fat, fuzzy dreadlocks that Nanny Ei was always threatening to chop off in his sleep. When he leaned over Maggie to kiss her good night, they brushed her forehead, softer than they looked, and filled her room with their loamy smell. It still remained one of Maggie's favorite memories, lying with the pressure leaking out of her ears and the bedspread soft and swirling pink and her uncle singing folk songs to her in the darkness: *I wish I was a headlight on a northbound train. I wish I was a headlight on a northbound train. I'd shine my light through cool Colorado rain.*

Kevin had a mystical hold on the memories of the people who loved him, a magnetic pull, and maybe this was the reason that although Nanny Ei had planned to stay in Bray until New Year's Day, she became anxious to get back to Chicago as soon as Christmas was over. On Saint Stephen's Day, the family took the train to Dublin and walked the holiday-abandoned streets along the path of the Liffey, which was black and oily, its concrete banks clotted with dark moss and the occasional silver of dead fish. The following day, Nanny Ei announced that she was worried about Kevin, about whether he got home okay, about whether he had gone to the hospital to get his nose set, about whether the transient women and burnout men with whom he associated were sleeping naked on her hand-patched quilts while she was out of town. There was another argument, of course, with Laura yelling and Colm shaking his head and Ronnie crying and Maggie quietly seething. Nanny Ei left the following morning.

Aíne returned from Kilkenny the same day and immediately called Maggie to put the screws to her to go on another double date with Paul. Maggie refused, until Aíne, near tears, confessed that her mother wouldn't let her spend time alone with Paddy and that she needed Maggie and Paul to act as buffers.

"You don't have to do anything you don't want to do," she begged. "You don't even have to *talk* to each other if you don't want to. You just need to *be* there."

"Why don't you just lie to her about who you're going out with?" Maggie asked. "That's what I would do."

"This isn't a big city like Chicago," Aíne sighed. "My mother's got spies all over the place. Can't you just come out with us for one night? I know the two of you didn't fall madly in love or anything last time, but Paul's a lovely fella once you get to know him. Smart, too. *Please?*"

And Paul *was* nice. He wasn't bad looking either. But then there was the matter of his cold, acrobatic tongue. Kissing had felt more intimate—more *physical*—than Maggie had anticipated. She'd been aware of the soft, mammalian puffs of Paul's nostrils, the tremor of his shaking hands. It wasn't something she thought she could fake her way through again, especially because, having experienced it, it just made her wonder all the more intensely what it would be like to kiss Eoin. Would it be different with every boy? Was kissing a boy the one true way to find out how you felt about them?

"Fine," Maggie finally agreed. "But if you think I'm going to make out with him again, you're crazy."

They met the boys at the carnival later that evening. The night was damp; a cold, briny wind blew in from the sea. They took shelter underneath the heavy canvas shell that protected the magic teacups from the corrosive winter air. Inside, it was dark and cozy as a tepee, the teacups immobile, skewered like huge marshmallows at the ends of their metal spokes. The hub in the middle of the ride was large enough for the four of them to sit cross-legged in a tight circle, their backs against the cold spokes, squinting to see the features of each other's faces in the darkness and listening to the wind batter the tarp outside.

"Look what I brought," Paul grinned, pulling a small bottle of whiskey from the inside pocket of his coat. "Who wants some?"

"I don't drink," Aíne sniffed, nestling into Paddy's lap.

"Yeah." Paddy folded his skinny arms around her. "Keep that stuff to yourself, Paul."

"Suit yourself, lads." Paul unscrewed the cap and took a swig, grimacing as the liquor spilled down his throat. "Maggie? Care for a nip?"

Back in Chicago, it was mostly the rich kids who spent their weekends getting sloshed on the stolen contents of their parents' liquor cabinets. As the daughter of a bartender, and a member of the hard-partying Lynch family, Maggie had never really seen the allure. But the events of the last few days had put her in a self-destructive mood.

"Hand it over," she said, ignoring Aíne's disapproving glare, and took a sip big enough to make her eyes burn.

"Strong stuff, isn't it?" Paul laughed as she wiped her eyes.

"It's not *that* strong." She took an even bigger drink, then, and forced it down with a straight face. It continued in this way: while Paddy and Aíne whispered and kissed on their side of the teacup's hub, she and Paul passed the bottle back and forth. In twenty minutes, it was empty. Maggie scooted closer to Paul, and taking her hint, his fingers crept across her back and came to rest around her shoulder. *Our first kiss wasn't so awful,* she thought. *I mean, it could have been a lot worse.* She experimented with resting her head on his arm. It didn't feel terrible. On the other side of the hub, Aíne was welded to Paddy with the needy grip of a skydiving pupil to her instructor. He began reciting to her some poetry he'd learned in school.

"*Te spectem suprema mihi cum venerit hora,*" he said, twining his fingers around hers, "*Et teneam moriens deficiente manu.*"

"That's Tibullus," slurred Paul. "We're in the same honors Latin class. Don't let him impress you, Aíne."

"But I know how to translate it, too," Paddy bragged. He turned back to Aíne and cleared his throat, looking deeply into her eyes in the way Maggie was sure he had practiced after seeing in a movie. "May I gaze upon you when my last hour has come, and dying, may I hold you with my faltering hand."

Aíne leaned in and kissed him. Maggie felt shot through with sudden jealousy—not because her friend had found love first, but because Aíne, for all her academic intelligence, was not the kind of girl to appreciate such poetry. What drove her was ambition, not passion. But Maggie, who had been raised on song lyrics as their own kind of poetry, felt tears in her eyes. She wiped them away fiercely. She'd die before she let them know what words meant to her. From her slumped position under Paul's arm, she called, "Don't make me *vomit*."

"I wouldn't expect you to appreciate Tibullus," said Paddy imperiously. "You're from a rough crowd, is what I've heard."

Maggie sat up.

"What's that supposed to mean?"

"It means I heard what happened to your uncle outside the Quayside. Got a right belting, I heard. And broke Rosie Horan's brand-new front door in the process."

"What do you know about my uncle, you nerdy little prick?" She scrambled to her feet, the liquor beating in her temples.

"I know he's a scumbag who likes to start trouble, and that he got what was coming to him, is what I know."

He smiled at her, a mean, goading smile, while Aíne watched from the safety of his dorky arms. Maggie grabbed the empty whiskey bottle from Paul's hand and threw it at Paddy's smug face as hard as she could. He and Aíne both ducked, and it shattered against the red polka-dotted surface of one of the magic teacups, spraying shards of glass all over the tiny space.

"Owww!" Aíne squealed, covering her face with her hands. A piece of broken bottle had knicked her in the soft indentation right below her eye, and blood began seeping from the wound.

"For fuck's sake!" Paddy yelled, nestling Aíne's face into his chest. "Mad bitch. Must run in the family, I guess."

"Maggie," Paul said, stumbling to his feet, his hair sloughing along the tarp roof, "are you all right?"

"Oh, I'm fine," she laughed, kicking some glass shards in Paddy's direction. "Never better."

"Maybe we should take a walk?"

"Anything's better than hanging out with these two losers." She threw open the tarp.

"You could at least say you're sorry," Aíne whimpered into Paddy's sweater.

"Yeah, well, I'm not." She looked back, once, then slipped through the tarp's opening and let it fall behind her. The whiskey's powers hit her square in the face when she and Paul emerged into the cold night. A wildness lapped in her chest, bringing out things in her that she hadn't known were there—*What's happening to me? Did I really throw that glass bottle and hurt my only friend?* Maybe it was a Lynch thing, striking out at the people you care about and not being able to apologize. Or maybe that was just a human race thing. *Maybe I'm just like Kevin.*

"Don't worry about the two of them," Paul said. "They aren't much craic anyway." He put an arm around her waist and they lurched through the tarp village. When they reached the Ferris wheel at the edge of the carnival, Maggie's head began to swim. She leaned up against the ride's cold iron base.

"I don't feel so good," she said.

"Are you going to gawk?" Paul asked.

"Maybe."

"See, I'm fine," he laughed. "Takes more than a little whiskey to get me drunk. I've been drinking with my older brothers since I was ten." He stood back to look at her face, to see if she was impressed by this fact. She tried to smile at him but her head hurt. He grabbed her waist and kissed her, his spit cold and wet on her lips. She kissed him back, her eyes drifting shut, her mouth lolling open. The wind came in icy blasts on her cheeks and forehead. She felt his cold fingers yank up her sweater and squeeze her breasts roughly. Above them, the empty Ferris wheel carriages creaked. He pulled her sweater off and then, after some fumbling, her bra, and dropped both pieces of clothing on the wet ground. Why bother spending twenty pounds on a lace bra from Brown Thomas, Maggie wondered, when the boy won't notice anyway? She could feel her nipples pucker and tighten in the salted wind. He began to suck them, hard, and she grimaced, looking over his head into the water and at Bray Head, silent and ponderous in the distance. It didn't occur to her to tell him to stop. With his free hand, he yanked at the button of her jeans, pulled down the zipper, and stuffed his hand down her underpants. He found her warm opening, and twisted two fingers inside. Her breath caught sharply as the tight tissue inside of her unknit itself and gave way. Then the strangest thing happened. The pain of what he was doing to her somehow made her feel better. A memory floated before her, of Samantha Steinle, a weird, quiet girl from her Chicago neighborhood who, in seventh grade, had taken Maggie into the bathroom stall during recess, unbuttoned the cuff of her school blouse, and showed Maggie the patterns of razor marks that she'd scored herself with from wrist to elbow.

"Hurting myself is the only thing that makes me feel better," Samantha had said. Now, with Paul's fingers twisting inside of her, his teeth on the thin skin of her breasts, she finally understood what Samantha had meant.

He pulled his hand from between her legs and she heard the dull clinking of his belt buckle, the sharp exhale of a zipper being undone.

"Put your mouth on it," he whispered into her neck, his forearm a heavy pressure on her shoulders, and she crouched on the wet ground, her naked spine facing seaward, the puddles soaking into the knees of her jeans. He put his hands on the back of her head and pushed her closer to his thighs so she was nearly choking on it, and then his whole body stiffened and he moaned in just the way she'd heard her mother and Colm moaning through the thin walls of their bedroom. To stop herself from vomiting, she spit it out on the wet ground.

Paul walked her home soon afterwards. He kept opening his mouth to say something, but she wouldn't look at him, so he didn't. In front of her house, he leaned in to kiss her good-bye but she ducked away and his lips landed on the cold shell of her ear.

"Well—I'll ring you, or something," he mumbled. Maggie

saw that he had not tucked his shirt back in, and that his shirt tails were all wrinkled along the bottom.

"Sure."

He turned, shambling toward the road with his hands in his pockets. In the morning she found a streak of bright red blood in the crotch of her underwear. She balled them up tightly and threw them in the trash. Then she took a long, steamy shower, even though she knew her mom would yell at her for using all the hot water, and she held her hands over her bruised breasts to protect them from the stinging water. She never thought she'd be one of those girls who gave her body to someone she didn't even like. But then, she thought, looking up at the tiled ceiling to stop herself from crying, wasn't that what growing up meant? Wasn't it just a succession of actions and incidents where you break your childhood promises to yourself and do the very things you always said you wouldn't do? And how many more promises would she have to break before she came out on the other side?

Though she was only six when it happened, Maggie could still remember the months before the breakup of her parents' marriage: the silent suppers, the late-night arguments, her dad slamming out the door and staying gone for days at a time, her mom spending spring nights out on the back porch with Joni Mitchell's *Blue* album and a bottle of white zinfandel to keep her company. So on the night before New Year's Eve, when Maggie awoke in the middle of the night, looked out the window, and saw her mother slumped on the back stoop with a glass of West Coast Cooler in her hand, humming along to "A Case of You" while the headlights of Colm's truck faded toward town, she was struck with the realization that maybe Kevin had been right. Maybe this time next year, they'd all be back home, curled up on the pullout couch at Nanny Ei's and watching the snow sift down over the crisscrossing alleys of Chicago. She'd grown to love the mountains and the fields of Wicklow, the smell of the sea, the way old and young mingled with each other in the pubs. She'd grown to love afternoons in front of Dan Sean's fire, the constant small talk about the weather, and the Irish poets she studied in Sister Geneve's English class. But these things, taken together, could not make up the fabric of a teenager's life. After what happened at the magic teacups, Maggie once again was friendless. Eoin, too, seemed like nothing more than a receding dream. If she didn't have anyone to miss in Ireland or Chicago, what difference did it make where she lived?

The thought of spending New Year's Eve with her mother and stepdad because she didn't have any friends of her own was plenty depressing. But on the morning of the holiday, Colm showed up at the Quayside with his toolbox and a sheepish apology and asked Rosie Horan if he could fix the door he'd broken in his brawl with Kevin. His penance made, Rosie forgave him, and the family made plans to ring in 1994 at the Quayside. Suddenly, the night's prospects didn't seem so dismal: Eoin might be there. With renewed hope, Maggie blasted *Nevermind* and put on her black miniskirt and the blue turtleneck that Nanny Ei said brought out her eyes. She curled her hair with Laura's hot rollers and rimmed her lashes in smudged black liner.

"Whoa," said Colm when she clicked out of the bathroom in her knee-high boots.

"When did my beautiful little girl become a beautiful woman?" Laura said, reaching out and tucking a soft curl behind Maggie's ear.

"Mom, don't," said Maggie, but she had to bite the inside of her cheek to keep from smiling.

The pub was sweaty and smoky and packed. The DJ played Tom Jones while women in sequined sweaters with hairspray-frozen updos and men in pressed shirts and good jeans waltzed together in the cramped spaces between tables, giddy to be dressed up and free of their children for the night. The Christmas lights that Colm and Kevin had ripped down had been replaced. Colorful strands were tacked neatly around the newly repaired front door. Tinsel was draped along the liquor shelves, and a table by the front windows held aluminum tins of ham and cabbage and fried potatoes.

"There's no other *kids* here," Ronnie sighed, shoving into the booth next to Maggie while their mother disappeared with Colm into the crowd. "What are we supposed to do all night?"

A pair of white-permed women spun past their table,

sloshing their glasses of Guinness and black currant onto the floor, singing along with great passion to "Delilah."

"Well, for starters, we can laugh at all the drunk people," Maggie said. She stood up and smoothed her miniskirt while a man in a yellow rugby shirt wandered past dreamily, a big piece of ham hanging from his mouth. "I'm going to get a Cidona. You want one?"

She made her way to the bar, ducking and dodging the impromptu waltzers, the women sticking New Year's crowns atop their hairstyles, the molten tips of cigarettes lolling from between fingers. She arrived to the counter just as Eoin emerged from the beer cooler balancing a stack of pint glasses. He was dressed, without regard for the holiday, in his usual Liverpool hoodie and track pants. He placed the glasses beside the sink, looked up, grinned at her, and lifted his hand in a small wave. Seeing him behind the bar, sleeves pushed up to elbows, thick, muscular arms sloshing glasses through soapy water, Maggie felt the painful throb of her bruised breasts, remembered the stinging wind at the Ferris wheel, the cold puddles soaking into the knees of her jeans. She shook away the memory and waved back.

"Move over," she said to Ronnie, sliding back into her booth with two glasses of Cidona.

"Who was that boy you waved to?" Ronnie demanded, sticking a straw in her drink.

"Jesus, you're nosy! He's just a friend of mine." Eoin's back was turned now, and he was bending down to open a case of beer. Maggie could see a thin strip of white skin along the waistband of his track pants.

"A friend as in a regular friend or a friend you *do it* with?"

"*What?*" Maggie looked at her little sister. "Where the hell do you learn this stuff?"

"School," Ronnie shrugged, sipping her drink innocently.

"Well, he's a friend as in a *friend*. Do you even know what *doing it* means?"

"Do *you*?"

"Drink your Cidona and be quiet," Maggie said. "I told you I'd explain all of this when you're my age."

Midnight came and went in a blur of hugs and fizzing champagne. Laura and Colm made out in the corner; Maggie and Ronnie sat in their booth and spun noisemakers above their heads. In the crush of the packed pub, Maggie looked for Eoin but couldn't see him. Maybe, she thought, if he was anything like her, he'd fled to the quiet, cold safety of the beer cooler to ride out midnight without having deal with the pressure of finding someone to kiss when the clock turned. As soon as the confetti had sifted to the floor, the tables were pushed back against the walls to make room for the set dancing. The band began the Siege of Ennis, and Laura and Colm dragged Ronnie and Maggie from their booth to pair off into sets of four.

"I don't know the steps!" Maggie yelled over the hitching of the fiddle.

"Me either!" Laura yelled, grabbing her hand. "Just stomp your feet and act like you do!"

She led Maggie out into the crowd, back straight, knee bobbing in time with the fiddle, and when it was time, she began to move, dragging her daughter along behind her. It was in these moments that Maggie loved her mother in the way she'd loved her as a little girl: Laura Lynch, her dark hair falling around her shoulders, her green, mascara-coated eyes laughing, her purple dress tight around her soft body, the radiant beauty who could fake the steps and nobody would ever know the difference. Her confidence was so powerful, it was easy to believe that her mom could fix everything in Maggie's life with a wave of her slim wrist.

"Follow my lead," Laura yelled over the music. The dancers began to move in synch, and it was true: only about half of them really knew the steps. But everyone was laughing and everyone was trying, and as they lifted their arms, twirled around, and switched partners, Maggie found herself thrown, chest to chest, with Eoin.

Laura spun off like a purple top, and the music reached its maximum clip, the fiddler working his bow, the accordion player pushing and pulling his instrument to keep up.

"I don't know what the feck I'm doing!" Eoin laughed, but he possessed an athlete's grace, and when he grabbed Maggie's hands and spun her, she was nearly lifted off the floor. She threw her head back and whooped, her hair flying behind her, her skirt spreading around her thighs like an opened umbrella. He put a hand on her back just as he'd done the night she'd met him in the field, clinging tightly to the fabric of her blue turtleneck, holding her steady as she twirled. By the last verse of the song, the crowd had worked itself into a sweaty, frothing roomful of joy; even Rosie Horan joined the dancing, leaving the clutter of glasses at the bar.

Then, the accordion player closed his instrument and the fiddler dropped his fiddle to his side, leaving behind no sound but a humming in the air and the panting of the people, and before anyone could even cheer, the whistle player stood, a wiry little man with deep creases in his forehead, and he played a long, sustained note that trembled in such a way that the wild joy of only a moment ago was replaced entirely with something else, a deep feeling that was not quite unhappy but that matched the strange mix of celebration and mortality one feels at the wintry ending of every closing year. At the sound of the trembling note, couples moved closer to each other as if drawn by an invisible force, and Maggie could feel the heat off Eoin's skin as he moved into her. His close-cropped hair held a sweet muskiness. She closed her eyes to avoid her mom's ogling or Ronnie's spying, so that she could forget everything but his body near hers and the spare, sad notes of the whistle.

Rosie took her place in front of the musicians. The dancers, still catching their breath from the Siege of Ennis, eyed one another and nodded in anticipation. Rosie began to sing along with the whistle:

> *A Róisín ná bíodh brón ort fé'r éirigh dhuit*
> *Tá Na bráithre 'teacht thar sáile 's iad ag triall ar muir—*

The Irish words were completely foreign to Maggie but still strangely familiar, like the time only a week after they'd moved to Bray, when she had walked past a woman on Adelaide Street who wore the same perfume as Nanny Ei. She felt Eoin's body tense, straining to listen. Rosie bowed her head at the end of the verse while the whistle played on. Maggie whispered, "Do you know what it means?" He nodded against her cheek.

"Tell me?"

She could feel him hesitate for a moment, but then he relaxed and pulled her closer to translate, his lips moving in her hair: "Little Rose, don't be sad for all that has happened to you." His hand moved up her back and she felt his warm palm through her thin sweater. His lips skimmed the ridge of her ear: "Over mountains did I go with you, under the sails upon the sea." She no longer heard Rosie singing, only the whistle and Eoin's voice against her ear: "Fragrant branch, every mountain glen in Ireland will quake someday before my Dark Little Rose will die."

The song ended in an eruption of applause and whistling. Rosie smiled and gave a little bow, picked up her bar rag, and resumed taking drink orders. Tom Jones came back on the speakers and the world inside the pub began to move again. But Maggie and Eoin were no longer a part of it. They stood still together in the middle of the close, smoky bar, and his lips moved away from her ear and found her lips. She felt his kiss in every cell of her body, trembling, legs weak, cheeks flushed. It was undiluted happiness, of a kind so intense she didn't think she could stand it much longer, it would break her open and reveal all her tender parts. She pulled away and met his eyes, which were bright and shining and seemed to reflect everything she had just felt.

"I've been wanting to do that since the minute I saw you," he whispered.

"Me too." Somewhere far away, as if in a dream, Maggie heard her mother laughing and the Tom Jones song asking, "What's new, pussycat?"

"Come with me." Eoin grabbed her hand and they slipped out the back door and into the cold dampness of the alley, and he kissed her again, the air sparkling around them with light snow, her back cold against the stone wall.

"I've got to get back in there and help my aunt," he said, his hands still in her hair. "But when you're going home, find me. I can steal away for a little while and walk you."

If, just one year earlier, someone had told Maggie that she would be spending the dawning hours of 1994 walking home along the Irish Sea hand in hand with a boy like Eoin, she would not have believed it. Just one year earlier, she'd sat sandwiched between Nanny Ei and Ronnie on the lumpy velvet couch, balancing a bowl of buttered popcorn on her lap and watching Times Square on the television while Kevin partied downtown with Selfish Fetus and Laura drank at Oinker's with a pest control technician named Stan. Just one year earlier, Maggie was untraveled and inexperienced; love was still an abstraction, kissing was a thing that other, luckier, girls got to do, and she had never even been on an airplane. Now she knew the feeling of moving lips against her hair, of clods of Irish sand sifting into her shoes, of being noticed and admired by another human being who was not a member of her family. Life was happening at an accelerated pace, and Maggie was finally ready to keep up.

Later, when they reached her front door, Eoin kissed her again, and she was grateful for the puffy layer of her winter coat so that he might not notice the way his kiss made her whole body tremble.

She let herself in the door, moving the front curtain aside so she could watch him walk away, hands in pockets, dark head bowed against the wind, the perfect boy shape of him heading back toward town along the path of the perfect sea. She lay awake for a long time reliving his hands, his lips, again and again and again. At last she slept, her sweater wrapped around her pillow, straining for the last bits of his scent that clung to its fibers.

She awoke to a gentle knocking on her bedroom door. Sunlight leaked in between her bedroom curtains. Maggie looked at the clock—it was already afternoon. She experienced the wonderful sensation of waking up groggy and remembering that the thing you wanted more than anything had really happened to you, that you didn't dream any of it. Was this what love was—when life was better than you'd even known to dream about?

The knock came again, and her mom opened the bedroom door, her eyes bloodshot. Maggie pulled her blanket around her thin tank top and sat up. Laura was looking at her in a curious way: Is this how mothers knew? One look at their daughters and they knew they'd fallen in love? Well, just this once, if her mom asked, Maggie would tell all. She would gush about Eoin, about their first meeting in the misty field, about how she could forgive all the moving and the strangeness and the upheaval of the past four months, because it had led her to him.

But Laura took one step into Maggie's bedroom, held her fingers to her mouth, and burst into tears.

Colm appeared behind her, squeezing her shoulders. His face was ashen.

"Ma? What's wrong?"

Laura began to wail in a strange keening voice that Maggie had never heard before—it was not like the bitter, quiet tears she'd shed after their father had left, and it terrified her. She noticed that Ronnie was standing in the hallway, clinging to their mother's pant leg as she'd done as a toddler. Her eyes were huge and wet and she was staring at Maggie.

"*Kevin*," Laura finally sobbed. "Oh God. It's Uncle Kevin."

"What do you want out of life?" I asked, and I used to ask that all the time of girls. "I don't know," she said. "Just wait on tables and try to get along." She yawned. I put my hand over her mouth and told her not to yawn. I tried to tell her how excited I was about life and the things we could do together . . . We lay on our backs, looking at the ceiling and wondering what God had wrought when He made life so sad.

—Jack Kerouac, *On the Road*

9

At the very edge of Montrose Harbor, on the north side of Chicago, there is a bird sanctuary. On summer mornings, as the pink sun rises over the hazy blue horizon of Lake Michigan, amateur ornithologists creep along the trails of waving dune grass in search of piping plovers and American avocets while the shadows of peregrine falcons wheel above them. Butterflies, their wings translucent in the nascent light, coast on the wind. The sanctuary is part of the city and not part of it, a finger of land jutting out from the shore, and being there, amid the tall pale grass and the air crisp with lavender, it's easy to forget that just over the ledge are acres of sand volleyball courts, kayak rentals, and a bar that serves twenty-four-ounce cans of Budweiser and all-you-can-eat baskets of shrimp.

When the bitterly cold midwestern winter descends, people mostly stay away from the sanctuary. The colorful warblers of summer are replaced by gray mourning doves, blackheaded gulls, and stoic, unblinking owls that swoop soundlessly through frozen bare branches and stand sentinel on the abandoned volleyball poles, surveying the emptiness of the beach shanties. In the winter, the inhospitable peninsula belongs entirely to the birds. It's as if, for a brief period of snowy time, humans no longer exist.

When Maggie was a kid, Uncle Kevin worked as a lifeguard at the beach next to the bird sanctuary. On hot summer weekends, her family would ride the Montrose Avenue bus across the city to swim in the polluted waves of his patrol. Maggie always felt so proud, seeing her uncle perched on the high white tower along the water's edge with a big orange buoy arranged across his lap and his dreadlocks pulled back in a gnarled tuft, watching over all the splashing people to make sure they were safe. The scar from his childhood heart surgery stood white and jagged against his tan chest, and made him look tough—like he'd lived through things. Everyone knew him there, from the neon-bikinied college girls who twitched their butts for him as they passed to the amiable schizophrenics who drifted down from the halfway houses in Uptown, pushing shopping carts full of cans and still wearing their winter coats. No matter how crowded it was, Uncle Kevin always staked out a nice spot for his family in the shade of his lifeguard chair. Maggie would rub sunscreen on Ronnie's fat baby legs while Laura lolled in a lawn chair with a copy of *People Magazine* and Nanny Ei chain smoked and people watched in a skirted bathing suit and sun visor, her legs bumpy with varicose veins.

It didn't matter that throughout the fall, winter, and spring, Uncle Kevin was always coming home with a fat lip or tussling with the police. Here at the beach, when you looked at him high on his white tower, so young and alive, with a face made for sunglasses and shoulders square with muscle, he was somebody special, somebody important. Being related to him, being loved by him, was the closest Maggie ever came to feeling like a celebrity. Even now, the family called the place Kevin's Beach—as if it was still an extension of him, even years after he'd let his lifeguard training lapse and been replaced with a water polo player from Northwestern University.

Parked on the lumpy velvet couch of Nanny Ei's apartment, weary from the seven-hour flight, Maggie sat and listened to her grandmother explain the details she'd left out over the phone:

that on the night of his death, in the first dawning hours of 1994, Kevin returned to the bird sanctuary. He parked AG BULLT at the harbor and walked through the snow-covered soccer field, past the rows of volleyball posts, all the way to the frosty water's edge. What had he seen, when he looked beneath the waves at the murky bottom, the oozy weeds twisting? Had he known even then that the heart beating inside him was getting ready to give way? Had he looked up, the sky above him like stained glass, a city boy seeing stars for the first time?

He'd gotten home before sunrise. His unsteady key in the lock woke Nanny Ei, who'd drunk a glass of champagne, watched the ball drop on NBC, and fallen asleep on the couch. He was more talkative than usual. He told her about the New Year's party in Rogers Park he'd gone to with some of his old lifeguard friends, about how on his way home he'd pulled over and walked through the sanctuary to sober up before he made the long drive home west across the breadth of the city. The moon, he reported, had been perfectly full, a dollop of cream in a black sky. *This is going to be a better year for you, Kev,* Nanny Ei had said. She'd stroked his head like he was a little boy. *1994 is going to be the year that things change.*

She let him sleep it off until 3:00 the next afternoon. When she went in his room, expecting to chide him for the reek of booze sweating off his pores, she smelled something colder, sharper, and when she lifted the cover, there was no gust of warmth—and she knew. It had finally happened: his heart had stopped. "Just went to bed and never woke up," was how Nanny Ei put it, her voice brittle. Maggie remembered him eating fries under the yellow lights of Harry and Rose's, how awful he had looked; how sick.

But still.

Who dies at twenty-six? This isn't a cancer ward or a soldier in a strange country. This isn't a car going a hundred miles an hour on an icy road, a deer stepping out into the highway just as you turn the curve. A heart defect—what a sneaky and clinical way to die.

At first, Laura had suggested going home for the funeral by herself. "We don't have the money for four plane tickets," she said. She looked so broken, slumped on Colm's couch sipping directly from a bottle of West Coast Cooler, that Maggie almost let it go without an argument. But her own grief was so consuming that trying to sympathize with Laura was like sleepwalking through someone else's dream.

"I'm going," Maggie said, taking the empty bottle from her mother's shaking hands. "I loved him more than anybody."

And maybe because Laura knew that was true, she relented. She put two flights on the credit card, and just like that, the very next evening, Maggie was sitting at her grandmother's house in front of the TV while Nanny Ei and Laura sat at the kitchen table, a box of tissue between them, picking out the readings for Kevin's funeral mass.

American television programming fell over her like an old blanket. She sat and flipped absently through the channels. There was *Cheers*. There was *Golden Girls*. There was local news about streets and neighborhoods she'd known all her life. Up and down she went, from CBS to NBC to ABC to WGN and back again. She thought of Eoin. Even in all the shock and heartbreak of the past twenty-four hours, her thoughts still returned, again and again, to that kiss. It now seemed so long ago. When would she see him again? Did he know that everything had changed for her? Was it okay to think about something—anything—that made her happy now that Uncle Kevin was dead? If he was up in heaven this very moment, and knew that in spite of her sorrow she still thought of kissing Eoin, would he feel betrayed?

"Nanny Ei?"

Her grandmother looked up from the mass booklet and took off her reading glasses.

"Yeah, honey?"

"Would it be okay if I went and sat in Kevin's room for a little bit?"

Nanny Ei looked at Laura.

"Do you think that's a good idea, Mags?" Laura asked.

"I won't touch anything."

"I don't see the harm in it," Nanny Ei said. "After all, you were one of the few people he actually allowed in that lair of his."

She could feel them watching her as she turned the knob on Kevin's door. The smell of his bedroom was thick with cigarettes and Old Spice deodorant. A small stick of incense sat on the windowsill with its long, white ash still intact. His bed was neatly made. Nanny Ei had smoothed the coverlet and tucked in the sheets after he had died in it and they had taken him away. His walls were covered with music posters: Nirvana, Soundgarden, Urge Overkill. Dinosaur Jr., Jimi Hendrix, Bob Dylan. The corners of the room were stacked high with books. Kevin had never been a good student and had barely graduated from high school, but he was a frequent visitor to the Mayfair branch of the Chicago Public Library, which was staffed by an old Belarusian who claimed to have been an English professor back in Minsk. They often went out drinking together, Kevin and Paviel, and the old librarian would give him book recommendations: the Russian greats, of course, but also the American writers who captured, as he put it, "the Spirit of Fuck You": Ginsberg and the Beats, Whitman, Vonnegut, Richard Wright. Kevin had once made Maggie a handwritten list entitled "Summer Reading Recommendations to Keep Young Nieces Off the Streets." It contained subcategories:

Books that Will Make You Believe in Communism

Books to Read When You Turn 17 + then to Reread with Totally New Perspective When You Turn 22

Books that Made Me Believe, Despite Ample Evidence to the Contrary, that Not ALL Women Are Completely + Totally Insane

Books that Made Me Believe that Maybe Human Beings Aren't Just Ugly Barnacles Attaching Themselves onto the Beautiful Hull of the World with No Purpose but to Make It Uglier

Maggie had tried to read one of these recommendations —*Tropic of Cancer*, which was listed under the category

Excellent Books with Excellent Sex Scenes

She had only been able to get through the first chapter. Now, on the nightstand next to his bed, she found a copy of *On the Road* with a pen stuck in the middle to mark where he'd left off. It was a book Kevin had talked about often, and it had appeared on her summer reading list under the simple category *Essential Reads*. Maggie sat on his bed and opened to the page where he'd stopped reading. A sentence was underlined in neat black ink:

I was surprised, as always, by how easy the act of leaving was, and how good it felt.

Maggie read the sentence a few times, wondering why he had marked it, whether he'd been thinking of Christmas morning at Colm's house, when he stood at the end of her bed and said good-bye to her. The words on the page blurred with her tears.

Before she left the room, Maggie went back and stood before his open closet, full of flannel shirts from the Salvation Army on Elston Avenue. *Those clothes are for homeless people*, Nanny Ei had scolded. *I can buy you nice new clothes at Kohl's. When you get your clothes at the Salvation Army, it's no different than stealing from the poor.* She leaned forward, put her face in the fabric, and breathed her uncle in. She felt him stronger than ever, then: waving to her from the wooden throne of his lifeguard tower, throwing his arm around her as they walked down Martello Terrace, leaning over the bar to talk to Eoin's aunt Rosie as if he'd known her all his life.

She thought of him standing next to her at the Metro, screaming along to the lyrics at the Smashing Pumpkins show: *tell me all of your secrets / cannot help but believe this is true . . .*

I cannot help but believe this is true.

She lifted one of the shirts from its hanger. It was gray and black plaid, the flannel pilled and threadbare: lived in. He'd often worn it, unbuttoned, over a ratty white T-shirt. She folded it and folded it again, stuffed it under her sweater, and snuck back into the front room. Her mom and Nanny Ei were still huddled over the funeral readings. Maggie knelt down next to the couch and opened her duffel bag. She lifted out the black dress she'd brought for the wake and placed the flannel at the bottom of the bag, gently, as if it still contained him, as if beneath the worn front pocket, she could still hear his heartbeat.

Before the wake, Maggie painted Nanny Ei's toenails. It was a ritual the two had shared since Maggie was in fifth grade and Uncle Kevin had forgotten to salt the icy back steps during a nasty cold spell. Nanny Ei had slipped a disc falling down the stairs and hadn't been able to bend down properly ever since. Laura had suggested she start getting pedicures, but Nanny Ei had dismissed nail salons as cesspools of foot fungus, and Maggie had been given the job. She didn't mind, though, because Nanny Ei didn't have old lady feet. They were delicate and soft—size five—papered in thin white skin, and they smelled like the lemon bath salts she liked to soak her feet in while she watched reruns of *M*A*S*H*.

"Honey, do me a favor," Nanny Ei said as she stuck her foot out and Maggie began brushing a coat of fuchsia on her baby toe. "Stay away from those bum friends of Kevin's at the wake."

"Okay, Nanny," Maggie nodded, fixing a smudge with the edge of her thumb.

"I mean it, missy." Nanny Ei pulled her foot away so Maggie had to stop what she was doing and look up. "The last thing I need to worry about before I bury my son is Taco or Rockhead or any of those other degenerates chatting it up with my beautiful granddaughter."

Maggie sighed and pulled Nanny Ei's foot back into her lap.

"Stop being crazy. Those guys are, like, ten years older than me."

"Exactly! Perverts and degenerates, every last one of 'em. Except maybe that Sullivan boy."

"Nanny! Kevin hasn't hung out with Sully since he quit Selfish Fetus to go to law school!"

"Is that right?" Nanny squinted at her newly pink big toenail. "Well, if that bastard thought he was too good for Kevin, he still better show his face at the wake. You *always* go to the wake, Maggie. Even when you don't want to. *Especially* when you don't want to."

She began to cry then, suddenly, and Maggie finished painting her toenails in silence.

The parking lot of Cooney's funeral home was freshly plowed, and mountains of dirty snow were pushed up as high as the chain-link fence. Nanny Ei turned off the ignition and they sat for a moment, listening to the car tick. Finally, Laura took a deep breath and looked at Maggie in the rearview mirror. Her eyes were puffy, but her hair was tied back into a neat bun and she wore a new shade of dark red lipstick.

"Are we ready, you guys?" She reached back and squeezed Maggie's hand. Maggie squeezed it back.

"Mom?"

"Yeah, babe?"

"You look really pretty."

Laura's eyes filled immediately with tears. Maggie realized, with a stabbing sense of guilt, how cruel she'd been to her mother since the move to Ireland. She reached into her coat pocket and closed her fist around Kevin's broken compass. If anything good had come of his dying, it was that they had all chosen, at least for now, to forgive each other.

They were the first ones to arrive, followed shortly by Maggie's uncle Dave, his wife, and their three boring children. As the oldest child in the family, Uncle Dave was everything that Kevin wasn't—Maggie had never seen him wear anything other than khakis and a golf polo—and for this reason, she had never trusted him. He had escaped into the Navy, married a wide-hipped woman named Marjorie, and now worked as a mortgage broker in Oklahoma City. He had three daughters—Caelynn, Taylor, and Kimberly, who were all around Maggie's age. They all wore headbands and cardigans and spoke with voices bleached of any regional accent. They only came to town once a year, and when they saw Nanny Ei, they hugged her with cold affection and called her "Grandma." Maggie was glad her cousins were there, though, because it was easier to concentrate on how much she hated them than to face the wave of agony that lapped at her heart when she saw the open coffin at the front of the room.

At first, she could not go look at him. Nanny Ei and Laura went up to the coffin together. They crouched on the velvet kneeler, held hands, and cried. They prayed. They whispered to him. Nanny Ei reached out and stroked his hair and put a rosary in his interlaced fingers.

When they were finished, Uncle Dave and Marjorie approached the coffin, and Maggie stared at the clean bottoms of Marjorie's ugly shoes. Then the daughters went up, all three together. They squeezed together on the kneeler, leaning over to stare at Kevin's face. Taylor, the youngest, whispered something and Caelynn and Kimberly snorted with sudden laughter. They crossed themselves hastily and scurried back toward their seats, while Maggie cracked her knuckles and glared at them, daring them to smile or laugh just one more time.

Before the doors opened for the public viewing, Nanny Ei came over and sat next to Maggie on one of the vinyl chairs near the back of the room.

"If you want to go up and say good-bye to him, I can come with you," she said.

Maggie nodded and let Nanny Ei take her hand and lead her up to the coffin. She felt like a very small child—frightened, weepy, everything in the world both new and strange.

He was there. It was really him. Maggie felt vaguely surprised—had she not really believed he was dead until now? She felt lightheaded, sick, and her legs crumpled into kneeling position. Next to her, Nanny Ei began to cry again, but Maggie couldn't. A blackness had filled her throat and chest, corking up every feeling. His long hair had been combed and tied into a ponytail. His face was as skinny as she'd seen it at Christmas, and the thick layer of makeup seemed to heighten that hollowness. He wore a ridiculous gray mock turtleneck—Maggie could not imagine why Nanny Ei would have chosen it, or where in his closet she'd even *found* it—under a black wool sport coat, also an unrecognizable garment that Kevin would never have worn. In his hands was the red Saint Theresa's rosary Nanny Ei had placed there. Maggie reached into the pocket of her dress and fished for the guitar pick she'd found on the carpet in his bedroom. She slipped it in the breast pocket of his sport coat.

I can't play the guitar, Mags, she imagined him saying to her. *I'm dead, remember? No need to be superstitious.*

But she wanted him to have it. The ancient Romans buried their beloved with offerings and objects, and Kevin had always loved the idea of Rome. He'd wanted her to see Nirvana at the Palaghiaccio di Marino. Had he known, in some elemental way, that he himself never would?

People began trickling in to pay their respects. There were the regulars from Oinker's, the ladies from Nanny Ei's Altar and Rosary society, and strange distant cousins whom Maggie had never met. There was a steady stream of young grunge heads, a gauntlet of cigarette smokers out in the front. Maggie stood in the receiving line next to her mother and Uncle Dave and Nanny Ei and shook hand after hand. Rockhead came, and Jeremy, and Taco, and even Sonia, the woman from the Smashing Pumpkins show, her hair blunt cut and platinum, black smudges around her eyes. Most of them were crying. They all said the same things, "I'm so sorry, I'm so sorry," but Nanny Ei was stony faced and hurried them along, managing, somehow, to hug them while still barely touching them.

After several hours of this, Maggie wandered off to the basement, where a linoleum kitchen hummed with refrigerated pop machines and mayonnaise congealed on a tray of drooping sandwiches. Her cousin, Kimberly, sat down next to her and took a roast beef.

"So," she said brightly, "how are things in Ireland?"

Maggie looked at the girl's placid, griefless face. She knew it was unfair to hate this cousin. How close, really, are most people with their uncles? But knowing this didn't make Maggie hate her any less.

"Things are shitty," she said. "Nice *headband*, by the way." She threw down the rind of her turkey sandwich, then pushed her chair away and walked up the stairs, satisfied at the insulted, open-mouthed look she'd conjured on Kimberly's face.

After the wake, Uncle Dave and Marjorie and the three cousins went back to their hotel and Laura and Maggie went back to the two-flat. Nanny Ei pulled out the bed for Maggie, and Laura poured herself a huge glass of wine. The two of them were up late into the night, smoking and drinking, and Maggie heard the bedrooms door close when the sun was nearly up, and in the morning when Laura emerged from her bedroom to get ready for the funeral, there was no trace of the sad beauty in her face from the wake the day before. She looked exhausted, hungover, defeated, and, for the first time, old.

A graveside burial in a Chicago January was not possible. The ground was frozen solid and would have required a crew of pickaxes to break the soil. Instead, after mass, they held a burial ceremony in a small chapel at the cemetery. The priest swung the thurible and the small room was filled with the heavy, sweet smell of frankincense. Maggie thought she might choke on it. And then it was over, and they were off to the luncheon in their long procession, and they left Kevin's body behind in the chapel to be buried when the ground thawed.

Kevin's body. That's all he was now—a thing. And soon enough he would be even less than that, a skeleton with a rosary entwined it its finger bones and a guitar pick stuck in its rotting sport coat. *Why didn't they just cremate him?* Maggie wondered. *Did they really think he'd rather be dressed up and stuck in a box?* Sitting in the backseat of Nanny Ei's Oldsmobile, she remembered the poem they'd studied in English class before Christmas break:

> I dreamed that one had died in a strange place
> Near no accustomed hand,
> And they had nailed the boards above her face,
> The peasants of that land . . .
> And left her to the indifferent stars above
> Until I carved these words:
> *She was more beautiful than thy first love,*
> *But now lies under boards.*

Reading it aloud to the class, Sister Geneve's eyes had begun to water. After she finished the poem, there was a heavy silence in the classroom while the girls exchanged glances, and the nun apologized, removing her reading glasses to wipe at her eyes. "I lost my mother when I was just around your age," she'd said. "This poem, it still gets me every time."

Remembering the anguished face of the old nun, Maggie

marveled at the lifespan of grief. Sister Geneve had to be at least sixty-five. That meant that her mother had been dead for fifty years. Half a century! And still, a poem could make her cry. She thought of Dan Sean, holed up tenaciously in his little hilltop house, refusing to leave the place where he'd lost his wife and infant daughter. Maggie had joined the company of Sister Geneve and Dan Sean: she was now a person who had to imagine a body she had known, a face she had loved, buried under boards, while over at the Montrose bird sanctuary, indifferent seagulls and winter birds gathered in the trees, and life continued for most things on the earth as it always had.

On the Saturday morning after she returned from Chicago, Maggie was just digging into her cereal in front of the television when the doorbell rang.

"I'll get it," Ronnie said, leaping off the back of the couch and disappearing down the hall. A minute later, she came charging back into the sitting room.

"It's for you," she whispered excitedly. "*Annnnd . . .*" she arched her shoulders and began moonwalking enthusiastically back and forth across in front of the TV. "It's a *boy!*"

Please let it be Eoin and not Paul. The thought began repeating itself in Maggie's head as she abandoned her spoon into her cereal and left Ronnie to her goofy dancing. She smoothed her hair behind her ears and headed, heart thumping, down the wood-paneled hallway to the front door. *Please let it be Eoin and not Paul please let it be Eoin and not Paul please—*

Eoin was leaning on the doorframe, his short buzzed hair backlit by the morning sun. His hands were stuffed in his tracksuit pants pockets.

"Hiya, Maggie."

Maggie suddenly remembered that she was dressed in a pair of pink pajama pants and that there were still white crusts of Clearasil all over her chin.

"I would've rang you," he said, "but we haven't got a phone at my Auntie Rosie's. She's got one at the bar, and she says that's enough."

"That's okay," Maggie said. She cupped her chin in her hand to cover up the zit cream.

Ronnie peeked around the doorframe of the sitting room, smiling apishly. She began gesturing toward the door in a manner that could only be described as humping, and Maggie furiously waved her away.

"Anyway. I heard about your uncle, the one who I met on Christmas . . . just wanted to tell you I'm sorry."

"Thank you." There was a silence, as if Eoin was expecting her to say more. "It sucks."

"So I was thinking of heading into Dublin today. I've got a few bits and pieces to take care of. D'you want to get out of the house for a while? There's a bus that leaves in an hour."

"Today? I mean, I was hanging out with my sister now but—"

"That's grand," he said quickly, stepping out of the doorway and turning to leave. "No bother at all. I guess I'll talk to you some other time."

"No!" Maggie nearly shrieked. "What I meant was, I just have to check with my mom, that's all. And maybe take a quick shower. Would you mind waiting? My crazy sister can keep you company."

As if on cue, Ronnie appeared at the front door and curtsied. She grabbed Eoin's hand and dragged him toward the sitting room.

"What's your favorite Saturday morning show? Do you want some cereal? Aren't you the boy from the Quayside? Do you *always* wear the same outfit?" As she led him away, Eoin turned back and winked at Maggie. She bit her lip and smiled, and one of Nanny Ei's cheesy sayings floated into her mind: *That boy could charm the pepperoni off a pizza.*

She knocked on her mother's bedroom door. "Yeah," came Colm's gravelly voice from the other side. Maggie opened it gingerly, hating to intrude on the sexual den of her mother and stepdad. But this morning, there was none of the usual languid spooning, of naked shoulders poking out from under the covers. Laura was lying puffy eyed and alone in the middle of the big bed, while Colm was stretched on the floor in a makeshift nest of blankets and pillows. By the looks of it, both had slept with their clothes on.

"So, I'm taking the bus into Dublin with some friends," Maggie said, leaning on the doorframe. Laura looked up sleepily.

"That's great, honey!" she said with creaky enthusiasm. "Your pal Aíne?"

"No, just some other kids from school."

"Wonderful! Well, if you need money there's a ten-pound note in my wallet."

"Thanks, Mom."

Always give your parents only the most vital information, Kevin's advice had been. The more you tell them, the more they ask. Maggie plucked the tenner from her mom's wallet and ran to the bathroom, locking the door behind her. She shampooed, conditioned, tore a razor across her armpits and legs, and scrubbed her face with Laura's fancy facial exfoliator. In record time she was clean, scented, and stubble free. She toweled off and stopped for a moment to rub the condensation off the mirror and examine the face reflecting back at her. *Why does he like me?* She leaned in closer to scrutinize herself. Sometimes she just got so sick of her own face: the green eyes she'd inherited from her mother that people sometimes complimented; the half smile and snub nose and pimply chin that people never did. *He can't actually think I'm pretty. Because if I'm pretty, then why have boys been ignoring me all my life?* She squirted some Colgate on her toothbrush. Down the short hallway to the sitting room, she could hear Eoin laughing at one of Ronnie's dumb jokes.

She spit out the toothpaste, combed her dark hair, and rummaged through her mom's makeup bag. She dotted some concealer on her chin, swiped blush across her cheeks and a mascara wand through her lashes, then blew her hair straight, so it fell to her shoulders in a smooth wave. She dressed in a pair of dark jeans, a black shirt, and the patent leather Doc Martens that Nanny Ei had bought her for Christmas.

"You ready to go?" she said, stepping into the sitting room.

"Yep," Eoin said, putting down the half-eaten bowl of Weetabix Ronnie had poured for him. Ronnie climbed over the arm of the couch and squinted up at Maggie.

"Why are you wearing *makeup*?"

Maggie silenced her sister with a murderous glare and wiped at the blush with the heels of her palms.

"Tell Mom I'll be home by dinner."

They sat next to each other on the bus and spent most of the forty-minute ride trying not to accidentally bump knees or arms. The electricity that had flown between them on the dance floor at the Quayside was now, in the daylight, just another reason for shyness. The bus stopped in the city center, where the streets were crowded with throngs of office workers and tourists, buskers and hustlers and gypsy women with hoop earrings and flashing gold teeth. They walked down the wide sidewalks of O'Connell Street, passing under the green hulk of Clery's clock. The air was fresh and cool, and as they headed toward Grafton Street they stopped at the O'Connell Street Bridge and peered over the edge as crowds of Dubliners rushed behind them. The Liffey was black and rushing, ever moving. Eoin reached out and took Maggie's hand. She realized, as she looked down at the water, that he was the only person in Dublin who knew her name.

They walked on, getting used to the feel and temperature of each other's hands, crossing rutted cobblestone paths and sidestepping small piles of trash, hunks of spat-out gum. People streamed by, dressed in every manner of clothing, from ripped tights and flannel shirts to power suits to multicolored soccer jerseys. Finally, when they'd reached the gates of Trinity College, Eoin stopped and looked up.

"The Campanile," he said, pointing up at the tower that sliced through the scudding clouds above them. "My mom used to take me to Trinity every summer when I was small." They headed through the iron gates and into the central square of the college, under the Campanile and up the steps to the Old Library, where a short, pear-shaped man in a navy-blue suit was taking ticket stubs from a small group of Spanish students.

"Well, there's a sight for sore eyes!" The ticket taker, delighted to see them, gave Eoin's hand a vigorous shake. He had a small, strawberry-colored birthmark on his cheek and when he smiled, it crinkled into a small slit beneath his eye.

"How are things, Donie?" Eoin gestured in Maggie's direction. "This is my friend, Maggie Lynch."

Donie bowed. "How do you do, young lady?"

"Hi," Maggie smiled.

"How's your mother keepin' these days? I haven't seen her in—oh now, about three years. Lovely woman, Mary. Lovely, lovely woman. I pray for her every day, even though she broke my heart." He put his fat, purplish hands to his chest and squeezed his face into a wink, the birthmark disappearing altogether in the folds of his face.

"She's good as can be expected, Donie," said Eoin. "Some days are better than others, I suppose."

"Well, send her my undying love and devotion, next time you see her," said Donie, dropping the Spanish students' ticket stubs into a box. "I assume you've come today to show this lovely young American the treasures of our cultural past?"

"Yep. Am I still eligible for the friends and family discount?"

"Wouldn't dream of accepting a cent from the great Mary Brennan's son." He winked again and waved them through, calling,

"Enjoy, now!" as they stepped into a cool, dimly lit room.

"Who was that?" Maggie asked.

"Oh," Eoin shrugged, "that's just Donie. Old friend of my mother's."

Inside the exhibit, tourists outfitted in rain jackets and hiking boots crept around glass displays while a security guard stood watch to stop anyone from taking pictures.

"What is it?" Maggie asked.

"The Book of Kells," Eoin said proudly. "The most beautiful book in the world."

They waited for the clump of tourists to move away and stepped up to the lit manuscript. The pages were thick, made of stretched animal skin and decorated with intricate, gold-ringed paintings of saints, their pious eyes rolling up toward heaven. A metal plaque next to the exhibit read:

THE BOOK OF KELLS IS BELIEVED TO HAVE BEEN WRITTEN APPROXIMATELY 1,200 YEARS AGO AT THE MONASTERY ON IONA, AN ISLAND OFF THE WEST COAST OF SCOTLAND. IN 806, VIKINGS RAIDED THE ISLAND, KILLING 68, AND THE SURVIVING MONKS FLED TO A NEW MONASTERY AT KELLS, COUNTY MEATH. OVER THE CENTURIES, THIRTY OF THE FOLIOS HAVE GONE MISSING, AS HAS THE JEWEL-ENCRUSTED FRONT COVER, LEAVING THE 680 PAGES THAT REMAIN TODAY.

Maggie squinted closer at the fine-brushed colors, painted with such painstaking love. An energy seemed to glow from the book. She imagined these monks, toothless and starved, bent over vellum by the light of a flickering candle, possessed by a wild faith that was beyond the understanding of the brutish Vikings. Why did they do it? Why spend all those countless hours making art when they certainly would have had their hands full keeping themselves fed and warm and clothed? Was it their religion that drove the monks on Iona? Or did art itself become their religion during those isolated years on that lonely outcropping?

"Maggie?"

She turned around at Eoin's voice. An impatient crowd of tourists had gathered behind her. She mumbled an apology and moved away.

"So," he said, "what do you think?"

"I love it," she said softly.

"I wish I was more like those monks. If I could dedicate myself to football the way they dedicated themselves to this book, I'd be playing for Wicklow before my eighteenth birthday."

"I wish I had that kind of faith," Maggie said. "But I don't."

Eoin shrugged. "It's 1994," he said. "Nobody has that kind of faith anymore."

They left the Book of Kells room through a pair of broad doors and stepped into a massive library that smelled of dust and wood polish, the papery oldness of a long-closed book. The ceiling was church high, and Maggie imagined men, centuries dead, splayed on ropes and pulleys, polishing the mahogany arches hundreds of feet above them. And the books. God, there had to be a million of them. And they weren't the kind of books you'd find in an American library—they were bound in muted tones of leather and aligned neatly in rows as high as the ceiling. Spindly wooden ladders leaned against the shelves at forty-five-degree angles; a plump librarian in pantyhose and flat rubber shoes had scaled one of them with the effortlessness of a Nepalese mountaineer. She was leaning forward, peering over her reading glasses, to pluck a book from a shelf nearly two stories high. Maggie loved that someone knew exactly where to find each book, and had the dedication to risk her safety to acquire it.

They left the library and stepped into the cool afternoon, wandering the college green among earnest students. The students seemed like modern manifestations of those monks: bookish, determined, dedicated to higher pursuits of the mind and spirit. Maggie could see why Aíne's great dream was to be a student at Trinity one day. They crossed back through the iron gates and bought sandwiches and chips from a shop across the street. Carrying their lunches, they returned to the college green, past the museum to the rugby pitch where Eoin's mother had taken him when he was small. They found a bench beneath a large beech tree and unwrapped their sandwiches.

"So, what were you thinking about back there?" Eoin asked.

"What do you mean?"

"Back in the Book of Kells room. You were a bit zoned out."

"Oh." Maggie bit into her sandwich, chewed slowly. "I was just thinking about artists."

"Like your uncle?"

"He was a great musician."

Eoin nodded. "My mom's a singer."

"Really? What kind of music does she sing?"

"Irish music. Traditional stuff. She used to have an agent and a CD and everything. But—well, all that's gone now."

"You don't have to tell me if you don't want," Maggie said, picking at a blade of grass, "but how come you don't live with her?"

"I don't mind." He stretched his legs out in front of him. "I'm not ashamed of anything." He spread a napkin on his lap. Maggie sat and watched, waiting for him to continue.

"Things were great when I was small," he began. "We had plenty of money and we lived in a nice flat in Dublin. I was alone a lot—she did a lot of touring, but I didn't mind because when she was away I got to stay at my Auntie Rosie's house, and my uncle Dan would teach me how to do the farm work, kick around the football with me sometimes.

"Then, maybe four or five years ago, things started to get bad. My mom started acting really strange. She'd show up hours late for her gigs, get in shouting matches with her manager over the littlest things. Everybody thought she was on drugs. Eventually, her agent and her studio dropped her." A leaf fluttered down from the beech tree that shaded them, landing on a corner of his untouched sandwich. He didn't notice. Maggie reached over and picked it off.

"By then we were broke, and we had to move in with Auntie Rosie and Uncle Dan. Mom began accusing us of things: saying that Uncle Dan was spying on her in the shower, or that I was sprinkling rat poison in her supper. Crazy stuff. She started hanging tack paper over her bedroom windows and she wouldn't eat anything home cooked, would only eat prepackaged cream crackers and canned soup.

"Then, a couple years ago, when Cork played Meath in the All-Ireland, she took me down to Croke Park for the game. We set up a little table near the stadium to sell copies of her CD for a pound a piece. This rich Cork fella—I'll never forget, he was wearing a suede jacket and a red and white scarf around his neck, he came up to our table and told my mom that he'd only buy a CD if she could sing him a Cork song. I'm sure he thought, by the looks of us, me with my messy hair and mom dressed in some ratty pink shell suit left over from the eighties, that she'd be a disaster. But the minute she opened her mouth and sang the first lines of 'The Banks of My Own Lovely Lee,' he saw that she was the real thing. A crowd gathered, and when she was finished, the fella bought a CD, then reached up and untied the red and white Cork scarf from around his neck and hung it on my shoulders. Being the bold little bastard that I was, I said, 'But I'm not a Cork man.' And he said, 'Well, do you want me to buy another one of your mommy's CDs?' And I said, 'No. I want to go to the match.'

"See, Maggie, Gaelic football is more than just a sport in this country," he went on. "It's, like, part of our national identity. And I'd been playing since I was a kid. But nobody had ever taken me to Croke Park before. And that's exactly what I told the fella—I gave him my sob story about growing up without a father, never having anyone to take me to a game. And just that easy, he reached into his jacket pocket and handed me two extra tickets. I nearly died right then and there."

"That's amazing!" Maggie laughed. "I had no idea you were such a little hustler! Was it a good game?"

"I'll never know," Eoin shrugged. "The minute the man walked away, my mom said, 'we can get good money for those tickets. We're touting 'em.' "

"Touting?"

"Yeah. I think Americans call it scalping."

"She *scalped* your tickets?"

"I begged her to let me see the game. I said I'd go by myself and she could sell the other one. I promised I'd get a job the next day and pay her the difference. But she told me to shut up and man the CD station, and off she went with the two tickets."

"That's *awful*," Maggie said.

"So I'm standing there at our table holding back tears and trying to hawk the rest of the CDs, and I'm watching her in that old pink shell suit, chasing after people with these tickets. With *my* tickets. And these two guards pass by. I call 'em over. I say, 'see that woman over there? She's trying to tout some stolen tickets.' I don't know why I did it. I knew that now, we wouldn't get any money, and I *still* wouldn't get to go to the game. But I suppose I was just so pissed off I didn't care."

"Did they arrest her?"

He shook his head.

"They told her to shove off. They said, 'If we see you around here again today, we're gonna lock you up.' And then they pointed at me. They said, 'That young fella over there, he's our lookout. So don't try anything.' "

Maggie raised a hand to her mouth. "So your mom *knew* you ratted her out? What did she do?"

"She got mouthy with them, and they took the tickets from her and they pushed her onto the street. She came storming back over to me, we packed up our table and the rest of our CDs, and we went back to Bray. She didn't say a word to me the whole bus ride home. She just sort of looked out the window. And when we got back to Auntie Rosie's, I watched the game on TV, just like I'd done every other year, and she went off to her bedroom and didn't come out for the rest of the night."

Eoin shifted his legs in the grass and began playing with his sandwich wrapper.

"That night I dreamed that I was drowning. I woke up, all in a panic, and shot up in my bed. There was this mirror on the wall across from me and there was a clear moon outside the window, so I could sort of see what was happening even though it was dark. I could see my face, and it was all purple, and above that, behind the headboard, I could see my mother's face. The expression on it was just totally blank, the same face you might wear watching an ad for laundry detergent. She was standing behind my bed and she had my red and white Cork scarf tight around my neck and she was strangling me."

"Oh my God," Maggie whispered. She reached a hand to touch him, but he seemed so far away, so alone with his memory, that she was afraid he might flinch at her touch. Her hand went back to her lap, to the forgotten sandwich gone soggy in its wrapping.

"I tried to scream and Auntie Rosie heard it. She woke up and ran into the room and knocked my mother in the head to make her let go. Uncle Dan called the police, and they took her away, and by the following week they had a diagnosis: paranoid schizophrenic. Sometimes she's well enough to come home and stay with us, but every few months or so she has another episode and back to the hospital she goes."

A soft mist had begun to steal over the mossy carpet of

the college green. Maggie finally found the courage to reach for Eoin's hand.

"I'm so sorry," Maggie said. "I didn't know."

He hung his head. "Now you think I'm some nut, I suppose."

"No." She shook her head and held his cold hand to her cheek for a long moment. "Families do horrible things to each other all the time—it's not your fault."

The mist had scattered all the students back to their classrooms and library cubbies. She and Eoin were alone, and Maggie felt like crying—for him, for herself, for the poor dead monks who couldn't save the jeweled front cover of the Book of Kells so that now, no one would ever be able to gaze at it under lit glass in the warm room of the Old Library.

"We've still got a couple hours to kill before the bus," Eoin said. "If you want—but it's cool either way—we could pay her a visit?"

"Your mom?"

"Yes. She's staying in the hospital just up the road, in Dun Laoghaire."

"Is that why you needed to come to Dublin today?"

He looked down at his sandwich wrapper. "I just didn't want to go by myself."

"I'll go with you," Maggie said. "Of course I will."

Our Lady of Perpetual Help Hospital was a short bus ride from Dublin, a gothic stone building set back from the road and surrounded by gnarled trees. It looked like the kind of place where delicate Victorian women may have gone, a hundred years earlier, to cure their nerves. Inside, the walls of the lobby were as blank and sterile as the outside had been turreted and mossy.

"How long has she been in here?" Maggie asked as they waited for the elevator.

"This time around, been about two weeks. Since right

before Christmas. Holidays are not optimal times for people with mental illness."

"Holidays are not optimal times for most people," Maggie observed. The elevator dinged, the doors slid open, and a nurse wheeled out a balding, jaundiced man, who was hunched over in his wheelchair and muttering to himself "One, two, three! One, two, three!" over and over again. Maggie's heart began to pound: she'd never been in a hospital before. Eoin remained stoic, but in the empty elevator, he stood closer to her than he needed to.

They stepped out of the elevator into a clean, carpeted hallway. A signpost on the wall read: FLOOR 8 PSYCHOSIS. Unmarked doors stretched in two directions. Eoin marched to the one on the left and pressed the buzzer. He waved at a small camera hanging from the ceiling and the door clicked open. Maggie hesitated.

"Come on," Eoin said, reaching back to grab her hand. "They don't bite. Well, some of them do. But they keep those ones in a different ward."

Maggie laughed weakly at his joke and followed him toward the sound of a bell-sweet soprano that was drifting down the empty corridor. The voice was singing "Raglan Road," perfectly on pitch, clear as rainwater, without the accompaniment of so much as a harmonica.

The door was ajar and Eoin knocked gently before pushing it open. His mother was sitting in a plastic chair, facing the window. She was dressed in a beige tracksuit, her thick back and large rump spreading across the seat. She wore a pair of gray socks and Adidas sandals, and her hair was tied up in a ponytail. The ponytail part was showgirl blond, but the roots were a faded, dull brown.

It was only when she stopped singing that she seemed to feel, as mothers do, the nearness of her child. She whipped her head around, revealing a once-pretty face gone droopy and stretched with rapid weight gain—the bloated side effects of steroids or heavy meds. A sheen of sweat stood out at her hairline and upper lip, where a faint mustache was apparent in the sunlight that slanted in through the barred window. Her star had fallen, that much was clear, but Maggie could see that Eoin's mother still possessed a faded glamour, the imprint of a memory of what she once was. She passed a hand over her lips as if ashamed at their chapped state, and pawed self-consciously at her hair. But if she was surprised or unhappy to see them, she didn't show it. Her smile was genuine, maternal: *normal*. She didn't look like the type of woman who could be capable of strangling her child.

"Hi, Mammy."

"Eoin, darling." She rose from her chair and wrapped him in a hug. He collapsed into her just a little, pressed his cheek to her hair. Touching his mother, Eoin's eyes fluttered closed. Maggie picked up a week-old issue of the *Irish Times* that was folded on the nightstand and pretended to read.

"Mammy, this is my friend, Maggie," he said.

"Hello, Maggie," Eoin's mother bowed her head politely.

"Hi, Mrs. Brennan," she said shyly.

"Oh, please! Call me Mary. You make me feel old. Please, sit down! You'll have some tea." She pointed at the bed, and Eoin and Maggie sat next to each other on the edge of it. She went over to a small dresser next to the sink and flicked on the electric kettle.

"How are you feeling, Mammy?"

Mary sat down heavily in her chair, sighing deeply.

"I'm good, I'm good," she said. "Everyone here is very nice. Except the night nurse, of course."

Maggie wanted to know more about the night nurse, but Eoin changed the subject quickly.

"We heard you singing when we came down the hall. Your voice is top-notch, Mammy. Sounds like the good old days."

She pulled nervously at her ponytail, girlish and pleased.

"D'you think so? I've been putting lots of lemon and honey

in my tea, trying to get my voice back. And I even gave up the fags. Haven't smoked in three days! The doctors here have arranged for me to put on a little concert this evening. Nothing too glamorous, of course. Just a little singsong in the canteen for the other patients on the ward." The kettle clicked off and she stood up and began to pour the tea.

"Well, that's great!" Eoin's voice had taken on an artificial quality, as if he was talking to a child prone to tantrums.

"Well, it's the least I can do for these poor people," she said, handing them their tea in thick paper cups. "You should see them—shitting themselves, wandering the halls half-crazed, babbling to themselves. It's awful. They're pure lunatics, most of them. But even a mad man can appreciate a bit of music, and as Jesus teaches us, we're meant to shine our light with the world—"

"Not hide it under a bushel," Eoin finished. "I know, Mammy. That's one of your favorites."

Mary beamed, reached over, and patted Eoin's cheek.

"My good boy," she said. "You always *listened* to your mother." She turned back to Maggie. "You see, I treat these little concerts as practice. I've got to keep my voice in shape for the bigger venues. Why, only next month I'll be giving a show at the Cork Opera House." She stopped, struck with an idea, and clapped her hands together. Her nails were long and pointed, and smeared with chipped purple polish. "You know what? The two of you should come! I'll call Eddie Naughton and get him to reserve you some seats!"

"That would be great!" Maggie said. "I've never been to an opera before."

"It isn't opera, though," Mary explained. "I sing traditional music. They've got Luke Kelly to accompany me on the banjo." She sipped her tea gleefully. "Can you believe it? The great Luke Kelly!"

Eoin, who had been twisting his hands together on his lap, began cracking his knuckles loudly, one by one. His Adam's apple bounced like a Geiger counter. He glanced at Maggie and shook his head nearly imperceptibly.

"What time's your show today?" Eoin asked with that same bright tone he'd been using since they'd arrived. "We'd love to stay and watch. I'd love for Maggie to hear you sing."

"Well, that would be lovely!" Mary smiled broadly. "What an unexpected treat. The show goes on right after supper—in about an hour. So you'll have to clear out for now. Even if it's just a practice gig, I need my privacy before I go on. I need to practice my scales, put on a little makeup and all that."

"Well, we'll leave you then, so." He put his cup on the dresser, leaned down, and kissed her quickly on the top of her head. "And we'll see you in the canteen in about an hour."

Mary walked them to the door. She put a hand on Eoin's cheek, searched his face with a pair of blank, gray eyes.

"My good boy," she said again, and now her voice was trembling, and she threw her arms around his neck. He hugged her back, and Maggie watched with a growing sense of shame. *How can he still love his mother, who almost killed him,* she wondered, *when sometimes I hate mine and I don't even know why?*

The hospital canteen was filled with late-afternoon light. It had high, arched, Plexiglas windows. The patients, murmuring quietly, were shuffling along the food line with their dinner trays. Young women in hairnets scooped turkey and parsley sauce, potatoes, and mashed turnips onto their plastic plates.

"I'm excited to hear your mom perform!" Maggie said, as she stepped into the canteen. "Will we eat dinner here, too?"

Eoin took her arm gently and held her back.

"There's no concert in the canteen," he said. "And no concert in the Cork Opera House. Luke Kelly's been dead for ten years, and my mother will probably never sing again for any crowd, not even this sad bunch." He waved a hand at the dining room. The patients were seated together at long tables, high school cafeteria style, but most ate with their heads bowed, content in their solitude, and Maggie was struck by how deeply lonely the sound of a fork scraping a plate at a silent table could be.

"I've found that the best way to keep her happy is to humor her," he said as they waited for the elevator. "We smile at each other and tell polite lies—and that's how I save our relationship." He shook his head. "I know it sounds funny, but you don't know what I would give to have a knock-down-drag-out *fight* with my mother, like a normal teenager!"

On the way back to Bray, Eoin slept, his head bouncing against the window. Maggie sat and stared out beyond him, at the gray sprawl of suburban Dublin. She thought about her own mother. It never occurred to her that she should be grateful for the screaming matches that had become, in the last year, a staple of their relationship. Eoin sighed in his sleep, nestling against the window. Beyond him, Maggie's face hovered in the reflection of the bus window. Earlier that day, in the steamy bathroom at Colm's house, she had wondered what Eoin could possibly see in her, an unremarkable girl who had been ignored by boys for most of her life. *But maybe it isn't about being pretty*, she thought, as the bus picked up speed on the N11. *Maybe it isn't even about boys.* After all, it wasn't a "boy," that foreign creature of big feet and low-pitched voice, who had come to her door on a Saturday morning and shown her the Book of Kells, who had sat on a bench under a beech tree and told her about the worst thing that had ever happened to him. It was a person. Eoin. And the sum of him was more than all the illusions and romantic notions she'd had in her early days in Bray when she went out for open lunch in search of "boys." She leaned her head on his shoulder, and he stirred to near waking, fumbling, in the darkness, for her outstretched hand.

In February, the eastern coast of Ireland experienced a rare event: a snowstorm. There were dire, apocalyptic warnings from the weathermen, people rushing off to buy canned goods, nervous talk on the streets. What ended up falling was a slushy four inches—mild, by Chicago standards, but the town council still closed the schools for three days. Maggie spent most of the unexpected vacation in her room. On the first day, she daydreamed about Eoin and listened to every single CD in her collection while the snow fell on the hills outside her window. On the second day, she daydreamed about Eoin and made progress on Kevin's list of *Excellent Books with Excellent Sex Scenes*: which is to say, she foraged through *Ragtime* and *The Unbearable Lightness of Being*, looking for the juicy parts. On the third day, she daydreamed about Eoin and leafed through Kevin's copy of *Lady Chatterley's Lover*, which she'd taken from his room on the night of his funeral. There, underlined lightly in pencil, she found the following passage: "He put his face down and rubbed his cheek against her belly and against her thighs again and again." The memory of Eoin's kiss came to her for the thousandth time, the feeling of his hand at the small of her back, and she began wondering what it would be like if Eoin were to kiss her belly and her thighs again and again. But then she remembered that this was Kevin's book, marked by Kevin's hand, and she slammed it shut, cheeks flushing, because those wavy pencil marks made her feel like he was in the room with her, listening to her secret thoughts and watching in affectionate disapproval: *Mags, you're supposed to read the* whole *book, not just the sexy parts, ya little perv!*

It was all too much—the grief for Kevin, the longing for Eoin, the overwhelming power of words. She needed air. She threw *Lady Chatterley's Lover* aside, pulled on her Wellingtons, and went out the back door to pay a visit to Dan Sean.

After three days of wet, heavy storms, the ground beneath her boots felt runny. Little rivers had appeared in the rocky hills and ditches, and even though it wasn't raining, Maggie's pants were saturated up to the thigh by the time she made it up Dan Sean's hill. He greeted her, as always, by motioning her into the high-backed chair next to the fire and hobbling over to the sink to put on the kettle. Woody, the dog, settled his dingy warmth across Maggie's wet lap while Dan Sean poured the tea and handed her a cup. Then, he humphed back into his chair.

"Some weather," he said, bringing his trembling cup to his lips. By now, Maggie understood the farmer's custom, and they spent ten minutes or so discussing the temperature, the cloud cover, the levels of precipitation, and whether cattle could be let out in this rain, before moving on to their real conversation.

"So," Dan Sean said, "how's your beau? The Brennan boy from up the road?"

"I need your help," Maggie said. "So I told you about how we went to Dublin and I met his mother."

Dan Sean nodded. "Shame what happened to that poor woman. What is it she's got?"

"Schizophrenia, it's called. Anyway, since then, we've hung out three times."

Dan Sean leaned forward in his chair and glared suspiciously at Maggie over the thick rims of his glasses. "What do you mean— *hung out*?"

"Dan Sean! It means, like, spent time together. Or, I don't know, courted or something."

"Good." He settled back into his chair. "I won't have you behaving like these young girls on television."

"*What* young girls?"

Dan Sean adjusted his Cossack's hat. "*You* know. The ones who get *up the pole*."

"Trust me, I'm not pregnant. We've *spent time* together, and that's all. Which is kind of the point I'm getting at."

Dan Sean held up an arthritic hand. "Where?"

Maggie began ticking off on her fingers. "Well, once, we went to Elvery's so he could buy a new soccer jersey; once, we met at the chipper after school and went for a walk along the water; and another time, I went to see him while he was working at the Quayside, and it was dead in there, so we sat at a booth and worked on our French homework together."

"French homework?" Dan Sean jabbed at the fire with a long iron poker. "Why have they got you studying French? *An bhfuil Gaeilge agat?*"

"Huh?"

"Exactly."

She sighed, and Woody snuffled in her lap.

"Dan Sean, you're getting off topic here! I have a *problem*. Don't you want to hear it?"

"Well, get on with it, then! I'm old—I haven't got all the time in the world." He poked the fire again, and a shower of sparks sizzled on the sooty hearth.

"You're so cranky sometimes." Maggie rolled her eyes. "Okay. So, me and Eoin—we laugh, we talk, we even touched knees under the table while we were doing our homework—I hope that doesn't make me a strumpet, in your book—but he hasn't tried to *kiss* me! Not since that night on New Year's Eve. He hasn't even looked like he was *thinking* about kissing me—and I'm beginning to think he just wants to be, like, friends."

Dan Sean listened to all of this wordlessly, blinking

periodically behind his black glasses. He folded his gnarled hands around his mug of tea. His Cossack's hat stood atop his small head like an exclamation mark. Finally, he spoke:

"So, he won't kiss you, is it?"

"That's right," Maggie said, running her hand along the dog's greasy back. "He won't kiss me."

"Well, that isn't good at all."

"I *know*! This is why I need some *advice*."

"It's a very simple problem to solve."

"What do I do?" She leaned forward, and the dozing dog tinkled his collar in annoyance.

"Wear perfume."

"What?"

"Perfume. It's simple. Men like women who smell good."

"But is it really that simple?"

"The problem with you young ones," Dan Sean sighed, "is that you overthink things."

While Maggie rolled this piece of advice around in her mind, she heard the crunch of gravel outside the window. An unfamiliar car was making its way up the driveway. It was an olive-colored Peugeot, with patches of rust and bald tires. A small old woman with a square of plastic tied around her white hair emerged from the car. Colm had warned Maggie that everyone in Bray knew each other, but she was still sort of shocked when she saw her English teacher coming up the walk.

"Oh, hello, Maggie!" Sister Geneve smiled brightly, untying the small knot beneath her chin. "I was *hoping* I might run into you up here. Dan Sean tells me that he's struck up a friendship with one of my Saint Brigid's girls."

"Maggie," Dan Sean yelled, his Cossack's hat quivering, "meet my niece, Geneve!"

"Your niece?" Maggie was incredulous. Sometimes it was hard to remember that not all old people were the same age.

"Well, technically speaking, I'm not his blood niece," Sister Geneve said. She went over to the sink and poured herself a cup of tea. "Dan Sean's wife, Nora, was my mother's sister."

"God rest her soul," Dan Sean mumbled, and the two of them paused to cross themselves. Maggie, hastily, did the same, and she remembered that winter afternoon when the old nun had cried reading the Yeats poem. *She was more beautiful than thy first love, / But now lies under boards . . .*

"But how . . ." Maggie trailed off. She remembered Nanny Ei's advice: never ask a woman her age, her weight, or her political affiliation.

"Dan Sean's ninety-nine," Sister Geneve said, reading her thoughts. "And I'm sixty-nine. Why, I'm a spring chicken compared to this old man!" She patted him affectionately on the arm and settled into a chair. "Would either of you have a little more tea?"

"I actually was just on my way out," Maggie said, lifting Woody to the floor and fumbling with her jacket. She stood up, her jeans sifting dried mud. "I have to help my mom with dinner."

This was, of course, a lie. The thing was, Maggie really liked Sister Geneve. But this was too weird. It was bad enough that her only friend was a ninety-nine-year-old farmer, but if she started socializing with teachers, too—nuns, no less—it was bound to leak at Saint Brigid's.

"Remember," Dan Sean called as she opened the door to leave, "*perfume*."

When Maggie arrived home, she found Ronnie parked on all fours in the sitting room, rump in the air, working on one of her puzzles.

"Eoin called you," Ronnie informed her. "He said to call him back at the Quayside. Is he your boyfriend?"

Maggie stood over the puzzle, squatted down, snapped a piece into place.

"Wouldn't you like to know. What time did he call?"

"Like twenty minutes ago. You smell like dog."

"Love you too, Ron."

She went into the kitchen and dialed the number, praying that Eoin's aunt wouldn't answer. It was embarrassing at the best of times to have to talk to the adult family members of the boy you were crazy about, but Maggie was quite sure that Auntie Rosie considered the Lynch family a bunch of drunken hillbillies after they had destroyed her bar on Christmas Eve.

"Hello, Quayside," the voice was soft and low and made Maggie feel happily adrift.

"Hey, Eoin."

"Maggie, how are things? Did you survive the snowstorm?"

"You'll have to come to Chicago with me sometime—I'll show you a *real* snowstorm."

"I'll have to take you up on that offer. In the meantime, what's your plan for this evening?"

"Don't have one." She twisted the phone cord around her fingers hopefully.

"Well, one of my mates just got his driver's license. Want to meet me here at the pub around seven? We're going to drive down to Greystones, maybe do a bit of bowling."

"Cool." She hung up, gave a happy little leap, then showered and dressed, brushed her hair loose around her shoulders, and smudged a thin strip of dark eyeliner against her lashes. She peered at the troubling acne that persisted on her chin and dabbed some concealer over it. There was only one last thing to do.

Hi, Kev, she prayed as she padded in bare feet into her mother's bedroom. *You met him once. I know you would approve. Please, please let him kiss me tonight.*

Her mother's mirrored dressing table was a mess of lipstick tubes, pots of eye shadow, nail polish, face creams, a package of Nice n' Easy Cocoa Brown hair dye. There was an ashtray in the shape of a seahorse that she was using as a jewelry holder, and curling school photos of Maggie and Ronnie stuck around the mirror frame. There were magazines and coupons and unopened mail. And there were several bottles of perfume. Maggie picked them up one by one, spritzing small bursts of jasmine, vanilla, and coconut into the bedroom, trying to find the perfect scent to make Eoin want to kiss her. When she picked up the last option, a squat, cheap-looking vial in the shape of a daisy, a plain white envelope beneath the clutter caught her attention—the fragment of her own name.

The envelope was hidden beneath several other papers. *Weird*, Maggie thought. *I barely ever get mail.* She moved aside the stack of papers that obscured the letter. It was postmarked December 31, 1993. She picked it up. When she saw the handwriting, that distinct boyish scrawl, the trembling slants and randomly capitalized *a*'s, her legs went weak.

She hid the letter under her shirt and locked herself into the bathroom. Trembling, she sat on the rim of the shower. Someone had already carefully opened the envelope with a knife. Maggie unfolded the notebook paper.

New Year's Eve, 1993

Dear Mags,

Of course by now you already know what I've
done + I want to tell you how sorry I am.
If I was a good Uncle, I would tell you it's
because of the drugs, how they've burned my
creative edge to ashes, + then this could
at least be a cautionary tale to you, a story
with a moral. But in all the ways I've disappointed
you, at least I will not lie to you now.
The truth is, the drugs aren't the problem.
My shitty band isn't the problem. My shitty
friends aren't the problem. The problem is me.
The problem has ALWAYS been me. My whole
life, the only thing I've ever managed to do
consistently + reliably is fuck up. The rest of the
world realized this years ago. You, my most loyal
fan, never realized it at all.

I look at you, Mags — God, you are so beautiful
+ so good. If I'm proud of anything in this life,
it's that, by some freakish whim of genetics,
a degenerate like me ended up an uncle to the
two loveliest nieces to ever grace this world.
I don't think I've even told you that —
Chalk it up to cowardice or Catholic repression
— so here it is now, + listen: I love you kid.
I love you, I love you, I love you.
Shine your light through that cool Irish
rain. Do all the great things that you

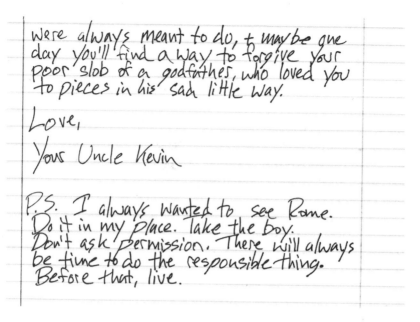

were always meant to do, + maybe one
day you'll find a way to forgive your
poor slob of a godfather, who loved you
to pieces in his sad little way.

Love,

Your Uncle Kevin

P.S. I always wanted to see Rome.
Do it in my place. Take the boy.
Don't ask permission. There will always
be time to do the responsible thing.
Before that, live.

Two tickets, printed on thick orange cardboard and paper clipped together, slipped out of the envelope and onto the bathroom floor. Maggie leaned down, her hands shaking, and picked them up. Nirvana, at the Palaghiaccio di Marino. Rome. February 22, 1994. In four days.

The air ticked. A single song thrush twittered on the drooping electrical line. What was that wake, then, but a giant cover-up? *Stay near me, Maggie. Don't talk to those bum friends of Kevin. I never liked them.* It made sense, now. Rockhead, Taco, Jeremy, even that blond girl from the Smashing Pumpkins show—they all knew. *They all knew, and I didn't. Me. His goddaughter, his niece, his Maggie. I was the only one who didn't know. And those bum friends of his would have slipped me the truth.* How had he done it, then? A rope? A razor? A small, determined step into the ice-frosted waters of Lake Michigan? Why did it feel like she was losing him all over again?

She went back into her mother's room. The perfume she'd sprayed hung thickly in the air: a funereal smell. She wandered, numb, into her own bedroom, crawled under the covers. She wanted to call Eoin and tell him she could not go bowling, but she didn't trust herself to speak, or even to leave her room. Ronnie came in, once, but Maggie turned to face the wall and pretended to be napping. She played Pearl Jam's *Ten* on her Discman from beginning to end and stared at the faded rose vines that crawled up and down her wallpaper. She waited, calm and singular of purpose as a sniper, for her mother to come home.

Around dinnertime, Maggie heard the key scrape in the lock. She placed her Discman next to her pillow and looked up at the ceiling.

"I will not cry," she said out loud. She threw her covers off and walked out into the sitting room, where Colm stood at the door untying his work boots.

"How did Kevin die?"

Colm froze. He looked up at her, his dark hair falling over his eyes.

"He died in his sleep, Maggie. You know that."

"No. Twenty-six-year-old men don't die in their sleep."

Colm kicked one boot off, then another. He stood there at the door, looking strangely defenseless in his socked feet.

"It was a heart defect, congenital. He had it since he was born. You know that—you saw the scar. Sometimes . . . these things just happen."

"Is there an autopsy report?"

Colm lined his boots neatly at the door, then sat down heavily on the couch.

"Look, Maggie. I am trying the best I can here. I know you are hurting. But it's not my place to—I wonder if maybe you should talk to your mother if you really want to sort out the details."

"Okay, then. I'm staying right here and I'm waiting for my mother to come home. I swear to God if she doesn't tell me the truth, then I will leave and never come back."

Colm sat there, his mouth half open, and raked his hand through his thick hair. Finally, he put his keys carefully on the end table.

"I'll let you wait for your mother, then. I never thought any of this was quite right." He got up, closed the kitchen door behind him, and made a hushed phone call.

Ten minutes later Laura arrived home, panting and flushed. She was still wearing her Dunne's apron. She hovered at the doorway as if deciding whether to face her oldest daughter, who sat like a small dark fortress on the paisley couch, or to run.

"Maggie."

"How did Kevin die?"

"Honey."

"Don't lie to me." Maggie's voice was all threat. "How did he die?"

Laura walked slowly toward her daughter, kneeled in front of Maggie on the sofa. Maggie reached beneath her sweater and thrust the letter out in front of her like a shield.

"Mags," Laura said. "Honey. You don't understand."

"No," Maggie said. "You stole this from me. He wrote it to *me*. Don't lie to me again."

Her mother's hands, damp with sweat, gripped Maggie's knees and black mascara tears leaked from her green eyes.

"I didn't want you to think of him that way, honey. I didn't want you to feel like he abandoned you. I didn't want you to admire or—or *romanticize*—what he did. Or to think that doing *that* is a way out when life gets hard. Because life is *always* going to be hard." Her mother was sobbing now, her shoulders shaking, her breath ragged. Maggie was aware, somewhere in the house, of a door closing. The soft burst of an engine coming to life. Colm shuttling Ronnie off somewhere, to spare at least one daughter from the truth. "Maybe it was wrong to lie to you, but I was trying to protect you. Me and Nanny Ei both. You've got to try and understand that."

"I want to know how he did it," Maggie said.

Laura dragged herself up, pushing off Maggie's knees, and sat on the couch. She breathed deeply, gathering herself to tell the story.

"He went to a party that night," she began, her eyes glued to the cloth bowl of apron in her lap. "He was drinking, he was doing drugs. He left the party and went home—everything that Nanny Ei said about that part of it was true. He went to the bird sanctuary; he saw the full moon. He told Nanny Ei about it and kissed her good night, and she went to bed. But what he did then—" she stopped.

"Tell me."

"He grabbed his blood thinner meds—you know, the stuff he takes for his heart. He went back to Jeremy's house and he took the whole bottle of pills. The party had mostly broken up by then, so no one was around. He locked himself in the bathroom. Jeremy broke down the door the next day and found him in the bathtub with his wrists cut."

She put her head in her hands.

"He did it there so Nanny Ei wouldn't have to see. God, there must have been so much blood. I can't think about it. I can't. I didn't want you to have to think about it either."

A razor. A bathtub full of thinned, watery blood. A small jar of pills meant to help his heart.

"Can you understand?" Laura said softly. "Can you understand why I thought it would be better just to lie?"

Maggie nodded, staring at the panels of the timber floor. She could not look at her mother. Laura kept talking, crying, the words tumbling out, the explanations. But Maggie had stopped listening. Had he already decided to do it when he'd come to Bray for Christmas? Had he joked with her and chatted with her and sang for her, all the while knowing—no, *deciding*—that he would never see her again? No. It wasn't possible. It was one impulsive act, made on an angry whim, fueled by drugs, gas-station champagne, and a whole lifetime of impulsive acts that had always, somehow, carried him safely into his next waking. That was the only explanation. Maybe he had experienced a moment of clear-headed panic watching the life pour out of his wrists, splashing at the tepid bathwater with weakening legs, just before he slipped away. Maybe he had been thinking, *Reverse this, reverse this. I want to go to shows at the Metro and make love to blond strangers and sing my throat to sandpaper. I want to play the Double Door and start a new band. I want to live. I want to fall in love. I want to see my nieces grow up.*

But no. Because he'd thought far enough ahead to write the letter. He'd been clear thinking enough to buy an international stamp and drop it in the mail.

This was what he had wanted.

That night, Maggie let her mother brush her hair and make her a hot chocolate. She didn't ask her why she had chosen to shelter her from this truth when she had never sheltered her from anything else. She let her mother tuck her into bed. She became as passive and blank as she'd been with Paul against the Ferris wheel.

As soon as she heard the shallow snores of her mother and Colm on the other side of the wall, Maggie pulled her duffel bag from under her bed, packed her necessities, propped open the window, and climbed out. She ran up the back hill, feeling the mud ankle deep, squelching into the instep of her Converse. Oh, starless Ireland, there was no way to look up and find her way, but now she knew it by feel, past the dark hulk of Auntie Rosie's house beyond the field, and up to Dan Sean's. She was high enough that the clouds had wisped away and the whole cup of Wicklow was there before her, the basin of the Irish Sea, the lapping shore, the black bulk of Bray Head. She stood for a full minute in front of Dan Sean's door, her hand wavering on the doorknob. She turned it. Locked.

She peeked in the front window. The only light inside was a circle of dying red embers in the huge brick fireplace. Dan Sean's rocking chair was empty, his blanket folded neatly on the velvet cushion. Even if he were to hear her ring the doorbell, Maggie couldn't bring herself to roust a ninety-nine-year-old man from his sleep.

In the muddy yard behind the house, a small shed stood surrounded by rusty farming equipment and bales of silage. Inside, Dan Sean's gray-spotted goat, Billy, lay sleeping on the straw. The February wind battered Maggie's thin jacket as she approached the shed. She crossed her arms and shivered. Never before had she felt so entirely alone. There was nowhere else for her to go: not home, not Eoin's, not Aíne's, not anywhere. *It can't get any worse than this, can it, Kev?* she prayed. *If you could just help me make it through tonight, I know things will never be this bad again.* She crept into the doorway and Billy swung her head around, the moonlight glancing off her beady eyes. She nickered, a sharp, insulted blast from deep in her throat. Maggie, shushing her, reached out a hand and pet the bristly spine at the ridge of her back.

"I promise I'll be out in the morning," she whispered. Billy glared at Maggie for another moment. Then, perhaps with an animal's innate sense of things, she swung her head away and snuffled back into the hay, leaving just enough room for Maggie to curl next to her. The shed was thick with the smells of mud and manure. Maggie pulled Kevin's flannel shirt tightly around her shoulders, covered herself with the dry straw, and snuggled into Billy's warm animal stink. The goat's rib cage rose and fell against her cheek, the quick heartbeat quivering beneath the spotted skin. Maggie didn't think she would ever be able to sleep, but as the shed warmed with the heat of their bodies, the sorrow and exhaustion of the night overcame her, and the small space soon fell away into a dream in which her fingers trailed through warm bathwater, searching for the upturned faces of all the people she loved.

Just before dawn, Maggie was awoken by a kick to the back.

"Jesus, Billy," she said, rolling over. "I get your drift." The goat responded by stepping on her, its hooves digging into the soft flesh of her stomach, and strutting out of the shed into the morning. It stood directly outside the doorway, glaring at Maggie with beady, malevolent eyes, and issued a forceful stream of urine that splashed off the mud and onto her jeans. Dodging the stream, Maggie climbed out of the shed on all fours and backed away from the resentful goat. Her muscles, clenched against the damp cold all night, were achy and stiff. She reached down to touch her toes, joints cracking, while Billy wandered off to search the yard for bits of garbage to eat.

The morning was cold and foggy, a hanging greenness in the air. The sleep had done Maggie well—she still felt shaken, but resolved. There was no going back. There was only Rome. For a month now, Maggie had been praying to Kevin instead of God, and finding that letter six weeks after his funeral and only four days before the concert made her feel like he had heard her prayers and answered them. She now believed, with an evangelical determination, that he would find a way to get her to Italy, too. She pulled his flannel tight around her shoulders, rubbed a kink at the back of her neck, and stood for a moment watching the sky lighten the peaks of the hills. Then, she unzipped her duffel bag and laid out its contents: the fifty-pound note Nanny Ei had given her at

Christmas, her Discman, her Liz Phair, Nirvana, and Selfish Fetus CDs, a few changes of clothes and underwear, Kevin's compass, a plastic bag containing a toothbrush, concealer, and black eyeliner, and finally, zipped carefully into the inner pocket, the concert tickets.

It was enough.

She went around to the back of Dan Sean's house and found that someone had unlocked the back door. "Dan Sean?" she called, turning the knob. It was early, but she knew he'd be awake. He was on farmers' hours, even now.

He was not in the sitting room, so she went to the metal bucket at the side of the fireplace and stoked the embers with some turf. It caught, and the fire filled the room with its earthy smoke. Maggie sat on the floor in front of the blaze for a while, closing her eyes while the glorious heat burned warmth back into her cheeks. Woody, joyful at her presence, came loping down the stairs on his two front legs, the cat darting past him and out the opened door.

"Mike?" The reedy voice traveled down the narrow staircase. "I'm up here."

Maggie hesitated. She'd never been up to the second floor of Dan Sean's house before. "Dan Sean? It's me, Maggie!"

She stood at the bottom of the stairs and listened. No response.

"I hope you're decent," she called, her hand on the railing. "I'm coming up!"

The upstairs was cold, dim, and low ceilinged. Mass cards lined the walls of the narrow hallway, which smelled of dander and stale bedding. A candle flickered inside the bedroom door, where Dan Sean was crouched on a faded velvet church kneeler before a shrine to the Blessed Virgin. Glass votives, their wicks burning high in the still air, lined the altar. In the middle was a statue, nearly four feet tall, of the Virgin Mary in her traditional blue robes, her eyes and palms pointing heavenward. Bunches of dried lavender and rhododendron were stuffed in plastic vases at the corners of the altar, and Dan Sean was halfway through his rosary.

Oh my Jesus, forgive us our sins, save us from the fires of hell, lead all souls to Heaven, especially those who have most need of your mercy. Maggie hovered at the doorway and waited for him to finish, his mumbled words ticking over the Hail Marys and Our Fathers, the Glory Bes, the Holy Mysteries. For the first time, she saw him without his Cossack's hat. His head was small and thin skinned, with bits of white hair horseshoed around his ears. He wore a pair of old-fashioned pajamas, unbuttoned to reveal a concave chest as brindled with liver spots as a horse's hide. *Hail, Holy Queen, mother of mercy, our life, our sweetness, and our hope. To you we cry, poor banished children of Eve; to you we send up our sighs, mourning and weeping in this valley of tears. Show unto us the blessed fruit of your womb Jesus. O clement, O loving, O sweet Virgin Mary.* He crossed himself, kissed the rosary, and dropped it back in its little silk pouch. Maggie went over to him. He put his arthritically puffed hands in hers and allowed himself to be helped up, but his eyes were glazed and far away. For the old, Maggie imagined, finishing a rosary was like leaving a concert was for a younger person—it took you a while to adjust back to the normal world. The religion of Dan Sean's generation, it turned out, was still religion.

"Put on the kettle and stoke the fire," he instructed. "I've got to get dressed."

She went downstairs and began preparing the tea. When he came down ten minutes later, he was neatly dressed in his suit and hat.

"Dan Sean," she said, stirring the milk into her cup, "I'm leaving town for a bit today. I wanted to say good-bye."

"Not back to America, I hope?"

She shook her head. "Rome."

"Ah!" Dan Sean clapped his hands together. "On a pilgrimage?"

"Well, I've never really thought about it that way, but yeah." She smiled suddenly. "A pilgrimage."

"Where are you staying?"

"I have absolutely no idea."

Dan Sean banged his mug on the little end table next to his chair. "Go into the other room and get me my address book."

Maggie found the stained leather journal next to a broken rotary telephone. When she handed it to him, he fanned her away.

"Christ above, there's a smell off you!"

"I know, I know," she said, lifting the dirty cuff of her sweater to her nose. "I slept outside with Billy last night."

"Well, what'd you do that for? Go in there and take a bath. I'll have this ready when you come out."

He pointed to the bathroom, and Maggie put down her tea and humbly obeyed, closing the door behind her. The bathtub was a simple corrugated basin, and when she turned on the ancient faucets they moaned, spilling warm water down rusty trails. She took off her clothes, folded them carefully, and huddled into the tub. Dan Sean's small shaving mirror hung from the faucet. In its reflection, her hands reached to the wooden windowsill for the box of Borax soap and poured it into the water. Without being able to see her familiar, teenaged face in the mirror, Maggie was able to admire her body for the first time. It was like watching the private movements of a stranger. The hands cupped the soapy water and washed the white neck, the lightly freckled shoulders, and the two round breasts, entirely formed and entirely hers. Water streamed over her skin as she rubbed Borax into her hair and washed it in the shadowy light from the frosted glass window. The hands then rubbed the belly, the thighs, between the thighs, and down to the toes with their paint-chipped toenails. When she was finished, she pulled the stopper and climbed out of the bath, her skin feeling as shrunken and clean as bleached laundry. She pulled on a clean pair of underwear, letting her hands linger over the drying heat of her own skin, and combed her wet hair with her fingers. When she emerged from the bathroom, dressed in a fresh pair of jeans and a Nirvana t-shirt, Dan Sean was waving a piece of paper at her.

"This is the address for the Chiese del Domine Quo Vadis," he said. "The Church of Lord, Where Are You Going. This is where you can see the soles of Jesus's feet imprinted in the marble. There's a convent hotel nearby, the Casa di Santa Barbara. You can get there by taking the bus towards Volpi. Tell Marta that you're my friend—she'll give you a good rate."

Maggie folded the note and put it in her pocket. She hugged Dan Sean's small, trembling frame.

"Thank you for everything." Her eyes stung with sudden tears.

"You can thank me by bringing me back some holy water!" he yelled.

"You got it, old man." She kissed the cool skin of his jowly cheek and stepped out into the yard, where Billy stood near the chicken wire fence chewing on a Crunchie wrapper.

"Thanks for your hospitality, Billy!" Maggie called as she passed. The goat responded by tossing her head, swishing her tail, and emitting a low, rumbling fart.

As Maggie headed toward town, the winter sunshine warmed the crown of her wet head, drying her hair in soft waves. For the first time since New Year's Day, she felt the heavy stone of grief in her heart begin to lift. She was scared and alone and hungry, but at least she was *doing* something: Closure. A pilgrimage. *Nirvana*.

At the train station café, she bought a sausage roll, a soggy gray oval of meat wrapped in a sheen of greasy biscuit. Biting into it, she was flooded with hunger. She realized that she had not eaten since the previous afternoon, when she and Ronnie had shared biscuits and currant bread before she'd gone up to Dan Sean's. Before the letter. Licking her fingers, she went back to the shop and bought a paper cup of tea and a chocolate bar—runaway food, the packaged provisions of the motherless. She bought a ticket to Dublin from the automated machine, popped Liz Phair's *Exile in Guyville* into her Discman, and sat on a bench waiting for the train. A hotel bellman whistled past, followed by a homeless woman with long, flyaway gray hair and a pair of young brothers in matching Limerick jerseys and hurling sticks slung over their shoulders. An African mother in yellow robes and a matching headpiece tried to navigate a stroller containing a screaming baby around the uneven pavement. As Maggie watched the woman, she realized, with a stabbing sense of possibility, how free she was. Unencumbered by family anymore, the world was hers. It would have been nice to say good-bye to Eoin, but she could always find a payphone once she got to the city. Maybe he could even come hang out with her at night, find her a place to stay, tell her where she could eat for cheap. She would only be gone a few days. Or maybe longer. She didn't know.

It was a forty-minute ride to Dublin. When she stepped off the platform at Connolly station, teeming with office workers and backpackers hoofing their huge multicolored packs and buskers singing Beatles songs, guitar cases opened at their feet and glittering with coins, Maggie felt the rush of urban chaos that reminded her of home, of the night Kevin had taken her to the Smashing Pumpkins show and they'd danced all night and in the morning, even the cars looked wilted and the sun was a pink wine stain across the jagged Chicago skyline, ushering in another perfect summer day.

There were plenty of hotels constellating from the streets that surrounded the train station, and even though most were shabby with flashing neon signs and gruff cashiers, the prices they advertised in their smudged windows were enough to eat up, in two or three days, the little money Maggie had—and that was before she found a way to hustle up the money for a plane ticket to Italy. Since she had nowhere else to go, she walked around for the better part of the morning, as far out as the posh, brightly colored doors and brick facades of Ballsbridge, and back into the city center. She walked through Trinity again, under the Campanile and past the Old Library, and then around again, until late afternoon, when lowering clouds threatened rain and the soles of her feet ached inside the slap of her thin Converse. There were all sorts of nice little cafés advertising their soup and sandwich specials on chalkboards outside their front doors, but Maggie had to be careful with her money and instead stopped for a hamburger at Supermac's. What she wanted, with an irrational pique of longing for someone who'd been a runaway for exactly twenty-four hours, was a Coke, but she asked for a cup of water instead, which was free, and which was given to her reluctantly by the bucktoothed manager who looked at her askance as she sat, hunched over her paper bag, devouring. It made her feel like a street urchin already.

She briefly considered sleeping in a quiet corner of Saint Stephen's Green and waking early in the morning to find her way out to the airport, but the incessant, bone-chilling February rain that had begun to fall made her reconsider. She was about to give up, return to the train station, and find a bench, when she walked past a backpackers' hostel, an open doorway with a garish pink sign: Nora Barnacle's—*Beds 4 Cheap*. A group of twenty-somethings stood clumped around the door, smoking hand-rolled cigarettes and speaking a language that sounded like blowing bubbles. They ignored her when she walked inside.

Behind the desk, a small, Slavic-looking girl with blond hair and a yellow warm-up jacket was sitting and staring at a tiny television.

"Yes?" She did not look away from her program.

"Um, what are your room rates for tonight?"

"Ten pounds. Fifteen if you want sheets and towel."

Maggie fingered the folded bills in her front pocket. How necessary, really, were sheets anyway?

"I don't need sheets." She pushed the money across the counter and the girl glanced at Maggie's small, threadbare duffel bag without comment. Maggie liked that. If this was a mind-your-own-business type of place, then she'd chosen well.

"Go up stairs behind me," said the girl, pointing. "Pick a bed that's open. Curfew midnight."

Maggie, suppressing a grin, thanked the girl and headed up the stairs. A curfew of midnight was no curfew at all—her mom had always made her come home at eleven, Nanny Ei, nine thirty.

The setup of the dorm was nearly identical to the Girl Scout camp in Galena where Maggie had been discarded for a week many years back when her parents had been, as they'd explained, "working on *us* for a while." The room was a large, spare loft, with high, narrow windows and rows of utilitarian bunk beds. The open bunks were indicated by their bare, striped mattresses, and others were made up with the scratchy white sheets that Maggie hadn't been able to afford. Some were covered with warm nylon sleeping bags that Maggie stared at enviously. Why hadn't she brought a warmer coat?

She found an unclaimed mattress near the windows and sat down. Scattered about the room were travelers poring over guidebooks or drinking beer, young people from all over the world. A few beds down from where she sat, a heavyset man with a perfectly shaped bald head and skin so smooth and gorgeously dark it was nearly blue—Maggie finally understood why the Gaelic term for *black man* was *fear gorm*, which translated to "blue man"—was sitting before a small audience, ankles crossed, his back curved over his guitar. He was playing "Brokedown Palace," a Grateful Dead song Maggie recognized from Kevin's hippie phase. She sat on her lower bunk with her bag in her lap and listened. *Fare you well, my honey, / Fare you well, my only true one . . .* They'd had to dig his grave with pickaxes, once the funeral party had been shepherded away to the warm banquet hall. Terrible enough if it had been visited upon him by fate, by a failed heart. But how could he have wanted that for himself? *All the birds that were singing have flown / except you alone . . .*

"Are you okay?"

Maggie looked up into the face of one of the most beautiful women she had ever seen. The accent was American, and hearing that nasal enunciation after months of Irish lilt gave Maggie a jarring flash of homesickness.

"Sorry," she said. "I was just listening to that guy play." The woman, who looked five or six years older than Maggie, had long blond hair that hung in tangles down to her waist, with pieces loosely braided throughout. She wore a soft-knitted sweater, the kind everyone back home called a drug rug. She glanced in the direction of the music and sat next to Maggie on the bed.

"That's Ehi," she said. "He's a friend of mine. Pretty good, huh? You play music?"

Maggie shook her head. "But my uncle does." *Did*.

"Well, Ehi can probably teach you some chords, if you're interested." She stuck out a hand, the fingers long and tapered, elegant. "I'm Ashley."

"Maggie." She shook the soft hand.

"I'm from California. Santa Cruz. Been traveling all over. Asia, Eastern Europe, North Africa—that's where I met Ehi. He's from Ghana, but when I met him he was a student in Cairo on semester break. I convinced him to extend it. We've spent the last six months backpacking Europe. Ireland's one of our last stops—we've got a couple more days here—then it's over to Scandinavia. Then, I guess, home." She looked over at Ehi, smiled absentmindedly. "I suppose that's where he and I will part ways."

"Is he your boyfriend?"

Ashley shrugged.

"As much as either one of us has ownership of the other, I guess. I haven't told him I'm headed home yet." She sighed dramatically. "I'm dreading it."

Ashley pulled a pack of Silk Cut Blues out of her sweater pocket and offered one to Maggie. Maggie didn't really want one—she'd grown up in a house of smokers, so the act had never seemed particularly rebellious—but Ashley, with her beachy hair and debutante's nose, had a quality about her that made you want to accept whatever it was she offered. Maggie took the cigarette and Ashley pulled out a Zippo and flicked open the flame. The foul taste filled Maggie's lungs, but with an iron will—and a lifetime of secondhand smoke—she suppressed a cough and exhaled in a gray cloud.

"So. What's your story?" Ashley asked, lighting her own cigarette.

"Me?" Maggie's mind raced, pausing on several different lies before settling on one that she thought Ashley would believe. "Well, I'm from Chicago. But I live here now—I'm just down in Dublin for a couple nights to look at colleges."

"Colleges!" Ashley laughed, exhaling smoke like a mod girl from a sixties movie. "You look like you're about twelve!"

"No, actually I'm eighteen." The cigarette had made the air buzz, and Maggie felt giddy and sophisticated. She *felt* eighteen.

"Well, I'm probably not the right person you should be talking to," Ashley said. "I dropped out. I thought I'd get my education through travel. I've been to over forty countries."

"What was your favorite?"

"Morocco, without a doubt. I grew up watching *Casablanca* and being there, I actually *felt* like Ingrid Bergman, you know?"

Maggie didn't, but she nodded encouragingly. It was so nice to have somebody to talk to—an American, no less—and she didn't want Ashley to leave.

"So, you here by yourself?" Ashley stretched her legs, which were long and tanned and covered with downy blond hair, and put them on Maggie's lap. She had chipped red paint on her toenails and a gold ring around her middle toe that tinkled with tiny bells.

"Well, for tonight," said Maggie. "But my boyfriend's going to meet me in a couple of days." She liked the way the word *boyfriend* felt on her tongue, even if it was a lie.

"Well, you should come out with us tonight, then," Ashley said. "There's nothing more depressing than sitting alone in an empty hostel on a Saturday night." She ran a hand through her tangled hair. "Meet us downstairs at the bar in an hour, okay? I'm going to go take a shower. I just had sex and I need to freshen up down there, you know?" She winked and sauntered off toward Ehi's bed, and in her departure Maggie was left to process this stunning bit of candor.

Maggie had an hour to make herself look eighteen, and the concealer and eyeliner she'd brought in her Ziploc bag weren't going to cut it, especially not with this crowd. She rushed down the stairs and out onto the street, where she found a small pharmacy a couple doors down from the hostel. She bought some cheap black mascara, a compact with blush and eye shadow, red lipstick, and a little vial of drugstore perfume.

Back at Nora Barnacle's, she stood before a shattered mirror in the communal women's bathroom and attacked her teeth with a glob of toothpaste. She tarred her lashes in the mascara, rubbed the gray shadow along her lids, swiped blush along her cheekbones and painted her lips a deep red. She put on the black cotton dress she'd packed for the Nirvana show and pulled on her boots, stuffing her money and her concert tickets into the ankle. On her way downstairs, she paused to look at herself in the bathroom mirror again. The makeup and the tight black dress made her appear not just older, but dangerous and urban. She felt that this was a self that she could inhabit, a person she could become. She tied Kevin's flannel around her waist. Her pilgrimage had begun.

Ehi and Ashley were already drinking at the hostel bar with a small, eclectic crowd of Europeans.

"Beer?" Ehi offered, his voice booming over the thin pop music that streamed from a speaker above the bottles of whiskey and rum. Maggie nodded shyly and he called to the bartender, who put a Heineken in front of her. She'd tried wine and port before, and even whiskey, but this was her first-ever sip of beer. It was awful.

Ashley appeared at her side. She'd wrapped her hair in some sort of red printed scarf, and she looked like a gorgeous gypsy from a Grimm's fairy tale.

"So, Chicago, tell me the truth. I *know* you're not here to look at colleges. Europeans don't *do* that. You're a runaway, aren't you?"

Maggie, to bide her time, swigged from the Heineken. It made her eyes water.

"Not exactly," she said finally. "It's more of a temporary thing."

Ashley smiled, flashing a perfect set of white teeth, and put a slender arm around Maggie's shoulder.

"You can tell me," she said. "I'm a runaway, too." She laughed, a light sound like the tinkling of her toe ring. "Do you know my dad is one of the most successful movie producers in LA? I mean, I went to the Buckley School. You've heard of it, I'm sure."

Maggie hadn't, but Ashley was not in the habit of waiting for people to answer her questions.

"And I know you might be thinking, poor little rich girl," she continued. "But honestly, having everything—it numbs your *mind*. So one day, I just decided to say fuck it! And I took a leave of absence from UCLA. My parents said they'd bankroll me for a year, help me find myself or whatever. First, I went to London, called up some people I knew. It didn't feel all that different from California, except for the rain. But then, I went to Poland. At Auschwitz, I felt—well, I felt a lot of things, obviously. But what I felt *most*: it was this feeling of neutered existence, like I'd been locked away in a castle all my life. Not that I *envy* people who have suffered. But don't you think that never suffering at all—is its *own* form of suffering?"

Well, you've obviously never lost someone you loved, Maggie thought. But she nodded politely and sipped her beer.

"The thing about traveling," Ashley continued, leaning her elbows on the bar, "is that it doesn't cure your wanderlust.

Tennyson says that 'all experience is an arch wherethrough gleams that untravelled world, whose margin fades forever and forever when I move.' And that's exactly what it's like. The more of the world you see, the more insatiable the desire to see more becomes. You're always reaching for the next place. You want more and more and more and soon enough you realize that you can't ever go home."

"I know what you mean," Maggie said. "I don't even know where my home *is* right now."

"Right?" Ashley tucked a loose blond strand back into the folds of her headscarf. "So, anyway, my parents gave me a year but I've been gone eighteen months. I'm actually fending for myself for once—I haven't spoken to my family in four months. And each day that goes by, I feel less and less like I can ever go back. I was studying fashion merchandising when I dropped out. Can you imagine? How can I go back and major in fashion merchandising when I've walked the slums of Calcutta?"

She paused, picked up her beer, closed her eyes, and took a long drink. Ehi came over, clapped an arm around each of them. His guitar was slung over his back.

"Who's this?"

"Ehi, this is Chicago! She's a runaway. She's a big fan."

Ehi grinned down at Maggie from his impressive height. His eyes, like Ashley's, were bloodshot and dreamy.

"Well, perhaps I will play for you later tonight," he said. His accent managed to sound both sophisticated and approachable. He waved an arm and the entire group finished their drinks and followed him out into the Dublin night.

The pack of them—Ashley and Ehi and the people who'd sounded like they were blowing bubbles (Dutch, as it turned out)— walked down through Temple Bar, where the nightclubs pulsed and spilled drunk, done-up teenagers onto the street, lining the curbs like finely plumaged birds. Ashley marched through them with the purposeful way of the beautiful, her face a sneer.

"This is where the amateurs hang out, the college kids from Boston who think they're all international because they got their very own passport last week," she explained. "You won't meet anyone interesting here." She linked her arm through Maggie's as they traversed the city, past the flower stands and street performers on Grafton Street and into McDaid's because one the Dutchmen, who was getting his PhD in Irish literature, wanted to sit at the barstool where Brendan Behan drank and perhaps in the process get some good vibes to help him finish his dissertation, which had stalled halfway through, at five hundred pages. He sat next to Maggie, lurching into her, his breath reeking of onion crisps and Guinness, and confided, "The whole thing is actually a heaping pile of shit: a reflection, really, of my entire grad school experience."

Eventually, they made their way back to Saint Stephen's Green. They walked past the Shelbourne Hotel, its tall, grand windows and curling staircase, and in the failing light Maggie could see elegant couples leaning together over glasses of red wine, finely dressed old women sitting in plush velvet chairs sipping champagne from crystal flutes.

"That's the kind of place I'd be staying if I was with my father," Ashley said as they walked past. "Only the finest for David Green. But don't you think the way we're living now—cheap hostel, cheap beer, good company, strangers who become friends by the end of the night—don't you think this is better? This, here, is *real life*!" She squeezed Maggie's arm in the crook of her elbow and guided her across the street and through the northeast entrance of the park while Ehi, the Dutch contingent, and a trio of Greek college students followed behind.

The park had fallen into shadow, the swans floating in the pond like white buoys. In the little gazebos, small groups of flannelled runaways huddled against the cold. Ashley found a spot beneath a circle of bare trees in the north end of the park. Ehi took a bright wool blanket from his guitar case and spread it on the ground. He picked at the instrument for a minute and strummed a few chords. Someone began passing around a joint, and when it came to Maggie, streaming smoke, she inhaled once, delicately, and held the sweet smoke on her tongue. Then she tried again, this time puffing harder. A heavy heat rolled down her throat, and she burst into a coughing fit. Ashley laughed and gently kneaded her shoulder.

"Not so hard," she whispered, her voice honey heavy. The joint came around again sometime later, and Maggie felt the sensation of limbs both heavy and weightless. The swans trailed silently in the water and the air beat around her like a pulse. Her hair blew in the wind, and bits of trash skittered by on the walking path. Ehi bent over his guitar, his fingers strumming a G chord.

"Any requests?" Ashley said. Her voice sounded far away. "Ehi can play whatever you want."

"Do you know 'I Know You Rider'?" Maggie spoke for the first time since they'd sat down. "It's, like, a folk song. My uncle used to sing it for me."

Ehi's fingers moved over his strings while he thought.

"I don't think I do," he said. "Sing a little bit of it for me."

"I can't sing," Maggie said.

"Come on!" Ashley said, handing her the joint. "Everyone can sing a *little* bit!"

The small band of Dutchmen and Greeks sat cross-legged on the bright blanket, making room for the runaways who had fluttered over like moths to the flame of Ehi's guitar. The pot had inhabited Maggie's brain and everything around her felt gauzy and pleasant, even the faces of staring strangers and the cold, cutting wind.

"Okay, why not?" She leaned her head back, her hair brushing the grass, her throat white and exposed in the moonlight, and began to sing.

I know you, rider, you're gonna miss me when I'm gone
I know you, rider, you're gonna miss me when I'm gone

I love you, rider, and I know you must love me some
I love you, rider, and I know you must love me some
You put your arms around me like a circle round the sun

Ehi had taken up the melody on his guitar and the runaways and Dutch PhD students stood up, bobbing their heads like the swans on the pond. Her voice was nothing special, but it didn't matter. She'd never sung for anyone before, had never even wanted to. Now, raising her voice above the wind, it felt like she'd been doing it all her life.

I laid down last night and I tried to take my rest
My heart was ramblin' like wild geese in the west
I wish I was a headlight on a northbound train,
I wish I was a headlight on a northbound train,
I'd shine my light through cool Colorado rain.

The city at night was a blooming thing, come to drink at the Liffey and the life spiraling from its banks, spreading all the way out to the battered rock at the edges of the country, the black mountains of Donegal, the rainy coasts of Kerry, the shores of Wicklow. They all called her Chicago, and that's who she became—a nameless nomad of Dublin, unmoored from her family and her past, from any life she'd known. A fine snow of downy confetti sifted from the sky, coating Maggie's eyelashes and hair as Ashley grabbed her hands and spun her around the blanket. They were both laughing. More joints were passed, small bottles of brown liquor. Hours or minutes later they meandered back to Nora Barnacle's along the narrow streets paved in bumpy cobblestone, the shooting stars of neon signs, singing Janis Joplin while their wild voices reverberated off the emptying streets. Maggie remembered climbing the rickety hostel stairs, Ashley's warm grip on her arm. She remembered Ashley's sweet breath over her, pulling off her boots and placing them next to her bed, helping her out of her clothes, peeling off her dress and tights and folding Kevin's flannel into a pillow beneath her head. She remembered feeling tired and sweetly anonymous. And then she was asleep.

She awoke in late morning, the rain beating on the thin roof of the dormitory. Her head throbbed. She was in her underwear, covered by someone else's sheet. Ashley's, she thought. *That girl is so cool.* She sat up slowly, rubbing the dried mascara from her eyes. There were a few other strangers scattered around the dormitory, sprawled in their sleeping bags, but the room was mostly abandoned. Ehi and his guitar were gone. Ashley's things, her bright green sleeping bag and North Face backpack, also gone. Maggie pulled on her jeans and reached into her boots to retrieve her money and her concert tickets.

They were gone, too.

13

Maggie dumped the contents of her duffel bag onto the bed and began clawing through them. Her brain rung from the liquor and the beer and the weed. She yanked up the mattress, got on her hands and knees, and crawled along the floor around her bed. What she found, through the blur of her tears, were dusty clumps of lint and strangers' hair, a half-melted tube of purple lipstick, and a scattering of mouse droppings. She shook out her Doc Martens again and again, knowing, even as she did this, that she was wasting her time. Had anything Ashley said been true? The rich girl stuff? The fashion merchandising? But then, no true street urchin would have teeth that nice. So maybe Ashley had just done it for the thrill. Or maybe this what she had meant by "fending for herself." *How could I be so stupid?* Maggie gagged, tasting the bile in her throat. She ran to the bathroom and kneeled on its cold tiles. She puked violently, saliva swirling lazily in the toilet. She wiped her mouth and straightened up to go look at her swollen face in the mirror. Her eyes were bloodshot, crescented by pink bags, "like two piss holes in the snow," as Nanny Ei used to say to Kevin when he came home from a drinking binge. She brushed her teeth and begged twenty cents off the Slavic girl at the front desk who, seeing the tears trembling in the corners of Maggie's eyes, dropped her Cold War act and slid the coins across the counter with a sympathetic smile.

"Bad night?"

Maggie nodded, and the tears spilled over and splashed on the counter. She wiped them away with her finger, went to the payphone, and dialed the number of the Quayside.

An hour later, she sat, duffel bag on in her lap, at a bench at Connolly Station. When the train from Bray pulled up and she saw Eoin's dark head ducking through the crowd, she opened her mouth to call out to him but instead dissolved into tears again. She collapsed into him, the warm detergent smell of his sweatshirt reminding her of home, of chores, of her mother.

He took her to get something to eat, and it took every ounce of Maggie's self-control not to devour her entire breakfast with her bare hands. Meanwhile, with gentle questions, he got the story out of her. She told him about Kevin's letter and her mother's confession and her night out with Ashley and Ehi.

"I have to get those tickets back," Maggie said. "It was supposed to be my pilgrimage."

"Tell you what," Eoin said, forking a tomato into his mouth, "why don't we stay in Dublin for another day? We'll scour the city for these two. If we find them, I'll go to Rome with you. Just like your uncle said."

"But even if we *do* find them—then what?"

Eoin shrugged. "We kick their asses and steal the tickets back. No bother."

"But what if they've already *sold* the tickets?"

"Then we kick their asses for the simple satisfaction of it, and we go home avenged!"

"But what if we try to kick their asses and we end up getting *our* assed *kicked*?"

"Who's gonna win in a fight—a couple runaways with fucked-up families and nothing to lose, or some rich California princess and her hippie boyfriend? I know who *I'd* put my money on."

"I don't know, Eoin. That hippie boyfriend was about six foot three."

Eoin rolled up his sleeve and flexed his forearm.

"That may be true," he said, grinning, "but only one of us was a champion under-twelve boxer in the Bray Athletic Club who retired, undefeated, before his thirteenth birthday."

Maggie laughed. "Well, that *is* pretty impressive," she said. "But what if we somehow actually find the two of them—*and* we manage to kick their asses, *and* we get the tickets back? Then what? How the hell are we supposed to get to Rome?"

"Listen, Maggie." Eoin leaned over their breakfast plates. "You came this far, didn't you? You wouldn't have run away in the first place if you didn't believe you'd get there somehow."

"I know." She put her hands over her face. "But part of me just thought Kevin would, like, show me the way somehow. I swear, sometimes I forget that he's actually *dead—real world* dead, not angel-in-a-fairy-tale dead—and that he can't help me anymore."

"Well, why don't you let me pick up where he left off?" He put his hands on hers and gently pulled them away from her face. "I've been working at the Quayside since I was fourteen. The only thing I ever spend my money on is *Shoot!* magazine and the odd visit to the chipper. I've enough for two plane tickets and then some." He pointed his fork at her. "*But:* you have to promise me that if we look for this Ashley girl and we can't find her, you'll get on that train with me tomorrow and come home, before your missing-person mug is splashed all over the cover of the *Irish Times*."

Maggie twisted her napkin into a tight band.

"I don't want to take all your money."

"You're not taking it. I'm going with you. I've always wanted to see Rome. And that's *if* we find them. It's a long shot."

"But what about school?"

He shrugged.

"Concert's on Tuesday, right? Today's Sunday? Say we find these two scumbags and we get on a plane tomorrow. We see the show, we fly back Wednesday, we miss three or four days of school, we catch hell for it. I guess you've just gotta ask yourself—would it be worth it, the trouble we get in, for this chance?"

Maggie threw her napkin on the table. "To me, it would be worth anything."

"Well, it's settled, then." Eoin wiped his last bit of toast through his eggs. "Search Dublin, find thieving American blonde and her African accomplice, kick ass if necessary, get tickets, head to the airport. No bother at all."

When they returned to the hostel, the Slavic girl was at her station, watching her eternal TV program.

"There's going to be two of us tonight," Maggie said.

"Ten pounds a person," the girl looked up from the TV and examined Eoin with interest. "Fifteen if you want sheets and towel."

Eoin reached into his pocket and slapped twenty-five pounds on the counter. "The lady will be needing some sheets. Me, I'm fine without."

"Eoin, you really don't—" began Maggie.

He held up a hand.

"Please don't question me when I'm being chivalrous."

Upstairs, the bunk Maggie had slept in the night before was still open.

"So," Eoin said, flopping across the bare mattress, "you have any idea where these arseholes might be?"

"Well," Maggie said, sitting down beside him, "Ashley said they were going to be in Dublin for a couple more days, and then they were leaving for Scandinavia. So I know they're still around. Last night, we all hung out near this gazebo in Saint Stephen's Green."

"Right so. We'll have a look there. But first, let's do a little detective work." He stood up, gave her his hand, and helped her up from the sagging mattress.

Back in the lobby, he leaned over the counter and grinned at the Slavic girl.

"Hi there," he said. "Ukrainian?"

"Polish," the girl said peevishly.

"Ah! That was my next guess. Name, please?"

The girl rolled her eyes, leaned over, and switched off her TV program.

"Grazyna."

"Grazyna! Lovely name. Well, I'll cut right to it, Graz. My name's Eoin, and this is my friend, Maggie." Maggie raised a hand in greeting. Grazyna nodded. "We were wondering if you remember a couple that stayed here last night: blond American girl and a big African lad with a guitar?"

"Yes, I remember. I see them leave very early this morning." Grazyna began to pick at one of her acrylic nails.

"Any idea where they might have gone?"

"Why you want to know?"

"They stole my stuff," said Maggie.

"*Cholera jasna!*" Grazyna said, abandoning her nail. She shook her head. "They seem so nice." Then, she added, "Nora Barnacle's is not responsible for lost and stolen items."

"We know that," Eoin sighed impatiently. "Do you know anything else about them? We don't want to cause trouble or nothing; we just want to get the stuff back."

"They stay here couple days. Every time they go out, they bring guitar with them. Maybe they're buskers. Try Grafton Street."

The afternoon had turned dismal—a sudden thunderstorm opened the sky and people hurried to their destinations under tented newspapers. Maggie and Eoin stopped in Penneys, bought a cheap umbrella, and slogged their way to Grafton Street, where pedestrians marched purposely ahead with sopped shoulders, certainly not in the mood to stop and throw change into a guitar case. The only street performer they could even find was a scruffy-looking mime, whose face paint was running onto his collar and who stood waiting out the storm in the doorway of an AIG bank. At first, he stayed obnoxiously in character when they asked if he'd seen a blond American and an African with a guitar, shrugging exaggeratedly and putting a finger to his lips. Finally, Eoin gave him some change and he dropped the act.

"Sure, I know those two. They've been playing in front of Boot's for the last week or two. Haven't seem 'em today, though. Ain't a very good day for it, anyway."

They thanked him and left, wandering around the street for a while, peering into shop windows in search of the thieves. Nothing. Eventually, they ducked into a pub and found a quiet table near the fireplace where they could dry off. Eoin helped Maggie out of her soaking jacket and hung it on the grate to dry. A girl came over with menus and they ordered soup, brown bread, and tea.

"We'll never find them," Maggie sighed. "I don't know why I was so sure we would. In a city of a million people! You must think I'm insane."

"I thought we would too," Eoin said. "I just had a *feeling*. We'll stake out that gazebo tonight. If that doesn't work, at least we can say we tried."

The girl brought the soup and bread, and Maggie poured the tea.

"It's absolutely vile outside," she said. "Nobody's going to be hanging around in the park tonight. They'll probably go to a pub, and there are, what, like a thousand pubs in Dublin? Impossible."

"Well, it's worth having a look anyway on our way back to the hostel," said Eoin, dunking his bread into the steaming soup. "Once I get an idea in my head, I like to finish things."

"That's one of the things I like about you," Maggie smiled at him. "I'm the same way."

After their dishes were cleared, the two of them sat in front of the fire, steam rising off their wet jeans. Later in her life, Maggie would always remember the coziness of that meal and Eoin's faith in their adventure. They were two near-orphans; fathers gone, mothers estranged, sixteen and seventeen years old. But as they finished the last of their tea, the need for words between them dropped away, and they were silent together, in the contented way of people who know they are no longer alone.

They left the pub just as the streetlights were winking on along Dawson Street and headed toward the gates of Saint Stephen's Green. The park rustled with dripping leaves and the shadows of urban animals. Maggie led Eoin to the gazebo, which stood white as a streetlamp next to a pond that even the swans had abandoned. The ground was littered with the remnants of the night before: wet cigarette butts, bottle caps, a trampled, muddy square of grass where Ehi had spread the blanket. Eoin squatted down and picked up the sodden burnt end of a joint. He held it out to Maggie.

"This is all from yesterday?"

She hung her head. "I never smoked weed before. It was stupid. I shouldn't have let myself get so messed up. I shouldn't have made it so easy for them."

Eoin flicked the joint into a puddle.

"Why'd I have to be so *stupid*?" She kicked a bottle cap, and it plinked into the pond. "Those tickets were the last thing he ever did for me, and I messed everything up."

Eoin put an arm around her shoulder and lifted the umbrella over their heads. "We'll see the show when they come to Dublin," he said gently. "I know it's not the same. But we'll do it."

Huddled under their umbrella, they came out of the park and walked toward Kildare Street. Up the road, the gas lamps of the Shelbourne Hotel glowed in the rain. The windows, iced in marble scrolling, leaked light and privilege onto the sidewalk.

"This is the kind of place Ashley said her father likes to stay at," Maggie said, peering into the gold-pillared lobby.

"Snooty bitch," Eoin muttered. He stopped short on the wet street. "Wait a minute!" He pointed. "Is that—?"

Maggie gasped and grabbed his arm. "Holy *shit*." Framed like a portrait in the picture window between two red baroque curtains were Ashley and Ehi. They sat together in high-backed velvet chairs, drinking from thick crystal scotch glasses: toasting, she supposed, their cleverness.

Maggie broke into a run, past the valets and the luggage racks. "Maggie, wait up!"

Eoin's gym shoes slapped on the pavement behind her as she shoved open the glass double doors to the lobby. Inside was such a shimmering fairy tale palace—so unlike any place she'd ever been in her entire blue-collar life—that she nearly turned around and walked right back out. Pinpricks of soft light glowed off crystal chandeliers, vases overflowed with cerulean puffs of hydrangea. A patterned marble floor was polished to a mirror shine. There was even a narrow yellow carpet that stopped abruptly at the eastern entrance of the Lord Mayor's Lounge. *Follow the yellow brick road.*

"Have you got a plan?" There was a faint pant in Eoin's breathing.

"No," Maggie said. "Just stay with me, okay?"

She took a deep breath and opened the lounge door. The room bustled with a well-heeled cocktail hour crowd—men in suit jackets and women in stiff velvet and heavy eye makeup. The carpet was Oriental plush and the bar counter was studded with silver bowls of almonds and sesame sticks. Elaborate three-tiered trays of tea sandwiches stood in the middle of the high-top tables and classical music piped from hidden speakers in the ceiling. Ashley and Ehi sat together by the window, laughing and clearly pleased with themselves for being young and bohemian in the midst of this starched crowd. Maggie marched up to them and stopped between their pink velvet chairs. Ashley, who was putting her glass to her mouth, flinched. A small "oh!" escaped her lips. She set the glass down.

"Chicago!" she said brightly, recovering herself. "What are you doing here?"

"I thought you said you preferred cheap hostels, cheap beer, and strangers to places like this." She heard the swish of Eoin's track pants as he came up beside her.

"I did say that, didn't I?" she laughed, nervously twirling a strand of her long, pale hair. "But it's our last night in Dublin and we figured we'd treat ourselves. Still a little rich girl underneath it all, sometimes."

"Give me my tickets."

"I told you," Ehi cut in. He was glaring at Ashley. He put his glass down on a coaster. It was embossed with the letter *S* in cursive writing. He looked tired, his face etched with the remnants of an argument, perhaps from earlier that day.

"What tickets?" Ashley looked up at Maggie and Eoin. "Did you lose something last night? You were pretty fucked up." She smiled at Eoin, her teeth Wonderbread white. "First-time weed smoker."

"Don't you fuckin' smile at me," Eoin growled.

"Now hold on a minute, mate." Ehi half-stood.

"And don't *you* call me mate, mate." Eoin rolled up his right sleeve.

"Excuse me. Can I get you something to drink?" A man with a trimmed goatee and a tailored pinstripe suit had materialized next to them. He held a clipboard in his hand and wore a brass nametag that said Manager.

"No, thanks." Maggie answered him, her eyes never leaving Ashley's face.

"Well, unfortunately, this lounge is for paying customers only." The manager pursed his lips at Maggie and Eoin, taking in their wet clothes and Maggie's threadbare duffel bag.

"Fine. We'll have two of what they're having."

"Glenfiddich eighteen year?"

"Sure."

The manager hesitated for a moment before slipping off toward the bar. As soon as his back was turned, Maggie reached out and gripped Ashley's arm so hard the tanned skin popped white between her fingers. Ashley's mouth twisted open in pain and surprise.

"Jesus. Relax, will you?"

Maggie squeezed harder.

"I can scream for help, you know."

"And I can break your pretty little nose."

"Okay, okay." Ashley's voice was small and pouty. "We already spent your money on these drinks."

"I don't give a crap about the money," Maggie said. Her face was an inch from Ashley's. She could see the tiny pores along the sides of her lovely nose, the pale lashes tipped in white. She could smell the expensive scotch rolling off her breath. "But I want those tickets back. *Now.*"

"I can't reach them until you let go of my arm."

Maggie released her grip, saw the receding imprint of her fingers on Ashley's flesh. Ashley reached down to the bag at her feet, her eyes darting around the lobby for an escape route. Eoin shifted his weight until he was standing right at the arm of her chair, so that if she wanted to escape she would have get past him. She knew better than to try. She unzipped the green backpack under her chair. Inside it, Maggie could see a stack of winking silver engraved with the Shelbourne *S*, and even a few stalks of cut hydrangea from the displays in the lobby. Ashley dug past these items and produced the tickets. Maggie ripped them from her hand and stuffed them down her sweater and into her bra. Then, she picked up Ashley's scotch glass. It was as heavy as a paperweight. She downed the last quarter inch of the liquor in one gulp. It burned hotly down her throat. She wiped her mouth and looked at Eoin. "You ready?"

"Yeah." He was fighting a smile.

On the way back out to the lobby, Maggie walked up to the manager, who was arranging their two glasses of Glenfiddich onto a tray.

"You might want to check that woman's bag," she said, pointing over at Ashley. "She's about to make off with some of your fancy nut bowls."

They walked out of the lobby and past the window just in time to see the manager stride up to their table and pull the stolen silver bowls from Ashley's bag.

"Do you want to watch the rest of the show?" Eoin asked as the manager took Ashley by the arm and waved over a security guard. Maggie shook her head.

"That's good enough for me."

On the walk back to the hostel, the tickets folded safely in Maggie's bra, she and Eoin were giddy with victory.

"You were amazing!" Eoin laughed as they ducked under awnings and jumped from puddle to puddle. "Drinking her scotch like that!"

"*My* scotch," Maggie reminded him. "Purchased with Nanny Ei's Christmas money. Glenfiddich eighteen year—that stuff is older than we are!"

"How did it taste?"

She grinned. "Expensive."

"Did ya hear that, everybody?" Eoin yelled to the startled strangers on the street. "Nobody fucks with Maggie Lynch!" Then he stopped right there in the middle of Grafton Street, whirled around, and kissed her in the rain.

It was late by the time they got back to Nora Barnacle's. Even Grazyna had gone home for the night, and a sleepy redheaded boy who looked practically prepubescent had to unlock the dormitory for them. They crept past the rows of sleeping forms, the cavernous room filled with the ambient sounds of breathing and rustling people. Maggie took off Kevin's flannel and handed it up to Eoin.

"You'll be freezing without sheets," she said.

"I'm no wimp," he protested, but he took the shirt and put it on. He helped her to make up her bed, then climbed up the ladder to the top bunk. Maggie crawled under the thin fabric and tucked herself up into a ball. She was freezing, and she could barely stand to think about Eoin above her, curled defenseless on a bare mattress. The springs creaked as he moved around, trying to warm himself. Ten minutes or so passed by. Then, he whispered,

"You still awake?"

"Yeah," she whispered back. The bed creaked loudly, his white feet hung momentarily above her, and he jumped down, landing with a soft thud on the tiles.

"You cold?"

"These sheets are pretty thin."

"Move in, then," he said. He raised his hands. "I promise to keep 'em to myself."

She lifted the sheet and he crawled under, close enough for her to smell his deodorant and the sweaty tang of his armpits. In the darkness, Maggie's eyes were wide open. She could see the deep grooves in the wall, the messages scrawled by travelers of the past: names and dates, hearts and crosses, song lyrics. The accumulated totem scratches of the ever-moving world.

Eoin reached over and pulled Maggie toward him, his arm a quiet promise around her waist, the heat of his body a radiant line down her spine. The want, the desire, crackled between them. But he didn't try anything and she didn't want him to; it was good enough, more than good, that he only lay beside her. Was it only two days ago that she'd wondered whether he would ever kiss her again? She remembered now the vial of perfume she'd bought at the drugstore next to the hostel, still unopened and unused in her duffel bag. Sometimes, even Dan Sean could be wrong about things. She drifted off to sleep with the Nirvana tickets pressed against her beating heart and Eoin's breath, warm and guileless, against her neck.

In a dorm with forty travelers, it was impossible to sleep in. They rose in the early morning to the zipping sleeping bags and gravelly voices of a Monday morning hostel, where travelers packed up to return to their real lives or their next guidebook destination. Eoin still had his arm around Maggie's waist.

"Good morning," he mumbled into her neck. His face, puffy from sleep, made him look younger than his seventeen years. A red pattern from the mattress was imprinted on his cheek. She reached, with her fingers, and touched the puckered skin.

"Sleep in for a bit," he whispered. "I'm going to catch the early train back home and get my money."

"Are you sure?"

"I most certainly am." He pushed a strand of hair behind her ear.

"What about your aunt?"

"She works at the pub Sunday nights. She probably didn't get home until one or two last night. She'll think I was sleeping. I'll just sneak back in through my bedroom window, get my money, and put on my school clothes. She'll probably even make me breakfast."

He pushed away the sheet, climbed out of the bed, handed her Kevin's flannel, and pulled on his shoes.

"You sure you'll come back?" Already, she could feel how much she needed him.

"Maggie." He leaned his arms on the metal rails of the top bunk. "Don't you trust me by now?"

"I do," she whispered.

He scratched at the rusting springs of the bunk bed with his index finger. "I can be your person, you know," he finally said. "I can be the person who won't hurt you."

She lifted the sheet.

"Come back under for a minute?"

He smiled, kicked off his shoes, and climbed back into the bed. Maggie pulled the sheet over their heads. The sun filtered through the thin fabric, illuminating a faint line of stubble along Eoin's jaw. It stirred Maggie in some primal way as yet unknown to her. He brushed the hair from her eyes, kissed her forehead, her neck, her lips, then eased out of bed again, winked down at her, and left for the train station.

At Dublin airport, they waited in a long line at the Alitalia counter, only to be told that the sole flight from Dublin to Rome was sold out.

"Sold *out?*" Maggie dropped her duffel bag at her feet.

"Yes." The ticket clerk, in her pert red and green neck scarf, smiled an empty smile. "Both today's flight and tomorrow's. I might be able to get you on for Friday morning."

"Haven't you anything else? It's *extremely* important that we get there as soon as possible." Eoin, trying a new tactic, was now affecting an upper-crust Dublin accent. His Saint Brendan's blazer and neat red tie made it sound almost believable. The ticket clerk clacked on her computer.

"I've one flight to Bologna," the woman said. "From there, you could take a train to Rome—it's about three hours. But the seats are not together." She looked at her watch. "And it leaves in fifteen minutes."

"How much?" Eoin pulled his wad of savings from the breast pocket of his blazer.

"Two hundred ten for the both."

"Can we make it in fifteen minutes?" Maggie leaned anxiously over the counter.

The woman picked up the phone. "I'll see if they'll hold the plane." While she waited for a dial tone, Eoin began counting out the money. The months, even years, of savings accumulated on the counter in small piles.

"Are you sure you want to do this?" Maggie asked.

"It's just money," Eoin shrugged, pushing it toward the clerk. "I've got my whole life to make more of it."

"You've got to hurry," the clerk said, hanging up her phone. "They'll only hold the plane a few extra minutes." She handed them their tickets. "Run."

"Let's go!" Eoin whooped. He grabbed Maggie's hand and they bolted toward the security gates, bags flying behind them, as Eoin sang out the anthem of the Roma club soccer team at the top of his lungs. *Roma Roma Roma! Core de 'sta città! Unico grande amore! De tanta e tanta gente! M'hai fatto 'nammora!* As they ran, they dodged the crowds of older travelers who stared after them, a few in sour disapproval, but most with half-nostalgic smiles, perhaps remembering the way they, too, had been when they were young and free and seeing the world for the first time.

They arrived at the gate, breathless, just in time for the final boarding call.

"See you in Italy," Eoin waved, and he went off down the aisle in search of his back-row assignment while Maggie climbed, apologizing, over a middle-aged couple dressed in matching windbreakers, and settled into her window seat. She fished around in her duffel bag for Kevin's compass and held its cool, calming weight in her palm as the jet engines roared to life. It was only when the plane began to taxi along the runway that Maggie realized the extent of what she and Eoin were doing. This wasn't a forty-minute train ride into Dublin. There was an ocean involved, and national borders. But as the plane lifted into the air and she watched out the window as Ireland fell away, rocky and impossibly green, giving way to deep blue water and then clouds, white as silence, she felt a sense of calm. She was above punishment now. Whenever it was she decided to return to Colm's house, she might be lectured or grounded or worse, but at this moment, she just couldn't get herself to care much about some hypothetical future. *Take the boy. Don't ask permission.* Those simple instructions were her only guiding principle now, the only command she felt she had to heed. The flight attendant came around with her cart, offering coffee and packaged biscotti. Maggie ate gratefully. The food was as good as anything she'd ever tasted.

It was raining when they landed in Bologna. The small airport stood encased in fog, and the plane had to park far from the terminal gates. Maggie carefully descended a slippery metal staircase and waited for Eoin on the wet tarmac. Around her, airport employees wore reflective gear and walkie-talkies and chatted with each other. Italian sounded like crescendoing, excitable Spanish, and Maggie felt an unexpected wave of homesickness for Chicago, where Mexican grocers and taquerias had peppered Lawrence Avenue down the block from their two-flat.

By the time they'd cleared customs, bought their train tickets to Rome, and settled into their seats, it was already early afternoon, but the fog did not begin to lift until the train was well out of Bologna. The winter sun whittled away the clouds, and soon, out the window of the train, they could see the outlines of mountains and white farmhouses in the distance as if drawn in with pencil and then erased. She and Eoin sat across from each other, knees touching, and watched the foggy countryside roll along. "I've never left Ireland before," Eoin admitted, his nose nearly pressed against the glass. "Even the cows look different."

Somewhere in northern Tuscany, the train went into a long stone tunnel, and when it came blasting out again the fog had finally burned off. The world was dazzling and clear, and they were there, she and Eoin, throttling through its magnificence. Unlike Ireland, the country of her ancestors, Maggie had never read about Italy, except during a boring seventh grade history project about Roman aqueducts. She was totally unprepared for its beauty.

Crumbling farmhouses stood between the crevasses of hills painted with endless lines of spindly winter grapevines. Bare persimmon trees lined the dusty roads near the train tracks. Cypresses, the mythical trees of the afterlife, reached in clusters into the wide sky, as black and streamlined as arrows. Maggie and Eoin sat and gaped, chins resting on the windowsill of their train compartment. It went on like that for hours: Arezzo. Cortona. Montepulciano. Hills, pale dirt, stone walls, rows and rows of mute cypress and tangled, regimented vineyards. Outside the train was all of this, and inside was Eoin, his knee warm against hers, and the reclaimed concert tickets, nestled against her heart in the cup of her bra.

By late afternoon the hills and farmland had given way to concrete buildings, the multiplication of human settlement. They were approaching the ancient city at last. It did not look the way Maggie had imagined it. As the train slowed, approaching Termini Station, they passed high concrete walls scrawled with colorful graffiti. On the other side of these walls stood tall apartment complexes with iron balconies where faded laundry hung to dry and old women lazed over the railings, smoking cigarettes and folding sheets. Through a haze of train exhaust, the women looked down at the people coming and going, flicking their cigarettes down into wilting vines.

Eoin had torn the Roman subway map from a Fodor's travel guide on sale at the airport book shop, a petty crime which had mildly scandalized Maggie, but in the dark stink of the station, with strangers jostling them and gypsies swaying by in flowered skirts shaking cans full of change, she was grateful for it. They found an open bench and sat down, gathering their bags under their legs.

"There are two subway lines here," he said, tracing the map with his finger. "The A and the B. It looks like we just need to take the A train and get off at Furio Camillo. The Jesus-feet church and the Casa di Santa Barbara are a short walk from there."

The afternoon rush hour had already passed, and the A train was quiet. Maggie and Eoin sat down beside each other, and as the subway jolted forward, they looked out the windows at the dark concrete maze of underground rail, their white, curious faces reflected in the glass. Ever since she'd known Eoin, Maggie had always been the outsider, he, the native. But here in Italy they were both strangers and foreigners. Here, they could hold hands and nobody would gossip. They could laugh through their bungled pronunciations and whisper their excitement in a mutually foreign tongue. They could be lost together, and in their anonymity, they had the freedom to be themselves.

As they climbed the stairs and emerged from the subway station, Maggie discovered that the Eternal City actually looked pretty ordinary. Bits of trash clogged the gutters, horns honked, and people in office clothes, their faces hooded by helmets, buzzed by on scooters. *But what did you expect?* she asked herself. *Crowds of toga-clad plebeians?* This was a real city, after all, not a movie set. The convent hotel was a few blocks from the station, a rambling old building with peeling wooden shutters and sandstone walls. It had a big front door made of frosted glass, decorated with etchings of Saint Barbara. Inside, there was a sleek concierge desk, decorated with bowls of winter jasmine, but the air still smelled nunnish, like boiled meat and old textbooks. A woman in a plain black dress and tight ponytail looked up from the newspaper she was reading when they approached.

"English?" Eoin asked, setting down their bags.

"Yes, may I help you?"

"We need a room for a couple nights."

The woman looked at them in silence for long enough to make Maggie squirm. Maybe she didn't understand English after all?

"Are you sharing a room?" she finally asked. She appraised Maggie with calculating disapproval from beneath a thick pair of eyebrows.

"Well, we were planning on it," Eoin said, looking confused.

"You are—married, then?"

"Oh! Of course," Eoin answered before Maggie even had time to look in his direction. "I'm Eoin Brennan and this is my wife, Maggie. We're here from Ireland for our honeymoon. We're neighbors of Dan Sean O'Callaghan. He recommended this place. Are you Marta?"

The woman's iron face broke instantly into a maternal smile. She swiped off her glasses.

"Ah, yes!" she said. "I am Marta! I know Dan Sean well—Ireland's oldest pilgrim, we call him. You are very welcome!" She leafed through a large ledger made of leather and wrote down a number. "Signor and Signora Brennan. We will put you in room 19. And many congratulations to you."

She handed them an old-fashioned key with ornate edging.

"May I carry your bag for you, Signora Brennan?" Eoin said, swinging Maggie's duffel over one shoulder.

"Oh, by all means, Signor Brennan!" They fell over themselves laughing behind the metal grating of an ancient elevator, which deposited them at the end of a dark, narrow passage lined on either side with plain wooden doors and ending, at the far side, with a large ceramic statue of the Madonna and Child, her robes the same azure color as the shrine in Dan Sean's bedroom. But while Eoin walked ahead, carrying their bags, Maggie's giggles gave way to a nervous counting down of room numbers: twenty-five. Twenty-four. *I'm staying in a hotel room.* Twenty-three. *With a boy.* Twenty-two. *Did I bring pajamas?* Twenty-one. *What if I snore?* Twenty. *Are we going to*—nineteen. Eoin stopped in front of their room and fiddled with the key. The Virgin Mary stood frozen on her throne adjacent to their door. Her blue eyes said nothing. In her head, Maggie remembered the words of Dan Sean's rosary: *Hail, Holy Queen, mother of mercy, our life, our sweetness, and our hope.* The key clicked in the old lock and the door swung open.

Their room was as plain and quiet as one would expect of a former nuns' quarters. A naked lightbulb hung from the ceiling, spotlighting the center of the room in bright white light and leaving the corners in darkness. The only decoration on the whitewashed walls was a simple wooden crucifix above the narrow bed, which was covered in starched white sheets and several layers of faded quilts. Next to it stood a desk with a small reading lamp. On the far wall was a window, shuttered by tight wooden slats. When Eoin went to open it, the cold air flooded in, and it sucked the door shut behind them. *We are alone in a hotel room together*, Maggie thought. Trying to appear casual, she flopped onto the bed and watched as Eoin unzipped his bag and began putting the small pile of clothes he'd brought into the top drawer of the dresser.

"So," she said, "what do you want to do tonight?"

He took two neatly folded pairs of underwear from the bag and Maggie looked away quickly, scrutinizing the buzzing lightbulb in the middle of the ceiling.

"Well," he said, closing the dresser drawer, "I've heard it mentioned that Italy has some pretty good food. Maybe we should go check out one of these Roman restaurants I've been hearing about all my life?"

"We *are* newlyweds, after all," Maggie laughed. "So I guess we do have reason to celebrate. Do I have time to take a shower?"

"Course," Eoin said. "I'm going to go downstairs and check out the rest of the lobby. Guidebook said they've converted the old convent infirmary into a hotel bar. This, I have to see for myself."

"I'll meet you down there?"

"Okay, then." He stepped forward, as if he was thinking about kissing her, but then, changing his mind, he stepped back again. Maggie was left in the middle of the tiny room leaning toward him, waiting to receive his kiss, as he fumbled, blushing, out the door.

The bathrooms in the hallway were shared by all the guests staying on the floor. When Maggie entered the steamy women's area, she saw three shower stalls covered in white plastic curtains, and two of them were occupied. The women behind these curtains had youngish voices, and were speaking in a language that Maggie could not identify. It was not Italian, though—Portuguese, maybe. Or even French. She couldn't tell. Stepping into the shower, she felt the thrill of excitement of an American on the European continent for the first time. She strained to listen over the pelting water to their lilting voices, the unrecognizable trills and drops in language, peppered occasionally by girlish laughter. The hotel had provided a tiny tube of lemony shampoo with Italian wording scrolled across the package, and she squeezed some into her hair, then lathered her body with a seashell-shaped soap that smelled of tangerines. After Dan Sean's corrugated tub, the little shower stall and the fruity toiletries felt positively luxurious.

She rinsed off, wrapped herself in a towel, and stepped out into the steamy haze of the white-tiled bathroom. The two women were standing before the sinks. They were both completely naked.

"S-sorry," Maggie stuttered, fumbling back toward her shower stall, but they just turned and smiled at her.

"Hello," one of them said. She turned back to the fog-glazed mirror and dabbed some makeup across her eyelids.

"Hi." Maggie pulled her towel closer and stepped shyly to the vacant sink between them. She ran her toothbrush under the water. She'd never been in the presence of such bold, unselfconscious nudity. She'd thought Ashley had been the most beautiful woman she'd ever seen in real life, but these women were practically otherworldly. They were tall and large breasted, with lean muscles coursing beneath their pink skin and rich thatches of pale pubic hair. Each woman had long blond hair combed seal-slick down her back. Their eyes were an ice-gray color Maggie had only seen at the bottom of pools. She did not know it was possible to have eyes that color.

But what was most fascinating about them—what she really couldn't believe—was the tattoos. Maggie always thought that tattoos were for sailors, like the faded anchor on the inside of her years-dead Grandpa Lynch's forearm. She had never seen one on a woman, let alone a woman this spectacularly beautiful. The one to her left leaned toward the mirror and applied eyeliner in studied, precise strokes, and her plank-thin back, with its perfect shoulder blades, displayed a huge tattoo of a naked female figure, hands splayed, with intricately feathered angel wings that spread in pale red ink all the way to the tops of the woman's shoulders. *Why does that look so familiar?* Maggie combed her lemon-scented hair and tried not to stare. Suddenly she realized: it was the same image that adorned the cover of the Nirvana album *In Utero*.

The woman caught her eye in the mirror and said, in perfect and beautifully accented English, "Toothpaste?"

"Oh—sure!" Maggie unclutched her towel to fumble with her travel tube of Colgate. She handed the woman the toothpaste just as her towel dropped in a pool around her ankles. Her cheeks flaming, she reached down to grab it. But then she stopped. *I may not look like these women, but I'm no little girl.* She kicked her towel aside, straightened her bare shoulders, and continued to comb her hair.

"I like your tattoo." She smiled at the woman in the mirror, resisting the urge to cover her own untattooed skin.

"Thank you!" the woman said, absently reaching back and grazing the tattoo with long fingers. "It's still a bit sore—I only got it finished last week."

"That's from the *In Utero* cover, isn't it?"

"Yes! Is everyone in America as in love with Kurt Cobain as we are in Norway?"

"Pretty much," Maggie laughed.

"I have waited years for this," sighed the other woman. She held out a long arm for Maggie to inspect. A fragment of lyrics was tattooed across the soft whiteness of her forearm: *I'm not like them / but I can pretend . . .*

This confirmed it: these were the coolest women alive.

"Are you in Rome for the show?"

"Yeah, I'm here with my boyfriend," Maggie said. "My uncle got us the tickets."

"Well, you must have a very cool uncle."

"The coolest," Maggie smiled, rummaging through her bag for her mascara. For a second, she forgot completely that Kevin was dead.

"The whole city is full of Nirvana fans," the woman to her left said. "It's incredible."

And it was. *Here I am*, Maggie thought, *in Rome, combing my hair next to two Norwegian models with Nirvana tattoos.* Meanwhile, downstairs, a handsome boy—a boy she'd called her boyfriend and it hadn't felt like a lie—waited for her at a bar that had once been a nun's infirmary. This time last year, she'd been a high school freshman, lonely and bored, sitting through Mr. Blackwell's English class and reading *Our Town* in her pleated school skirt, staring out the window at the gray Chicago winter, a winter as drab and endless as her adolescence.

"See you at the show!" the Norwegian girls waved, covering themselves with minuscule towels and heading out to the convent hallway.

In the empty bathroom, Maggie put on her makeup and her tight black dress and dabbed her drugstore perfume on her neck and wrists. She zipped up her bag, dropped it off in room 19, and took the ancient elevator down to the main floor.

Eoin sat at the bar counter in the shadow of a large potted plant. He was drinking a bottle of Italian beer. He'd changed out of his Saint Brendan's uniform and put on a pair of jeans and a dark sweater. His close-cropped hair was neatly combed.

"You look so handsome." It was an old-fashioned thing to say, and far more straightforward than Maggie had intended. It had just come out of her, a remnant of the confidence high she was riding after her meeting with the Norwegians. But before she could qualify it with a friendly slap on the back or a careless laugh, Eoin swallowed the last of his beer and stood up.

"And you look beautiful."

At the front desk, Eoin asked Marta to recommend a place for dinner. She circled a spot on their map—"a short walk, very romantic for newlyweds," she explained—and the two of them walked hand in hand down Via Monserato until they found the restaurant by its hand-stenciled sign hanging from an arched stone doorway.

The narrow room at the front of the restaurant was a butcher shop crammed with slabs of cured meat, some with the bristles still attached; barrels full of hooves; thick wheels of cheese behind refrigerated glass, and links of sausages hanging in chandeliered loops above the ceiling. The closest Maggie had ever come to such a place was the Mars Cheese Castle, off Highway 94 on the way to Milwaukee, which despite being not nearly as rustic as this place, had still always managed to fill her with horror and vows of vegetarianism. But here, as they followed the bowlegged butcher, with his stooped shoulders and bulbous, scarred knuckles, through the barrels of molding cheese and casks of fermenting wine, out into a covered courtyard with cool dark tiles and tiny lights crisscrossing the ceiling, the magic of Rome began to sink in. Maggie suddenly became aware of the power of her long, young legs, the short hem of her dress, even the flaky mascara that fringed the green eyes she'd inherited by her mother. Her heels clacked on the stone tile as she moved across the floor, and she felt not just Eoin's eyes but the eyes of all the men in the restaurant watching. *So this is what sexy feels like*, she thought.

The butcher handed them menus on stained paper. Maggie had more experience with Italian food than Eoin did, having gone to Taylor Street with her father in those lost early years when he still made the attempt to be a part of their lives. But even she could only recognize two items on the menu: ravioli and pizza. The butcher's wife, a tiny woman with a large, fleshy nose and men's brogues came over to take their order.

"What's the drinking age here?" Maggie asked Eoin.

"What drinking age?" he laughed. "This is Europe, Maggie." He pointed at the word *vino*. The old woman nodded pleasantly and brought them a carafe of red table wine. "See?"

They clinked their glasses together.

"To Uncle Kevin," Eoin said.

"To Uncle Kevin." The wine was earthy and sweet, the color of rubies.

The butcher's wife came over with their pizza. It looked like anything Maggie had seen back in Chicago, but it was covered in shreds of deep green lettuce and curls of a pale purple meat that looked like it had been shaved off the sides of one of the big pig shanks hanging from the wood beams above them.

"What is that?" Maggie pointed.

"No idea." Eoin picked up the largest slice of the pie and stuffed it in his mouth. "When in Rome," he said through a mouthful of food.

It was the best pizza Maggie had ever tasted. The meat was salty and flavorful, the crust charred and crispy, the cheese creamy and mellow. And when the ravioli came, pillowy noodles filled with ricotta and drizzled in melted butter and chopped sage, she and Eoin fell into a prolonged silence so they could give it their full attention.

"This is the best feckin' stuff I've had in my life," Eoin mumbled, his mouth full.

"This time tomorrow," Maggie said dreamily, "we'll be standing in front of Kurt Cobain."

"Maggie, I have to warn you," he said, forking the last piece of pasta onto his plate, "I'm not into this grunge stuff like you are. Remember, I grew up listening to my mother's music and not much else."

"It doesn't matter! Great music is great music, no matter if it's Irish or country or grunge or *whatever.*"

"I'm just sayin', I might not like it."

"You don't have to try to like it," she told him. "You just have to stand there and listen. It will do all the work. It will get you, I promise. I've only been to one concert in my life, and it, like, blew me open." She'd only had half a glass of the wine, but it was making her feel elastic, profound. "My uncle took me to see the Smashing Pumpkins at this place in Chicago called the Metro. I'll take you there one day, maybe. Even if you don't know much about the band, you'll still love the show, I promise."

Perhaps the wine made him feel the same way, because he suddenly reached across the table and put a hand on hers.

"I love *this*," he said quietly. "All of this. The wine. The sage sauce. Italy. You. It's all perfect."

Maggie blushed. "I love it, too."

Dessert was a simple pot of custard. It was cloud light and perfectly sweetened. Maggie was quickly realizing that the Italian food she'd eaten back on Taylor Street had really not been Italian food at all.

They were stuffed to the point of sleepiness, but going back to the hotel was not an option. "We're in Rome, for feck's sake!" Eoin pulled out the map and began studying the crisscrossing lines. "We need to see the sights!"

They followed the wide, crooked path of the Via Del Corso, where stylish Italian couples in tailored black coats and smart shoes headed to parties and restaurants, cupping cigarettes and carrying bottles of wine under their arms. The wind snapped their coats, but compared to Chicago in February, it felt like a spring wind, and drier than most Irish days, too. As they searched for the Via Frattria, noses in the folds of their map, the sound of running water cut through the honking horns and scooter motors and stopped them short.

They were standing in front of the most magnificent fountain Maggie had ever seen. It was practically the size of half a city block. The water's mist hung in rainbows on the dark air, and she could taste its stony moss on her lips, feel its coolness on her nose and cheeks. Marble figures of muscular gods and goddesses with upturned eyes seemed to dance in the fountain's flow, and at the surface of the pools, lit up by soft blue floodlights, copper coins winked at the bottom like flashing treasures.

"Trevi Fountain," Eoin said. "I learned about this in art history class. You're supposed to throw a coin in the water, and it means you'll come back to Rome one day."

"You got any change?"

He rummaged in his pocket, found a few coins, and together they tossed them. We *will* return to Rome one day, Maggie promised herself silently. She stood and watched their coins plash into the water and sink to the bottom, letting her mind fill with all her hopes for the years ahead, some old and familiar, some newly born to include the boy standing next to her. There was so much to hope for, in fact, that her heart hurt just thinking about all of it.

Back in their sparse little hotel room, Eoin kissed her under the stacks of thin blankets. Maggie could feel the swell of him press against her thighs beneath his jeans. Outside their slatted window, a sleety rain pattered against the shutters.

"Is this too much?" He kissed her neck.

"No."

He moved his hands down her sweater, tracing the outline of her breasts, and skimmed his fingers over the sheer fabric of her tights. Her knees began to shake.

"We should try to get some sleep, Eoin," she whispered, because suddenly it all *was* too much—the foggy vineyards in Tuscany, the sage ravioli, the sweet wine, the rain at the window, and his fingers on her thighs; too much goodness and newness to take in over the course of one solitary day.

She closed her knees together and his hands slipped away.

"You're right," he said. "Sorry."

"Don't apologize." She curled into him and he put an arm around her waist. They fell asleep like that, still dressed in their dinner clothes, to the sound of the wind clattering the old wooden shutters.

In the morning they found a nearby café that served cheap pastries and espresso in tiny ceramic cups. They sat near a window and watched the city come to life. The Norwegians had been right: Nirvana fever had descended on Rome. Gangs of young people milled around, the boys with stringy hair and slouchy flannels, and the girls in Docs and smudged purple eye makeup. There were mohawks and wallet chains and band T-shirts; pierced noses, black lipstick, bleached blondes, and baby doll dresses. Some people hid behind sunglasses, others shouted happily at strangers, still wobbly from the previous night's debauchery. Everyone was smoking.

After breakfast, they went to the church of Domine Quo Vadis and San Sebastian to get Dan Sean his vial of holy water. There they saw pilgrims approaching the imprints of the Lord's feet on their knees, kissing the steps, crying into the dirt. Maggie thought of the monks on Iona, painting the pages of the Book of Kells with painstaking, loving strokes. She put a coin in the metal donation box, lit a votive candle, and genuflected. *I wish you were here to see this, Kev*, she prayed. The candles glowed red with all the tiny prayers of the faithful, filling the corner of the quiet chapel with filigreed, hopeful light.

Back at the hotel, Maggie gave Eoin her Discman so he could listen to *In Utero* while they got ready for the show. He wore his usual attire: Liverpool hoodie and track pants. She loved that he was so stubbornly himself, and that he didn't care about grunge or Nirvana. She loved that he was here not because he liked the band, but because it meant something to her. She went down the hall to shower and change, and when she came back to the room, dressed in her black dress and tights with Kevin's flannel tied around her waist, she lay down on the bed next to him. As afternoon descended into evening, they sprawled there side by side, loosely holding hands, and listened to the rest of the album together.

At Termini the atmosphere was feverish, festive. Buses were shuttling people out to the Palaghiaccio di Marino for five thousand lire a person. Maggie and Eoin waited in line and boarded the next one that came through where no one, not even the bus driver, was over the age of thirty. Someone had brought a portable boom box and was blasting "Lithium," while people screamed along and snuck sips from the bottles of Peroni they'd smuggled in under their jackets. There were Italians, Greeks, Germans, and Spaniards. There were Albanians, Armenians, and Turks. People shouted to each other in unrecognizable languages but they all knew the lyrics of the songs. Maggie's life, all that was familiar, had shrunk itself down to the dark-haired boy by her side. They grinned like fools when the Venetian strangers across the aisle tried to make conversation in broken, excited English. When the bus pulled into the massive parking lot and the Palaghiaccio di Marino appeared in a wash of lights, the bus erupted into cheers.

They dissolved into the massive crowd, Eoin holding tightly to Maggie's hand, and lined up at the entrance. Even the uniformed workers tearing tickets at the turnstiles looked excited. They followed the signs to their seats, zigzagging up and up and up the concrete ramps, past vendors selling beer and little bags of anise candy, until they reached the nosebleed level, stepped through the heavy velvet curtains, and were in the main auditorium. Their seats, so high they were nearly flush with the concrete back wall, were at the crest of a tidal wave of moving bodies, and at the far end of this ocean stood the stage.

"Are you ready?"

Eoin nodded, and the last thing Maggie saw before the lights went black was the liquid whites of his eyes. There was a momentary hush, and then the stage lit up and the Jumbotrons snapped on, displaying the shambling figure of Kurt Cobain, twenty feet high on the screen, and the hush exploded into the deafening chorus of five thousand screams. Maggie's hands fluttered involuntarily to her heart. She felt the way she imagined Dan Sean must feel at Lourdes, at Medjugorje, the way those pilgrims at the church of Domine Quo Vadis felt as they rubbed their fingers through the cool scoop of marble where Jesus Christ, they believed, had dug his heels. She could feel Kevin as a living presence by her side.

The band opened with "Radio Friendly Unit Shifter." In the dark, sweaty, cavernous hoard, among thousands of strangers who sang along in their accented English, who lit new cigarettes off the dying embers of old ones, Maggie felt weightless, floating away from all that limited her, her life growing louder and louder—more shaped, more possible—along with the music. She didn't need drugs to find transcendence. She didn't need beer or whiskey or wine. The music was enough. She jumped loosely to it, closing her eyes, opening them, wiping the sweat off her face with the cuff of Kevin's flannel. She screamed and applauded until her voice went hoarse, and then kept screaming, even though all that came out was a joyous gurgling sound. During "Smells Like Teen Spirit," she grinned over at Eoin, whose eyes shone in the steamy darkness, who had joined the impromptu mosh pit that was forming in their row and growing more and more aggressive, carnal, as the set went on. They were jostled and pushed, tripped and fell onto the sticky floor between the seats, and were lifted up by strangers' hands. All the while, Kurt Cobain sang himself raw. Between songs, Cobain joked with the crowd, sneered a little at them, at himself, at everything. The Jumbotron was merciless on his pixelated face; he looked haggard, haunted, over it all. He was two days past his twenty-seventh birthday. The band played twenty-three songs before smashing their instruments, their energy peaking and coagulating, deafening, on and on until Maggie touched her wet ears to check for blood. It was only sweat. The lights burst on, and just as quickly as it had started, the band left the stage and it was over. She and Eoin crashed into a soaking hug. They had just witnessed something important. *The anthem of our generation.* The crowd, still trembling and half-deaf, coming down from their visions, their religious encounters, began to pour out of the theater, pushing, shoving, screaming in Italian, tossing half empty cups of warm beer.

Maggie and Eoin followed the chaotic exodus out of the arena and were caught at a bottleneck crush of fans near the exit. Maggie lifted her chin to breathe and clung to Eoin's hand. It had begun to rain again. People stomped, shoved, shouted in Mediterranean languages. Police barked unintelligible orders from megaphones, and finally, there was a great push of bodies, and they stumbled free into the parking lot, which was lit up by the miles of headlights from cars streaming out of the parking lot and back to real life.

"Where do we go for the shuttle?" Eoin shouted over the crowd.

"I don't know!"

The lawn in front of the Palaghiaccio was slick with mud, and people were sliding through it on their bare bellies. They stopped a security guard to ask for help, but he didn't speak English. Neither did anyone else they asked. The buses began to crawl out of the parking lot one by one.

"Shuttle? Termini?" Eoin asked random people, but the hordes of drunken fans just grinned at him and shrugged, rambling off into the night. Just as they were about to give up and spend the rest of their money on a taxi back to the city, Maggie saw, in the darkness, the white-blond hair of the tattooed Norwegians.

"American!" called one of them, waving at her. She wore jeans so shredded they clung to her long legs by a few patches of fraying white thread. Maggie grabbed Eoin's sleeve.

"Those are the girls I met in the bathroom of our hotel," she said. "They speak English!"

"What did you think of our Kurt?" asked the woman in the torn jeans. "Wasn't he magnificent?"

"I can die happy now," said the man she was with, who came up behind her and put his big hands around her waist. He had cropped white hair and a metal bar through his nose.

"We're looking for the shuttle," Eoin explained. "Do you know how to get back to Termini?"

"The *shuttle*? Who needs this *shuttle*?" laughed the man. "We can take you anywhere you want!"

Maggie looked over at Eoin. He shrugged and gave her a look that said, why not?

The Norwegians' Volkswagen van was painted black—even the windows—and inside, all the seats had been ripped out. The floor was covered in dirty red shag carpet. Maggie and Eoin sat down against the back door while the rest of the Norwegians crammed in after them, sitting cross-legged around the perimeter of the van. The man with the bar through his nose gunned the engine so that Maggie could feel it hum beneath her butt. After they were on their way, the *In Utero* girl, who introduced herself as Bente, lifted a corner of the shag rug and produced a small baggie of white powder. She sniffed delicately from the small scoop of her black-painted pinkie nail, passed it to the girl in the torn jeans, then leaned her head back and let the cocaine drift up her aquiline nose. Maggie felt queasy. She wanted to tell them to stop, that they were all going to die, that they were too beautiful and young to snort drugs up the collapsing vessels of their pretty noses. But what was the point? This is what people did at rock shows, and probably what they had always done. She and Eoin sat together and watched. Bente offered the coke to Eoin first and he declined, mildly, in that judgeless way of his, able to say no without sounding prudish. She held it out to Maggie next, who waved the drugs away with a polite shaking of her head. Bente shrugged, and passed the bag down the line, leaving Maggie wondering: If Eoin had accepted the drugs, what would she have done? And if Bente had offered them to her first, what would she have said?

"We're going to a party on the other side of the city," Bente explained. "Do you want us to drop you off somewhere?"

"How about the Coliseum?" Eoin said.

The driver with the bar through his nose, whose name was Luther, screeched to a halt a short while later in front of Rome's most famous ruin. It stood, gaping, half-crumbled and half-perfect, seeming to have burst forth from the past, a fist through the earth of this magic city. They waved good-bye to the Norwegians and stood in the shadow of a wall that had once held lions and warriors, people so long dead that no one had missed them in a thousand years. A moon, white and round as a Communion wafer, hung in the sky and glowed through the hundreds of empty arches. All around them, cars sped by, honking and swerving. Tourist-trap restaurants blinked with specials for pizza and gelato, but all of these modern distractions seemed as flimsy as cardboard. The moonlit air felt weighted with history.

"It makes me feel so *small*," Maggie said. "Well, not me. But my *life*. You know?" Eoin nodded, but he did not quite seem to be listening. He stared up for a while, then turned away from the enormous ruin to find her eyes.

"Why are you looking at me like that?" She tucked her hair behind her ear self-consciously, suddenly shy.

"I love you, Maggie," Eoin said. He held his hands out to her, palms up, a defenseless, surprised gesture. "I mean, I really *love* you."

"And I love *you*." She grasped his outstretched hands. It was as true and simple a thing as she'd ever said. She was glad he'd said it first, though, because she knew that she never would have, and the very act of saying it had made it even truer. Somewhere above them, a low peal of thunder rumbled and a fork of white lightning threaded the sky. He kissed her so hard that her back scraped up against the cold, ancient stone, as if the past was pushing back at her, as the past does. The rain began to fall then, and cold drops slithered down the back of her neck. She slipped out of Eoin's arms and untied Kevin's flannel shirt from around her waist. Reaching up, she knotted it around one of the metal bars that surrounded the ground-level arches.

"What's that for?" he asked.

"Didn't the Romans leave, like, offerings to the gods?"

"Are we pagans now? Dan Sean would *not* approve."

"No. But the thing is, I don't need it anymore." Maggie stepped back and put her head on the wet curve of Eoin's shoulder. They stood in the rain and watched the shirt tail spin gently in the wind. *"I was surprised,"* she murmured, *"as always, by how easy the act of leaving was, and how good it felt."* It was a prayer, she knew, that Kevin would understand.

Back at the hotel, rain drummed against the wooden shutters. The soft beam of streetlight from Piazza Farnese filtered in through the slats as Maggie and Eoin lay down on the little twin bed with its faded, starched sheets and thin quilts. His eyes hovered over her collarbone and he was peeling off her wet black dress. She was totally and completely unafraid. She tugged at his sweatshirt and pulled it over his head. This wasn't something he was doing to her, or even something they were doing together. They were making something, or beginning something, or finishing something. Her bra fell away to the linoleum floor, his pants were kicked to the end of the bed, and the rain shook the shutters.

He moved on top of her and their lives became this moment, contained in the sheets, something that no one else would ever know, a secret to keep forever, the feeling of him inside of her. Afterwards, as they lay together, their heartbeats returning to normal, they heard the Norwegians returning from their party, drunk and crashing down the hall, singing "Pennyroyal Tea," while outside were the mazes of streets and tangles of parked mopeds, ancient temples and fading frescoes. Rome was under their nails, in their hair, and Maggie knew that when they awoke, they would never be able to wash it out: and that even if they could, they would never want to.

Early the next dawn, just as the sun broke through the dome of smog that blanketed Rome, Maggie awoke, naked and spooned in the warm crescent of Eoin's body, to a pounding on her door.

"*Carbinieri!*" A voice yelled from the other side of the door. "Police!"

Eoin jolted awake beside her.

"What in the name of—" He sat up, reaching blearily for his underwear. A reedy, familiar voice floated from the other side of the door.

"Maggie, please!"

It was her mother.

They were fully awake now, diving around the room, gathering and pulling on their clothes. The tiny space smelled of sweat and a palpable scent that Maggie was sure her mother would recognize. She had smelled it in Laura and Colm's room on many mornings after the bed had creaked and moaned.

Dressed, she took a deep breath and looked back at Eoin who was sitting, eyes wide, at the edge of the bed. She opened the door. There was her mother, travel worn and baggy eyed, Colm, smoldering and silent, and two police officers. Laura yanked Maggie's arm and pulled her into a rough, sobbing hug. The men looked away from her noisy crying. Dust motes helicoptered in the bars of sunlight that filtered from the cracks in the shutters.

She held Maggie against her chest, then pushed her away.

"You goddamn little *fool*," she bawled. She reached up and slapped Maggie across the face, hard, so that the dust skittered away, and for a moment, the room was filled with the pure, harsh light of a cold Roman sun.

Kiss
The mouth
Which tells you, *here*,
Here is the world.

—Galway Kinnell, "Little Sleep's Head Sprouting

Hair in the Moonlight"

They drove to Saint Brigid's in silence. Maggie was grateful for the pinging rain and the slap of the windshield wipers that cut through the quiet as Colm's old van splashed through the foggy streets and pulled into the car park. Morning classes had begun, and Maggie was sure she could feel the eyes of the girls in the second-floor classrooms staring down at the top of her umbrella, whispering about the American girl who broke the rules of comportment, ran away to the Continent with a boy, and was now going to get expelled for it. Girls who got kicked out of Saint Brigid's were marked for life. It wasn't the cool kind of rebellious, the kind that showed you knew how to dance on the edge of the line without crossing it, like cursing within earshot of a teacher or punching little hoops of silver through the cartilage of your ears or showing up to school on Monday with a hickey on your neck. Expulsion destroyed your reputation utterly. Maggie almost felt sorry for Aíne Keogh, who had probably worked herself into a tizzy, hoping that none of the other honors girls would remember that for a brief period during fall term, she and Maggie Lynch had been friends.

Laura had gone to Penneys the night before and bought an outfit especially for the hearing: a pair of black slacks and a conservative gray blouse that gapped at the buttons, straining over her large breasts. The cheap sateen material of the blouse creased along the back and arms from where it had been folded on the store shelf, making Laura look exactly like what she was trying *not* to look like: a blue-collar woman putting on airs, a nervous plaintiff on court TV.

"Let me do the talking," she said now, opening the heavy wooden door at the school entrance. "If there's one thing I learned when *I* was in high school, it's how to tangle with a nun."

The meeting was held in a small conference room with cracked leather chairs, a long mahogany table, and stone statues of Saint Emily, Saint Brigid, Saint Veronica, and Saint Anne standing guard in each corner. Outside, rain dripped from the heavy eaves of the courtyard trees.

Sister Joan, the principal, was the first to enter. She carried a file folder with Maggie's name on it, and her face, which protruded from the starched black folds of her wimple, had the exact shape and texture of a cabbage. She was followed into the room by Sister Geneve, the faculty representative. Maggie didn't know whether Sister Geneve was on her side, but she felt calmed by the presence of her teacher, whose heavy cabled cardigan, shapeless trousers, and white, tufty hair lent her a gentle, grandmotherly air that contrasted with Sister Joan and her stiff judge's robes.

"Thank you for coming, Mrs. Lynch," said Sister Joan, extending a hand to Laura, whose smart, self-possessed march through the linoleum halls in her new clothes and sensible black pumps had immediately crumbled in the principal's presence. Maggie remembered her mother telling her that when she was a high school student at Holy Redeemer in the 1970s, the Blessed Virgin Mary nuns—Big Vicious Mamas, she'd redubbed them— used to pick on her, and that once, in sophomore-year geometry class, a fat Canadian transplant named Sister Edward had shoved Laura right out of her desk and into a bookcase for waving out the window at a pair of sailors who were crossing Sheridan Road. Sister Edward and the other Big Vicious Mamas must've detected Laura Lynch's barely concealed vitality—the full lips, the dreamy gaze—

and foreseen her fate: pregnant before her teenage years were up, abandoned a few years later without a ring on her finger or a dress of yellowing lace shoved to the back recesses of her closet. And now she had to stand before another pair of Big Vicious Mamas to defend the product of her shame, her dark-haired daughter, for behaving in much the same way.

"Hi," Laura shook Sister Joan's hand limply, ducking her head and looking much like a girl herself.

"Please," Sister Geneve said, indicating two of the leather chairs, "sit down."

They took their places around the empty table.

"The purpose of this hearing today is to discuss whether Saint Brigid's is the right place for Margaret as she continues her secondary studies," Sister Joan said. She opened the file folder and began to read. "Margaret has missed a week of classes, and because all of these absences were cuts, she is not allowed to make up any of the work. As a result, she is failing several of her courses. That is the first issue. The second is Margaret's conduct while absent. It's our understanding that your daughter went, unaccompanied, to Italy with a student from Saint Brendan's. She shared sleeping arrangements with this boy for several nights." Sister Joan peered over the rim of her bifocals at Maggie.

"Margaret, it may seem unfair to you that we are going to be talking about your conduct *outside* of school when deciding whether to keep you as a student here. But at Saint Brigid's, character is just as important as academics—far more important, actually—and we have to think about what it will mean for the climate of our school if we allow you to remain a student here after some of the choices you've made over the past few days. What message will that be sending the other girls, the underclass girls? Now, Sister Geneve and I are not here to hear your confession—that is the business of yourself, your family, and God. What we *are* here today to do is give you the opportunity to tell your side of the story, to help us understand why you should remain a student here. To speak plainly, your job today is to convince us that we should not expel you."

Maggie nodded. Under the table, her mother groped for her hand and held it tightly.

"To be clear, Maggie," Sister Geneve added softly, "we *want* you to be a Saint Brigid's girl. This is your chance to tell us why you deserve to stay. It's not meant to feel like an inquisition."

"Okay."

"Sisters, before we start, I do want to tell you a little bit about our family situation," Laura began in a quaking voice. "I'm not trying to make excuses or nothing, but I just think maybe if you knew what Maggie's gone through over the past couple months . . ." She trailed off. Laura was a career bartender, used to getting her way by flirting, sweet-talking, wisecracking, or, when all else failed, handing out a complimentary shot. Here, all of her reliable tricks were powerless. While she looked to the ceiling beams for inspiration, Sister Geneve began picking at a loose thread at the cuff of her sweater and Sister Joan regarded her without expression from between the folds of her wimple. "My little brother died suddenly over the Christmas holidays," she finally continued. "Maggie was his goddaughter. They were very close. He committed suicide on New Year's Day, back in Chicago. I didn't want Maggie to know—it was so awful—so I told her he'd died of natural causes."

"Natural causes?" Sister Joan wrote something in Maggie's file.

"Yeah. See, he had a bum heart. A congenital defect. So I thought she'd believe it. I wanted to believe it myself, you know?" Laura paused now to reach into her purse and produce a balled up tissue. She honked into it while Maggie looked away, staring fiercely into the blank, stony face of Saint Anne.

"So, you lied to her?" Sister Geneve's voice had a delicate, neutral quality that didn't need to be judgmental in order to make its point. Maggie had seen her walk down the hallway before the opening bell and say nothing more than "Good morning," leaving in her wake a sea of upper-class girls who unrolled their skirts back to the required length of an inch above the knee and went sheepishly off to class.

"I don't know whether that was the right thing to do," Laura said quickly. Maggie could see the tiny crescents of sweat soaking the cheap material under her mother's armpits. "I don't like lying. I know that lying is a sin. But I wanted to protect my daughter from—I mean, Kevin was Maggie's *hero*. An uncle, a brother, a father and a best friend all wrapped into one. We *all* loved him so much. He was crazy and funny and he read all these books, you know, these big four-hundred-pagers with tiny print . . . he was just this—*force*.

"But like you said, this isn't an inquisition. I did what I did and that's that. The thing is, Kevin gave Maggie those Nirvana tickets. So going to Rome—for her, it was about a lot more than just a stupid concert." She took a breath. The crescents of sweat were now seeping into full moons beneath her arms.

"My point is, she's a good kid, okay? And she's been through a lot this year. I mean, if you were gonna expel every teenager who did something stupid, who would you have left? Maybe the valedictorian and a couple kids from the chess team?" She tried a laugh, which echoed emptily off the plaster walls of the sparse room.

"I'm sorry for your loss, Mrs. Lynch," said Sister Joan. "And you too, Margaret. Grief can be its own temporary form of insanity. How we handle our suffering speaks to our character as well. Margaret, do you have anything you'd like to add?"

Maggie looked up from her lap at the two nuns who sat and waited for her to say something.

"I was wondering," she began, the words coming out in a rush, "is Eoin up for expulsion, too? Because I heard he was. And it's not his fault. It wasn't even his idea, and—"

"We're not here to discuss his case," Sister Joan cut her off. "Saint Brendan's is a different school than ours, and we can't comment on their business." Her thick bifocals made her eyes look like two coffee beans, pupilless, cold. Maggie felt like screaming. She had done this to Eoin. She was poison; she had ruined his life.

"Maggie." Sister Geneve leaned toward her across the table, the string of her unraveling sweater curled around her wrist. "You can't control what happens to your friend. Right now, you need to be fighting for yourself, for *your* future."

"But—"

Under the table, her mother used the toe of her sensible pump to kick Maggie in the leg.

"*Honey,*" she hissed.

"*What?*" Maggie glared at Laura and turned back to the nuns.

"I mean, I guess you're going to do whatever you want with me," she said quietly. "But before last week, I had pretty good grades."

"That is true," Sister Geneve nodded firmly. "Maggie is a quiet but diligent student. She writes very movingly about poetry."

"I love Yeats," Maggie said. "I thought of that poem you taught us when I was at my uncle's funeral."

"What poem is that?" asked Sister Joan.

"It's called 'A Dream of Death.' " Maggie ran a finger along the wavy lines of wood grain on the surface of the table, the way they spread out and came together in parallel lines, marking age. "He wrote it for this woman he loved, about her being buried in a foreign place, and about her grave being marked with cypress trees." She paused. "When we were in Italy, on the train going through Tuscany, we saw them—cypress trees. The roads are lined with them, like gates or something."

"And here's me, thinking all she cared about was music." Laura smiled, that open, American smile that laid too many cards on the table, the one that showed the missing molar. There was a silence. Finally, Sister Joan straightened her papers.

"Well, if you don't mind stepping out for a moment, Sister Geneve and I are going to discuss this in private. We'll call you back inside when we've reached a decision."

"Thank you," said Laura. They all stood up and shook hands again. "I just want to say again, that, you know, Maggie really is a good kid. Her father left us when she was very young, and ever since then, she's been my little helper, my little woman." She hung her head. "Sometimes, I think she's more of a grown-up than I am. And—and I think stability is what she needs now. She's already had to start over once."

"We'll keep that in mind," Sister Geneve said. "We know Maggie's a good girl."

Back in the hallway, they sat in an old pew and waited while the nuns conferred.

"Jesus Christ, talk about an interrogation!" Laura fanned herself. "Goddamn nuns think they're so much better than everyone else. Brides of Christ my *ass*." Maggie sat next to her and chewed her nails. A clock ticked loudly above their heads. Ten minutes later, Sister Geneve opened the door and leaned out.

"Pardon me, ladies? If you could come back into the office." Maggie and Laura followed Sister Geneve back into the conference room and sat down.

"Maggie, we've taken into consideration your unique circumstances," began Sister Joan. "Normally, this kind of behavior would warrant an expulsion. But as Christians, we must always practice compassion and forgiveness. And we'd like you to remain a student with us at Saint Brigid's." Maggie sighed. She felt like an iron weight had just slid from her back. Laura slumped back in her seat, produced the tissue and proceeded to dab beneath her eyes.

"However, this is going to be a conditional reacceptance," Sister Joan continued. "One, you're going to have to work very hard to pull up your grades. You can't miss any more school, and you're going to have to do very, very well in all your courses. If you fail any of them at the end of term, we can't reinstate you."

"Okay," Maggie said. "I can do that."

"Good. The second condition is that—and we're going to need your support on this, Mrs. Lynch—we don't think it will send a good message to the community about our girls and our school if you continue to be seen tipping around with that boy. We want you to give us your word that you will end your relationship with Eoin Brennan. You're not to see him anymore while you are enrolled at Saint Brigid's."

All three of the women turned toward Maggie to observe how this news would settle. She closed her eyes for a moment, willing herself not to cry, but when she opened them, the tears streaked down her face anyway. *Why does my body not know the difference between sadness and rage? Why do I always have to cry when I'm furious? Why do I have to act like a little girl who just got her lunch box stolen instead of standing up for myself and telling them where they can stick their fucking rules?*

"Of course!" her mother's bright voice cut across the silence. "You know, I was going to suggest that anyway! They're just too *young*. There's nothing worse than getting involved too deep with someone when you're that *young*—trust me, I would know." She put a sweaty hand on Maggie's shoulder. "Honey, do you understand what this means? No more phone calls, no more dates, no nothing. Can you promise that?"

Maggie opened her mouth. The saints, Anne and Veronica and Elizabeth and Brigid, stood at attention. She felt their maddening, beatific, stony half smiles, daring her to jump from her seat, point her finger in Sister Joan's wimpled face and say the kinds of things that good girls and saints never said. And she would have done it, except that she felt the infinitesimal weight of Kevin's letter folded up, as it always was, in her jacket pocket.

Take the boy. Don't ask permission. There will always be time to do the responsible thing. Before that, live.

There will always be time to do the responsible thing. What did he mean by that—was this that time? What would he say to her now? Where did her loyalties lie—with the dead or the living? In her life, Maggie had loved two men. One was a few blocks away, standing before a review board at Saint Brendan's. And one was now a memory—uncut hair, eyes of burnout blue, seat back in AG BULLT careening down Lake Shore Drive on a bleary summer Saturday morning, cigarette dangling between his fingers and the sun rising blood-orange above Lake Michigan.

And so she made her choice. She heard herself speaking as if possessed, as stony and passionless as the statues in the corner:

"I promise."

Maggie returned to school the next morning. She refused her mother's offer of a ride, and left extra early to walk the mile into town, hoping that she might run into Eoin in the quiet chill of the seaside morning when the eyelids of corrugated aluminum were still pulled down over the storefronts and the Saint Brendan's boys gathered on the misty football pitch to practice their drills before school.

"You'll meet someone else," Laura had said after the hearing, smiling at Maggie apologetically over her West Coast Cooler. "I know it doesn't feel that way, but you will."

But to Maggie, love was like art—you went after it with a singular ferocity, like the monks on Iona, scratching away at their illuminated pages. You didn't just move on to some other thing.

She arrived to school before most of the other girls in her class were even out of bed, gathered her books, and headed toward her French classroom. The teachers began filing in, carrying umbrellas and cups of instant tea. As she sat in the hallway and waited for Ms. Lawlor to unlock the classroom door, Maggie daydreamed about where she and Eoin would move one day when high school was finally over: somewhere anonymous and huge where no one knew who they were and no one cared. Tokyo, maybe, or Rio, or Mexico City.

"Well, hello, Ms. Lynch." Ms. Lawlor smiled blandly down at Maggie as she turned her key in the lock, balancing a file folder in one hand and a sausage roll in the other.

"Hey, Ms. Lawlor." Maggie scrambled to her feet and slung her bag over her shoulder. "You want some help there?"

"Thanks." Ms. Lawlor handed her the folder and her napkin-wrapped breakfast. "I trust you can ask a friend in class to catch you up on what you've missed?"

"Of course," Maggie said. There was no point in explaining that she had no friends—that kind of personal over-sharing would only come off as cringingly American. As she followed her teacher into the empty classroom, she was struck, as she had been many times since Kevin's death, with the cruel, odd truth that when your life implodes, it shatters nothing but your own insides. Ms. Lawlor, with her hair-sprayed bun, chalky rouge, and ill-fitting wool pants, looked the same as she always did. So did the posters on the wall declaring *"Je parle le français pour dix bonnes raisons!,"* the pictures of the Champs-Élysées, the framed reproduction of Renoir's *Girl With a Watering Can*. All of this was a realization to Maggie that her life was its own tiny matter, and that the rest of the world carried on, oblivious and impervious to her aftershocks.

She sat in the back row and took out her notebook, waiting anxiously for her classmates to arrive. When the bell rang, Aíne and her new friend, Bea, were the first to walk through the door.

"Good morning, Ms. Lawlor," their bright voices called in unison. When they saw Maggie, they stopped short. She lifted her hand in a small wave, but the girls sat on the other side of the room, as if Maggie's delinquency might infect them. Class began at 8:00, and Maggie took notes furiously, not just to catch up on her conjugations but to keep her mind off the gossip that bubbled around her.

That was how it went, from French to physics to history. Maggie kept herself busy taking notes, ignoring the stares of her classmates. In her free moments, she doodled absently in the margins of her notebook and wondered where Eoin was, what he was doing, whether he had returned to Saint Brendan's, whether was thinking of her. The morning dragged by, and as she headed to the canteen for lunch, Maggie realized that she was about to become one of those high school clichés she'd always just managed to avoid: the pariah who eats lunch by herself. But just as she was about to sit down at an empty table next to a row of garbage cans, telling herself to keep her head up and show them how little she cared, the unthinkable happened: she was approached by a smiling Nigella Joyce.

Maggie had been a student at Saint Brigid's for six months, and in that time had never been even a remote blip on Nigella Joyce's radar. And why should she? Nigella was the most popular girl in her class. She always led the charge to town in warmer months when the hunt for boys was on, and rumor had it that she was not a virgin. This fact no longer impressed Maggie, who, after Rome, could quietly count herself among that crowd, but Nigella was reported to have slept with at least four boys, one of whom was twenty-three and a star halfback on the Kilkenny County hurling team. But because she was so stunningly beautiful—endless legs, bouncy, vivacious hair, and heavily made-up eyes that somehow conveyed both innocence and distilled sex, Nigella was exempt from the high school judgment machine. Unpopular girls who were reported to be promiscuous were dismissed as "slappers" or "hoors." But someone like Nigella seemed endowed by the Creator to have fingers inside her, hands in her hair, mouths on her thighs. For her, sluttiness wasn't a source of shame, but a birthright.

"Maggie, where are you going?" Nigella demanded, her rose-cheeked face pouty and concerned.

"I—I was just going to sit down to eat," Maggie said, putting her tray down on the empty table.

"Come sit with us!" Nigella said, slinking in the direction of a table where the powerbrokers of third class were opening their lunches.

Maggie hesitated before picking up her tray and following the pert flap of Nigella's skirt, reminding herself that she'd been among *real* women—in Dublin, in Rome—and she didn't need to feel so grateful for this sudden and unexplained act of goodwill from a girl who was, at the end of the day, just another high school teenager with good hair and polished nails. But she had just come so close to the bottom of the social food chain, a lonely misfit bowed over a limp ham sandwich, that despite her best efforts at cool nonchalance she tripped along behind Nigella's heels toward the popular table like an eager puppy. On the other side of the lunchroom, Aíne and the other honors girls watched sourly.

"So," Nigella asked as they took their places, "is it true you ran away to Rome with some fella who works at the Quayside?"

"Well, not exactly," Maggie said, peeling the crust off her sandwich. "We didn't run *away*. We went there for a Nirvana show."

The girls tittered.

"That is *so fantastic.*"

"So," Nigella said, "did you two fuck or what?" She propped her chin on her hands expectantly. Maggie looked around the table at their glittering, greedy eyes, the word *fuck* a piece of bloody meat dangled in the water.

"No," she said quickly. "It wasn't like that at all." That word didn't come close to describing what she and Eoin had done together. And besides, her memory of Rome was not something she was going to waste on these girls.

"Well, I just think it's so romantic," said Fiona O'Connell, biting into a shiny pink apple. "So *chivalrous.* The way he sacrificed himself for you!"

"What do you mean?" asked Maggie.

"The *deal* they offered him," Fiona said impatiently.

"What deal?"

Nigella Joyce leaned in even closer, so that Maggie could smell her lip balm.

"Wait a moment—you don't *know* about it?"

"No."

"They offered him the same deal they offered you—but he refused! He said they couldn't tell him who he could be with or who he should love. So they kicked him out of Saint Brendan's!"

In unison, the table of girls sighed at the romance of it all, drooping over each other like wilting flowers.

"I'd steer clear of those Saint Brendan's boys if I were you," Fiona warned. "You're their enemy number one right now. It's not so much that everybody loved Eoin Brennan—but he was one of the best footballers on their team."

Maggie didn't care if every boy in Bray despised her. It only mattered whether Eoin did. She thought about running to the nurse's office, pretending she needed to call home, calling the Quayside instead, asking Auntie Rosie if it was true. But if it was, then Auntie Rosie probably hated her now, and so, most likely, did Eoin. After all, she'd gotten him caught up in the drama of her life, and as a result, she'd shamed him and derailed his future. That night in Rome, as they lay together under the blankets, skin to skin and listening to the rain, she'd read him Kevin's letter. Her only hope was that he would remember it now and understand why she'd done what she'd done. Pressed up against the ancient walls of the Coliseum in the rain, he'd told her he loved her. Did he still? He'd forgiven his mother once; could he forgive her now?

18

In the seven months that Maggie had lived in Bray, she'd grown to love Dan Sean O'Callaghan and his little cottage on the hill. It had become an emotional monastery for her; a place where she could sit across from the old man with a mug of tea or hot port in her hands, the dingy cat on her lap, the turf fire blazing and the clouds low outside his curtained windows. He always gave Maggie the best advice—he was so far removed from his own teenage years that he was always able to look at her problems with perfect objectivity and healthy perspective. When it came to romance, he explained, the old ways are usually the best ways. When five weeks had come and gone and the only place Maggie had seen or spoken to Eoin was in her daydreams, Dan Sean advised her to write him a letter. "Short, plain, and honest," he told her. "You can give it to him at my birthday party."

Because, of course, Eoin would be there. Everyone would be there. Dan Sean was everybody's friend and neighbor, but he was also a holdover from an older time, a protector of the old ways, from long before modernity had roared across Ireland with its cranes and its cable TV. His hundredth birthday party was a celebration not just of Dan Sean but of all the things that had transformed the island in his lifetime—and no one in town was going to miss it. On top of that, one of the perks of growing old in a country as small and familial as theirs was that every citizen who lived to be a hundred received a government check for one thousand pounds on his centennial birthday. Dan Sean had already divided these proceeds into three accounts: one, for a summertime pilgrimage to Lourdes; the second to the parish church, and the third, to pay for a party with Guinness, champagne, and a three-course dinner at the Beaufort Hotel. Nearly everyone in Maggie's corner of Bray was invited: and that meant that she would finally get her chance to tell Eoin how she felt.

A few days before the party, while she sat sprawled on the carpet, slogging through her physics homework, someone knocked softly on Maggie's bedroom door.

"Yeah?"

Laura stuck her head in the room, holding a white package close to her chest.

"Can I come in, honey?"

"Sure." Maggie looked up from her notes.

"I got you a dress from Clery's." She put the package on Maggie's pillow. "Thought you might want something new for Dan Sean's party."

"Cool. Thanks, Mom."

"You're welcome." Laura lingered in the doorway of Maggie's room. Her hair was pulled back into a ponytail, and she wore a Chicago Bulls sweatshirt over an old pair of jeans. She'd put on some weight since they'd moved to Bray, a result of fried breakfasts and sugary wine coolers, and the extra pounds had made her face moony and round, a little slack around the cheeks and neck.

"Mom?" Maggie said. "You okay?"

"Maggie, I need to talk to you."

"Okay."

"About something important." Laura sat down on the carpet and began fiddling with the zipper on Maggie's backpack.

"Okay."

"I want to be honest with you from here on out. I learned my lesson."

"*Okay*, mom." Maggie kept her voice casual, but she could feel her heart pounding. Serious talks were never good.

"Honey, I know you've had a lot on your mind lately, so I wouldn't expect you to notice what a mess I've been these last few months." Laura took a deep breath and began flapping her hands in front of her eyes. "Sorry. I told myself I am *not* going to cry, and I'm not! Okay. Restart button." She stuck a finger to the side of her head, as if she was turning on a computer.

"*Mom.*"

"Okay. As you know, your father took off when you were very young—when we were all very young. And it wasn't easy, raising you and Ron on my own."

"Well, you weren't *really* on your own, Ma. You had Nanny Ei to help you out. I mean, she lived right upstairs."

"Maggie, you of all people should have realized in these last couple months that a mother's love is a blessing, but it can't be a stand-in for the other kind of love. And when I met Colm last year . . . he was so *good* to me. He just *loved* me so damn much. I think it's safe to say that we both got a bit swept away. And we've been *trying* to make it work out here. We really have. But he's younger than me, you know. I don't know if he was really ready for all the responsi*bility* that comes from marrying a woman with two kids. And then we lost Kevin. When something awful like that happens, it just makes you *think*. About the importance of family. I mean, Nanny Ei's all alone in Chicago now. Uncle Dave is in Oklahoma City and we're here, and well, it's really the responsibility of the daughter to look after—"

"Mom, you're rambling," Maggie said gently. She put her pencil down. A sick feeling was gathering strength in her gut.

Laura began flapping her hands again and blinking tears away.

"You're right. You're right. I'm just going to spit it out: things have been shitty for me since the funeral. *Real* shitty. We've talked about it—me and Colm—and we've *tried*. But everything's been so different. *Ireland's* been so different. I miss home. And Colm, he adores you and Ronnie, he really does, but he also misses, you know, his old life. His space. His freedom." She sat up and bit her lip. "So I guess what I'm trying to say is—we've decided to call it quits."

There was a silence. "Are we moving home?" Maggie finally asked, in an even, artificial voice, trying to rein in the emotion that was trembling up her throat. She'd only lived in Ireland for seven measly months. And yet, her life in the States sometimes felt like it had been an extended rehearsal for her real life, which was here in Bray. What would a Chicago uninhabited by Kevin even *be* like? A city encased in ice for half the year. A city six thousand miles away from Eoin.

"I thought you'd be happy about this, Mags." Laura stood up and began to pace the small expanse of Maggie's bedroom. "I mean, I have to sort a few things out first, but my thinking is, you and Ron could finish up the school year here and be home in time for the beginning of the summer. Summer in Chicago, Mags! The festivals! The beaches! Ice cream trucks! Mexican food! God, don't you miss *Mexican food*? I swear I would commit serious crimes just for a decent steak taco and *actual* guacamole." Maggie picked up her pencil and began tracing a circle in her notebook, darker and darker lines spiraling out from the center in a little lead tornado.

"Maggie, look at me," Laura went on. "*Talk* to me. We'll be back in our apartment, back to our normal lives, by the end of June. I already talked to Mikey Collins. He said he'd give me my old shifts back at Oinker's, no problem. Nanny Ei can't wait to have us back. The poor woman, you can't believe how lonely—"

"What if I said no?" Maggie asked the question without looking up, scribbling at her tornado until the page ripped.

"Honey—"

"No, I'm serious." She threw down the pencil and scrambled to her feet to face her mother. "What if I told you I'm not leaving?"

"Maggie, all you've done the past seven months is mope around the place, lying in bed with your door closed and hiding behind your headphones! And now all of a sudden you love it here?"

"Mom, last summer you made this big announcement, and because *you* were in love, me and Ronnie had to pick up our whole lives and move across the freaking ocean. And we did—without even complaining! You told us that even if it seemed crazy, one day we'd see that when you fall in love with the right person, then you do what you gotta do to be with that person. You were so sure that Colm was the one. How do you change your mind like that?"

"It's not just about Colm, Maggie," Laura said. "You have to understand. Nanny Ei is on her own. The guilt I feel—"

"Bullshit. *Bullshit!*" Maggie shouted. "I love Nanny Ei just as must as you do. But this is about you and Colm and you know it! But guess what, Mom? You brought me here, and I fell in love, too. I know you think I'm too young, but I'm not the one who changes boyfriends every five seconds, okay? I love Eoin, and now you want to take that away from me because *you're* bored with your latest fling? Do you know how selfish that is?"

"Oh, Maggie." Laura passed a hand over her face. "I thought you said you were done with that boy."

"I never said that! I only promised not to see him again so I wouldn't get kicked out of Saint Brigid's. Do you really think I wouldn't break that promise in a second if I ever got the chance?"

Laura sat down on Maggie's bed with a heavy sigh. "Maggie, you are sixteen years old. There will be other boys."

"Well, of course that's what *you* say. But maybe I don't want to grow up to be a slut like you!"

Laura stumbled to her feet, holding her stomach as if she'd been punched.

"One day," she said, turning just before she left the room, the tears forming in the corners of her green eyes, "you'll understand how much you just hurt me." She closed the door softly and Maggie was alone again. She picked up the box her mother had left on her pillow, lifted the dress from the paper tissue and held it in front of her mirror. It was gray wool with a short, flared skirt and round buttons down the chest. It was the kind of dress that Maggie might pause to examine for a moment in the mall and then abandon in favor of something edgier. This fact, more than anything else, was what made her start to cry. It must be hard to be a mother. All those years of knowing everything about your daughter, of dressing her and bathing her and being intimately acquainted with her every need and want, and then one day you wake up and realize you don't even know what kind of dress to buy her at Clery's.

The next afternoon, Maggie walked up the hill to Dan Sean's. She asked him if she could borrow forty pounds, and he gave it to her, no questions asked. "Pay me back soon, though," he said. "I'm almost a hundred, you know. I haven't got time to charge interest." Then, she rode Colm's bike into town and went into the betting office. She put the forty pounds on the counter. "You're just in time," the bull-necked bookmaker told her as he handed her the receipt. "We're about to sell out."

She decided to wear the dress from Clery's to Dan Sean's party because even though she was still furious at her mother, she felt sick over what she'd said, and wearing a vaguely ugly outfit to the party of the year was still easier than apologizing directly. When she came out of her bedroom, dressed in black tights, black boots, and the gray dress, Laura's lips twitched into a smile, and Maggie was both annoyed and moved at how little it took to make her mother happy. It was exhausting, hating and loving her all at once, but Maggie had not forgotten Eoin's wish: to have a mother who was well enough to fight with. Laura Lynch, for all her faults, could always be counted on for that. Maggie slipped the letter she had written into her purse, slicked on a deep shade of mulberry lipstick she'd bought at Boot's, and went outside to wait in the car.

The party began with a mass in Dan Sean's honor. Maggie had a hard enough time following along with the readings and the homily and the plodding rituals on an average Sunday, but knowing that Eoin was standing somewhere in the pews of the little stucco church, sharing her atmosphere, alive in her orbit, made it practically unbearable. This was made even worse by the fact that Colm had insisted they sit up near the front, and Maggie couldn't search the crowd properly without turning around and craning her neck. The best she could do was stand up straight, keep her shoulders back, and hope that he was watching her, the thin backs of her thighs, the long sweep of her dark hair.

Afterwards, at the Beaufort, Dan Sean sat enthroned in a large rocking chair next to the fireplace. He still wore his Cossack's hat and three-piece suit, but had a festive red ascot knotted at his neck. A receiving line snaked past a long table stacked high with wrapped gifts. In the banquet room, the men lined up in their dress clothes along the polished mahogany bar, drinking pints elbow to elbow while the women gathered in small clumps with narrow glasses of champagne. Ronnie ran around in her yellow dress, playing games with the other girls from her national school. It would always be a source of envy and pride for Maggie, watching how easily her little sister made friends. There were plenty of girls from Saint Brigid's there too, wobbling around on brightly colored high heels, and on the other side of the room the Saint Brendan's boys congregated in their crisp sweaters and dress pants. As far as Maggie could tell, Eoin was not among them. Both groups eyed each other, but it wouldn't be until the DJ set up his speakers and the liquor had been snuck, later in the night, when they would go to each other. Maggie remembered the gang of teenagers she'd seen at the carnival a week after she'd moved to Bray—how foreign they'd looked to her, how intimidating. Their faces were now at least familiar, but she felt as invisible to them now as she did then, and even less welcome. She'd had so many chances to start over, to be normal, and she'd somehow managed to ruin it all.

By the time the dinner bell rang, Maggie had seen nearly everyone she knew: Nigella Joyce and the other queens of third class, Aíne and Paddy—still, by the looks of it, madly in love— horrible Paul with his horrible overhanging eyebrows, Sister Geneve and Sister Joan. For a brief, thrilling moment, Maggie was sure that Eoin had finally arrived when she saw Auntie Rosie, decked out in a pale lavender suit and matching hat, enter the ballroom on the arm of her husband, Dan. But it appeared that they had come alone. Maggie watched them as they ordered a drink at the bar, waving to friends, and when they sat down for dinner, she saw with some relief that their table was all the way on the other side of the room. God only knew what Auntie Rosie thought of her: the American stranger, always hidden behind a pair of headphones, whose uncle was a suicidal drug addict, whose family drank and smashed up her bar, who had somehow convinced her handsome, upstanding nephew to run away with her and in the process, managed to upend his future. Maggie slumped low in her seat, hating herself. As soon as the soup course was finished, she excused herself to the ladies' room. Standing before the mirror, she saw that the burgundy lipstick she'd worn had faded, leaving a dark, clownish ring around her lip line. She wiped her mouth with a tissue and wondered why she'd tried wearing that dark, grungy lipstick in the first place. It wasn't who she was. Sometimes, being sixteen felt like one giant looped film of fuckups big and small. But when she was with Eoin, life hadn't felt like that. In a weird way that she couldn't explain, loving him had made her love herself a little more.

Back at the table, she could barely eat her dinner. Why didn't he come? Maybe it was a practical reason, like a football game he couldn't miss, or maybe he had to cover at the Quayside while Auntie Rosie came to the party. Or was it more than that? Was he ashamed at his expulsion, did he not want people whispering about him? Or was it the thing she dreaded most of all—did he not come because he didn't want to see her? Because he hated her for selling him out and accepting the terms of her reinstatement while meanwhile, he'd been made the fool by standing by her and getting kicked out of school? She ran her fingers through her carefully straightened hair, the silky strands suddenly superfluous and vain. She'd gotten all dressed up for nothing.

After dinner there was dancing. A band played jigs and reels and ceili sets. The dance floor filled with parents and grandparents shuffling inward and outward, switching partners, and stamping their feet along with the pulse of the accordion while the teenage crowd, still separated by gender, began circling closer to one another. Maggie sat at the dinner table and drank so much lemonade she thought she might puke.

After the band played a final set, Dan Sean, seated at his throne, began to nod off, and Mike and some of the other neighbors carried his gifts out to the car. The DJ arrived to set up his strobe light and fog machine while the older dancers drifted toward the tea table. Fleetwood Mac's "Everywhere" blasted from the speakers.

"I *love* this song," cried Laura, hopping from her chair, West Coast Cooler in hand. "Who's dancing with me?"

Colm got up without a word and sauntered off in the direction of the bar. She glanced after him, her smile wavering for just a moment before turning back to her girls.

"I will!" Ronnie pushed away her plate of sherbet and grabbed her mother's hand.

"That's my girl! Mags? What about you?"

Maggie smiled and shook her head. "No thanks. You guys go ahead."

"Suit yourself!" Laura put her glass in front of Maggie. "Watch my drink!" The two of them sashayed off to the dance floor, which had now been taken over by the younger crowd. The young men, ties loosened, pulled the women around in their brightly colored Saturday night dresses, and in the spattering light they flashed past like schools of exotic fish. Maggie sat and watched her mother and sister spin together through the iridescent fog. Laura had squeezed into an old red dress, and even if it strained around the new paunch of her midsection and was spackled across the bosom with spilled champagne, there was a buoyancy about her that drew the eyes of the crowd: the radiance of a faraway citizen who was soon going home. Ronnie, who was as hardy and adaptable as a spider plant, had accepted the news of Laura and Colm's breakup in stride and was now waving her arms and whipping her braid from side to side with joyous abandon. Whereas Maggie had trouble feeling at home anywhere, Ronnie made a home for herself anywhere she went. She had even acquired the edgings of an Irish accent, which, of course, was bound to be a hit when she returned to Chicago to begin sixth grade. As they whirled past, laughing and singing along to the song, Maggie was filled with a grudging pride: this was her family and her people. For as much as they drove her crazy, they were still pretty okay.

"Sure looks like they're havin' fun out there, doesn't it?"

The voice, and the talcum-powered scent that trailed behind it, belonged to Sister Geneve.

Maggie looked up at her teacher. Even though it was the party of the year, Sister Geneve wore no makeup. Her face was as plain and soft as an old baseball glove. She had replaced her usual knit cardigan and shapeless slacks for a cheap pants suit and a dull silver brooch in the shape of an owl.

"You don't look like you're much in the mood for a party," the old nun said.

Maggie shrugged.

"Is it because he isn't here?"

Maggie looked at Sister Geneve suspiciously. Was this some sort of trap?

"Well, even if he was, I wouldn't be allowed to talk to him," she said finally. "Remember?"

"Yes, I do."

"Oh."

"How are you feeling about all that, anyway?"

Maggie shrugged, dragging a finger through her melted ice cream.

"Not good, if you want me to be honest."

"I always want you to be honest, Maggie."

Maggie glanced up from her ice cream. The soft, worn face seemed to invite confession.

"Okay, then. I don't regret what happened in Rome. I know you and Sister Joan wanted to make me feel sorry for what I did. But the only thing I'm sorry about is that I hurt Eoin, that I ruined his life and got him expelled."

Sister Geneve blinked. If Maggie wanted to shock her with this admission, it hadn't worked.

"Maggie, they were looking for a way to expel him anyway. His family can't afford his school fees. I've never been a believer in the kind of Christian charity practiced by the board members at Saint Brendan's." She put a hand on Maggie's arm. Her palm was papery and warm. "It isn't your fault, pet. He's going to be all right, I promise. He's already enrolled at a vocational school in Greystones."

"But why isn't he here tonight?" Maggie's eyes filled with tears. "I had something important I needed to give him."

"Nothing illicit, I hope?"

"*No.* It was just a note."

"I see. Well, then maybe I can help." The nun's gray eyes were soft and neutral behind the octagonal glasses. "I see him around from time to time. He works over there at the Quayside. Sister Alphonsus and I stop there for tea sometimes on our way home from bingo Sunday nights."

"You know Eoin? You've *seen* him? How is he? Does he look okay? Did he ask about me?"

"I know him to see him. That's why I said I could help."

"Is this some sort of trick? You trying to set me up or something?"

"No." She smiled and patted Maggie's arm. "It's just that you look like such a sad sack, and I have a soft spot for poor lost creatures. Give me the note, and I'll get it to this fella."

"You won't read it?"

"No."

"You won't tell Sister Joan?"

Instinctively, they both glanced around the ballroom. Sister Joan was drinking tea with several of the more pious older ladies of the parish at a table near the back door. Sister Geneve leaned close to Maggie's ear.

"I won't tell a soul. But I'll only help you this one time. I'm not going to act as your secret messenger after this. I've read *Romeo and Juliet*."

Maggie hesitated. But what were her other options? It was this or nothing at all. She took the envelope out of her handbag. It contained one ticket to see Nirvana at the Royal Dublin Society on April 8, and a folded-up piece of notebook paper.

Dear Eoin,

"I don't care for praise, my love,
    Only let me be with you,
and pray let me be called idle and lazy.
Let me gaze upon you when my last hour has come,
    And dying,
may I hold you with my faltering hand."

That's Tibullus. I thought if I stole the words of an ancient Roman to tell you that I love you, maybe you'd think of the place where we threw the coins into Trevi Fountain and maybe you would forgive me.

I'll be standing at the gates of Beweley's Hotel, across from the RDS, an hour before the show starts. If you love me, too, I hope you'll meet me there. If you hate me, I'll understand. Either way, I'll be waiting.

Love,

Maggie

She had made up her mind. If he didn't show up, she would go back to Chicago at the end of the school year without a word of complaint. She would make a place for him in her memory, cordon off a small portion of her heart and daydream from time to time of the way the morning sun brought out the red in his hair when it filtered through the wooden shutters of the Casa di Santa Barbara. And eventually, she would move on. She would silence the voice inside of her that said if she lost Eoin, her life would always be less than what it could have been.

And if he did show up?

Well, that was something else entirely.

"I'll take it from here," Sister Geneve said, standing up and slipping the envelope into the breast pocket of her pants suit. "Trust in God that what must be, shall be." She nodded toward Laura and Ronnie on the dance floor. "Now go enjoy the party."

19

Spring had come to eastern Ireland at last. Rainy days gave way to hours of flooding sunlight, and purple flowers bloomed along the hills. Wooly new lambs leaped and played in the fields, and pale yellow furze grew heavy over the guardrails of the highways. Sister Geneve had delivered her letter to Eoin at the Quayside after her Sunday bingo night. He hadn't opened it in front of her, so she had no information for Maggie other than to confirm that he had received it. All month, Maggie had wondered why Sister Geneve had offered to help her. She knew that nuns were supposed to be selfless and all, but this wasn't exactly giving alms to the poor: it was aiding and abetting a lovesick teenager. And even though Maggie was grateful for Sister Geneve's kindness, she wondered, didn't that break the rules of nun conduct to go against the orders of one's superior? Didn't they take a vow of obedience? There was only one explanation that made sense: Dan Sean had put her up to it. So on the night before the concert, Maggie went up to visit him and find out.

As she climbed the hill toward Dan Sean's cottage, she stopped to turn her face to the warm sun. The passing of the seasons made her wonder where she would be in a year, in ten years, in twenty years. Would she sit one day at a small stool in the Quayside on Saint Stephen's Day, Eoin older now, maybe with thinning hair or a belly gone soft, touching her gently on the shoulder before he stood to buy her a drink? Or would her life double back to where it had begun, and would she be living in a bungalow in Jefferson

Park or a two-flat in Albany Park, working for the city, married to a cop, watching Bears games on television while outside the air filled with the smell of burning leaves? At Colm's house, Laura had already begun packing boxes. She'd shipped home all of her summer clothes; there was no staying any longer than she needed to. Colm was barely home these days. He drank at the pub, slept on the couch in the sitting room, and puttered in the shed for hours. Once, Maggie had seen him walking down Adelaide Street with a freckle-sprinkled woman dressed in pair of nurse's scrubs. They were laughing together. When he saw Maggie, he stopped laughing.

"It isn't what it looks like," he'd said. "Your mother—" he sighed. "Emma, this is Maggie, Laura's daughter."

"*Oh*," was all the woman had said.

When she got to the top of the hill she could see through the window the turf fire illuminating Dan Sean, and there was a figure of a woman sitting next to him. A white puff of hair and octagonal glasses. Sister Geneve leaned over to Dan Sean, caressed his face with the back of her white hand. This in itself might not have struck Maggie as terribly odd, but it was the way the nun looked at him—the same longing look that she'd once seen on her mother's face when Colm came home from work covered in sweat and cement dust; the look that Aíne wore when Paddy recited Tibullus to her under the canvas tent at the Magic Teacups; the look she imagined must have been on her own face when, in the morning of a Dublin hostel, Eoin had said, *I could be the person who won't hurt you.* It was an ageless look, as innocent and hopeful on an old woman as it was on a girl of sixteen. Everyone visited Dan Sean O'Callaghan: it was a duty, a care, an act of respect. But Sister Geneve visited him because she was in love with him.

Maggie remembered the explanation. *I'm not his niece by blood, technically.* Though Maggie had not known it at the time, this had been a justification.

She scrambled behind Billy's shed when she saw the two of them rise from the chairs, and Dan Sean wrapped Sister Geneve's jacket around her shoulders. A few minutes later, the tiny nun emerged from the front door, the old man holding steady to the crook of her elbow. He held on to her as they picked their way down the front path. When they reached her rusty Peugeot, he stopped to lean down and stroke the puffy white hair at the crown of her head. Sister Geneve said something Maggie couldn't catch, and then she reached up to Dan Sean's jowly chin, standing on her tiptoes on the flagstone, drew his face down to hers, and kissed him: a lingering, gentle kiss that flouted and defeated their old age, their frailty, their worn bodies. When they separated and he made his measured progress back up to his front door, Sister Geneve got in her car and looked around her as if reacquainting herself with the trivialities of grass and stones, before starting the ignition and heading down the hill.

Maggie slumped against the shed door. *That's why she gave Eoin the letter. She knows what it's like to love someone when the whole world's against it.* How the town would have loved that scandal: a widower and his dead wife's niece! A niece who also happens to be a nun of the Order of the Blessed Virgin Mary! But then, thought Maggie, what was so ridiculous about that, really? We love who we love. We have as little control over that as we do over anything.

On April 8, the day of the concert, school went by in a torturous blur. Maggie watched the clock until she thought she'd go crazy. At lunchtime, she sat with Nigella and her popular crew, smiled placidly as they one-upped each other with their bawdy talk of blowjobs and nightclubs and clothes. When they finished their sandwiches and Nigella announced they were going out to the chipper to scour for boys, Maggie made a polite excuse that she had to meet Ms. Lawlor to go over a French assignment. Instead, she went into the bathroom stall with her Discman and listened to *Nevermind* with her eyes closed. *Uncle Kev,* she prayed, *I'm sorry to keep bugging you about this. Just one more reminder: please, please, please, let him be there tonight. It's kind of important.*

On the walk home from school, Maggie stopped at a shop and bought herself a ninety-nine, her first of the season. A warm breeze blew from the ocean, and the gulls wheeled and called in the harbor. It really felt like spring. In front of O'Connell's Electronics, a small crowd of longhaired boys with skateboards under their arms had gathered in front of the television sets. Probably some big soccer game, Maggie thought. Or is there a horse race on today? As she walked past them, licking her ice cream cone, she glanced up at the window at the six television screens all programmed to the same channel. She saw six identical images of Kurt Cobain's face: the matted blond hair, the cleft chin, the eyes both mischievous and sad. It was all she'd been thinking about since she'd woken up, and seeing his face on the screens like that was a little bit like wishing for snow and looking up and seeing it fall, beautifully and out of nowhere, from the sky. Then, at the bottom of the screen, she saw the headline:

NIRVANA FRONT MAN KURT COBAIN, 27, FOUND DEAD IN SEATTLE HOME

One of the boys with the skateboards was crying soundlessly. But there were other sounds to occupy the silence: tires on asphalt, women chattering to the babies they pushed in strollers, the deep call, out on the water, of a ship. And the sea, always the sea. Maggie touched the crying boy's arm.

"How?"

"He shot himself." The boy held out his palm to her, offering a cigarette. The five of them stood there, then, smoking in the bright spring air. Nobody said anything. One by one, the four boys flicked their cigarettes into the street, dropped their skateboards to the pavement, and wheeled away. Maggie had never seen them in Bray before, and after that day she never saw them again. It was as if they had walked in straight from the water and out again, a band of new wave psychopomps shuttling the souls of the dead across the wide sea line to whatever it was that lay beyond.

Because she didn't know what else to do, Maggie walked home, finishing her cone. She unlocked the door, put her backpack down, and took a shower. When she came out, wrapped in a towel and combing her damp her, Colm called to her from the kitchen.

"Did you hear the news? That Cobain lad is dead."

"He shot himself," Ronnie, parked inches from the television, said. "In his greenhouse."

"Yeah. I heard," Maggie said numbly. "I can't believe it. Gone too soon. He had his demons, I guess." The words fell out of her mouth like stones. They meant nothing. Colm stood in the kitchen doorway, his mouth half open, as if to offer some comfort. But the connection with Kevin was so obvious that mentioning it would have been crass. Maggie got dressed and put his letter in her pocket as she always did. She dabbed perfume on her neck and in the crooks of her elbows, where the veins were plump and ready. She moved through the house like a haunted spirit. She surprised herself at how little she wanted to cry.

She called her mother at Dunne's and told her she was going out with friends for the night. Then, she walked the mile back into town to catch the bus to Dublin. As soon as she got off at the Merrion Road stop, she knew that something special had occurred. Outside the RDS hundreds of fans stood soaked in the spring rain, milling about and hugging each other as if at a wake. Under the dripping trees, people played guitars. Someone had brought a CD player, wedged it high between the bars of the front gate, and was blasting Nirvana albums. They were teenagers and dropouts, grungeheads and misfits, the sad-eyed faces and fringe members of Maggie's generation. The rain seeped into the fabric of their flannels, gave off the wooly smell of wet dogs. A pair of drunken boys walked around taking a poll: where were you the first time you heard "Smells Like Teen Spirit"? That was an easy one: Nanny Ei's kitchen, eating canned chicken noodle soup in the failing light of a December afternoon. Uncle Kevin coming home from his job at the Christmas tree farm, smelling of sap and pine. *You've got to hear this song, Mags. Holy shit have you got to hear this.* Turning off *Wheel of Fortune* on the little countertop television set and plugging in the CD player. Nanny Ei saying, *Well, if that's music, then you can toss me a microphone and call me Aretha Franklin.*

As the wet sky purpled into evening, the street outside the RDS took on the air of a festival. A few disinterested guards patrolled, arms folded, leaning against police horses. Smoke hung in the air; joints were furtively passed. Someone distributed narrow white memorial candles with paper lips to catch hot wax, and people pulled out their lighters, cupped palms to protect the pinprick flames from the rain. A stranger gave a candle to Maggie and she held it in her hands, a gesture as hopeless as everything else about suicide, she thought. *Maggie, if you ever feel bad enough to even* think *about doing something like that, please promise you'll tell me,* Laura had begged. But Kevin's suicide had not had that effect on Maggie. It didn't make her want to die but to live. *That's why I went to Rome,* she thought to herself. *And that's why I'm here now.* She passed through the crowd, down the block, and found the tall iron gates of Beweley's Hotel. On the other side of the gate, past the green expanse of lawn, there were warm squares of light where older people who didn't care about Kurt Cobain were dressing for dinner. Night fell in earnest; the streetlights flickered on.

If he doesn't come, I'll go back to Chicago with Mom and Ronnie in June because that is what I'm meant to do. What must be, shall be.

If he doesn't come, I won't fall apart. I won't cry. I'll have my answer. It finishes here.

Then, a ballooning panic: *Oh God, what will I do if he really doesn't come?*

And the converse thought: *Oh God, what will I do if he does?*

If he does, I stay. I apply to be a boarder at Saint Brigid's. Or I move in with Dan Sean. I make Bray my home, because I choose life: not convention, not convenience, not obedience. I choose love.

The faces of all the people who passed by her were blurred by nighttime. She stood against the gates and breathed the stench of cigarettes and weed and candle wax and far away, on the edge of the wind, the mossy breath of the Liffey. It occurred to her that Kurt Cobain would have hated this. Nobody here at this makeshift wake—herself included—had known him. They had only known something that he made. It was not the same thing. *In the years ahead,* Maggie promised herself, *wherever I go and whatever happens, I only want, once and forever, to be really known to someone.*

Seven o'clock. Had Cobain been alive, the show would be starting. Eight o'clock. Still Maggie waited at the gates of the hotel, clutching her ticket in her palm until it was nothing but a pulpy ball. Rain seeped into her pockets. *This is dumb,* she told herself, scanning the faces in the crowd. *What am I waiting for?* But she gave it ten more minutes. Then, twenty. A half hour. At nine, she realized he was not going to come. *What must be, shall be.* She pulled her hood around her face and began to walk back to the bus stop.

All those people who stood in their flannels in the rain would always remember that on the day Kurt Cobain's body was found in a Seattle greenhouse, they came to the RDS in Ballsbridge with their meaningless tickets, to pay tribute. But only one among that crowd would remember, too, the young man with short cropped hair that turned red in the sun, who wore a Liverpool sweatshirt and old track pants, who dodged the glowing candles and the mourners who held them, his gaze leveled on the shining gates of Beweley's Hotel, running with all the power and determination of the athlete that he was. They would not remember the girl who had begun to walk away; just another grunge girl with pretty eyes drowning in too much black liner and a hood pulled around her wet face, who, hearing her name shouted over the music and the exhale of smoke and the traffic on Merrion Road, had stopped for a moment and gazed up at the sky, mouthing a prayer, before turning around. They would not remember that when the boy hugged her he held her so tightly that she dropped her candle into the mud and it burned out with an imperceptible *hush*, and her hands grazed the prickly hair at the nape of his neck, the beautiful inverted daub between the tendons, the living parts of him, and that they kissed in the open way of people who only wanted, simply and completely, to be known to each other. She was going to stay. She was going to stay, and she was going to love Eoin, always, because that's what living people do. They shatter and rebuild, shatter and rebuild, shatter and rebuild until they are old and worn and stooped from the work of it.

EPILOGUE:
MAY 1995

As tradition dictated, the visitation was held in Dan Sean's sitting room. The big open hearth crackled with a turf fire, filling the room with a rich peat smell. A warm amber light flickered across the brown-faded pictures on the walls, snapshots that chronicled the spread of Dan Sean's life across the twentieth century. The room grew close as the neighbors gathered, buzzing quietly with tea and whispered catch-ups, while Mike O'Callaghan and his wife walked around shaking hands and accepting condolences. Then, everyone quieted and bowed their heads while Father Boyle began the rosary and the Ecclesiastes—*a time to weep and a time to laugh*—and waved curls of sweet incense over Dan Sean's casket.

Outside, they lined up on either side of the stone path. Mike, Colm, Eoin, and some of the other neighbors hoisted the pine box onto their shoulders and carried the old man's body out of the house, as he had instructed. The wind was calm, and it rained, but it was a quiet spring rain with sunshine winking between the clouds, and it made everything sparkle dewy and green. As the procession descended the mossy hill, Billy the goat stared at them with black, derisive eyes and nickered once before resuming her never-ending snuffle around the yard in search of Crunchie wrappers.

Though Maggie mourned, she did not feel sad. This sorrow wasn't hers to feel. It belonged to Sister Geneve, who trailed behind the coffin in her black pants suit, the little plastic shawl tied around the plume of her white hair, and cried softly into a handkerchief. Later, at the funeral reception, the neighbors would talk about what a surprising spectacle of emotion the stoic old nun had given. How odd that a woman who'd seen plenty of death in her lifetime could barely keep it together during Father Boyle's eulogy, sobbing like a teenage girl for a man of 101 whose death was, in the last months of his decline, practically a blessing! Only Maggie knew why Sister Geneve wept. But she never told anyone, not even Eoin.

After Cobain's death, Maggie had returned to Chicago for the summer with her mom and Ronnie. Nanny Ei got her a job working for a friend's catering company, and she spent three sweaty months standing under the tents of street festivals, manning a deep fryer and selling beer-battered turkey legs and butter-dipped corn to the sunburned masses. That July, she had received a letter from Saint Brigid's, informing her that she had been accepted as a boarder on partial scholarship—and that the rest of her fees were being paid for by an anonymous donor. Maggie knew with absolute certainty who that donor was, but no matter how many times she asked him, Dan Sean, a stubborn old Irishman to the last, would never admit to it. In September, her family heaved her giant red suitcase into the trunk of Nanny Ei's Oldsmobile and drove her to O'Hare.

"If you don't wear aqua socks in the shower, honey, you will sentence yourself to a lifetime of Plantar's warts," Nanny Ei said solemnly as they stood in front of the Aer Lingus departure gates.

"And for the love of God, try to drink a glass of milk every once in a while," Laura added, putting a tender hand on Maggie's cheek.

It was the closest they could get, these tough blue-collar women, to telling her how much they would miss her.

Back in Bray, the new school year began, and her relationship with Eoin grew. She shared everything with him: not just the secrets of her body, but also the quieter things that burned softer. There were weekend bus rides out to Wexford to climb the lighthouses that dotted the craggy lip of the island; there were nights when she snuck him into her tiny dorm room at Saint Brigid's and they lay sprawled side by side on the carpet, listening over and over to *(What's the Story) Morning Glory*, trying to decide if it was okay to be obsessed with Oasis when everybody else in Ireland was, too. Weeknights they sat at a back table in the Quayside, drinking Cidona and drilling each other on French history in preparation for their leaving cert exams. This is what they were doing, in fact, on a mild May evening eight months after Maggie's return, when Dan Sean dozed off in his velvet-backed chair, a copy of the *Irish Times* folded in his lap, and never woke up.

After the funeral mass, everyone went for pints at the Quayside. Eoin's mother, released from the hospital, showed up in a new dress and freshly dyed hair. She sang "The Hills of Glenswilly" at Mike's request because it had been Dan Sean's favorite. Eoin's face burned with pride when she brought the house down, and this made Maggie ache for her own mother back in Chicago, but by now she knew enough not to mistake this aching feeling for regret. Later, two fiddlers from Shankill took the stage, and Maggie danced with Eoin on the same floor where it all began for them. And when the trays of potatoes and ham were eaten, the pints drunk, the ashtrays emptied, and the sky faded to a rich, velvety purple, she and Eoin slipped away. They walked hand in hand along the strand, breathing in the fishy wideness of the sea, pausing for a moment to gaze up at the spindly hulk of the Ferris wheel. A warm breeze was blowing down from the hills and the crab traps bobbed in the water.

"I haven't been on that thing in a long time," Maggie said.

"What do you think?" Eoin raised an eyebrow at her. "Feel like going for a ride?"

They approached the booth at the water's edge and bought two tickets.

"First riders of the season, you two," grunted the ride operator as he pulled the safety bar over their laps. "Might be a little squeaky."

The machine hummed to life, jerked their carriage forward, and swept them slowly toward the twilight, groaning with rusty effort.

"Is this thing safe?" Eoin peered over the side at the ground below, where the carnival workers were hoisting white tarps from the rides and rolling back the corrugated aluminum from the gaming booths.

"Who knows?" Maggie grinned. "Better hold on tight."

She felt the warm pressure of Eoin's knee next to her own as they creaked higher and higher, the briny air dewing their faces. When they reached the top of the arc, they could see the far-off lights of Dublin glimmering beyond the darkening hills to the west, and to the east, the vast, lapping Irish Sea. They remained like that for just a moment, suspended hand in hand above the hills and rooftops, their faces flooded with sunset, before the Ferris wheel whined and jolted them back to the safe, familiar earth.

ACKNOWLEDGMENTS

I'd like to give thanks to:

The wonderful team at Elephant Rock Books: Cassie Sheets, Amanda Schwarz, Emily Schultze, Amanda Hurley, and, most particularly, Jotham Burrello.

The Fiction Writing Department at Columbia College Chicago.

Mom and Dad, for being my first and best teachers, Nora and Dan for their friendship and superior musical taste, and Jackie, for Selfish Fetus—cooked up on a napkin at Burnside Brewing in Portland, Oregon.

Most of all, thank you to Denis for your fact-checking and advice about all things Irish, your read alouds, and your love.

THE CARNIVAL AT BRAY

A NOVEL

READING GROUP GUIDE

Elephant Rock's Cassie Sheets discusses the writing of *The Carnival at Bray* with author Jessie Ann Foley. Learn more about Jessie at jessieannfoley.com.

Cassie Sheets: What's the genesis of *The Carnival at Bray*?

Jessie Ann Foley: A few years ago, I took a day trip from Dublin to Bray. When I walked out of the train station, one of the first things I saw was this carnival at the edge of the Irish Sea. It was summertime, but chilly and overcast, so nobody was around, which imbued the whole place with this forlorn feeling. I thought that it would make a great setting for a story, and I wrote a little description of it in my journal. At that point, I had this cool setting, but no characters to put in it. A couple months later, it occurred to me that the obvious inhabitant of a lonely place like this carnival would be a lonely person—and Maggie was born.

CS: Did you draw on any other personal connections when choosing the locations?

JAF: I grew up in Chicago, and when I was younger I had a summer job renting out volleyballs at Montrose Beach. Business was very slow, so I spent 95 percent of my time sitting on a lawn chair, reading. Sometimes, when I got bored, I would lock up the volleyball trailer and go for a walk through the bird sanctuary, the place where Kevin goes on the night of his death. On these walks, I got the same feeling I had in Bray when I saw the carnival. I knew it would be a great setting for a story. For me, place is a trigger for storytelling. You can always create characters, but it's only when you put them somewhere that they become real. I've also spent some time in Italy and Ireland, but not enough to ever assimilate to either culture. That's why it made sense to me to write Maggie as someone who was struggling to belong.

CS: Did you find you needed to do additional research on Ireland as you were writing?

JAF: Well, the original draft of *The Carnival at Bray* was a short story that I published in the *Chicago Reader* Fiction Issue in 2010. If I had known then that I was setting myself up for the task of writing an entire *novel* set in Ireland, I might have made things easier for myself and kept Maggie in Chicago. But then, she wouldn't have met Eoin. I'm Irish American, but as Maggie learns in the first chapter, that identity has very little to do with what it means to be actually Irish. But my husband, Denis, is from County Kerry in the southwest of Ireland.

CS: And he helped you bridge that gap?

JAF: I couldn't have written this book without his help. I drove him insane with constant questions: What do you call those bales of hay covered in plastic? What is the hurling equivalent of a quarterback? When you were a little boy and your dad brought you along to the pub, what did he give you to drink? Things like that. The poor guy even read all the bits of dialogue from Irish characters out loud to tell me if they sounded authentic or not. I was so nervous for him to read the first draft of the book, because I knew I was going to make ridiculous mistakes. He was polite enough not to make fun of me.

CS: Music plays an important role in this story, and is one of the many interests that tie Maggie to her uncle Kevin. How did music influence you while writing this book?

JAF: While I was writing and rewriting the novel, I listened to a lot of nineties music: Nirvana, Smashing Pumpkins, Liz Phair, the Lemonheads, Dinosaur Jr., P. J. Harvey, and the sound track from *Singles*. I'm in my early thirties now, old enough to understand the nostalgic pull of bands you loved when you were a kid. This music from the early nineties just *means* so much more to me than any other music I've ever listened to. That's not to say I like it the best, or even that it conjures specific memories. At a certain age—maybe fourteen or fifteen—it's so much easier to be amazed by things, to be impressed by things, and I miss that. Listening to that music from my old Case Logic CD books reminded me of my capacity to be amazed, shaped, exposed—and I think that was really good for my writing.

CS: Maggie is also a reader, and Kevin's book lists are another way he guides her. What books did you read at Maggie's age?

JAF: My sister is two years older than I am, and she has always been a voracious reader. I often read books she had lying around. I remember when I was about fourteen, she was reading *Lady Chatterley's Lover*. I thought it was so dorky because, based on the cover art, it looked like something super boring that I'd be forced to read in Brit lit class. But then my dad, who's also incredibly well read, started grumbling that she was too young to be reading something like that. He didn't tell her she *couldn't* read it exactly, but he was definitely not happy that she was carrying it around with her. Well, of course, then I was totally intrigued. I was too lazy to actually read the whole book, so just like Maggie did, I skimmed it to see what my dad was talking about. And sure enough, I got to the chapter where Mellors meets Connie in the hut and I was like. . . *"whoa."* I didn't think people even *did* stuff like that back then. I don't know what I thought—that we were all a bunch of cold-blooded egg-laying reptiles until my generation came along and spiced things up?

CS: So you were a bookworm?

JAF: When I was in elementary school, I tore through books like crazy. I even snuck them into church with me. In high school, my priorities changed, and I became more concerned with obsessing over boys and sneaking beer into parties. I tried to play the rebellious part, but the only times I remember actually *being* happy during high school was when I was sitting by myself, reading.

CS: Your day job is teaching high school English. How did being around teens five days a week influence the way you got Maggie's thoughts and voice on the page?

JAF: I don't know if it affected me in any conscious way, but teaching high school, being surrounded with teens all day, does help you remember what it's like to be young. A lot of adults are disgusted by, mystified by, or straight up afraid of teenagers. I certainly wouldn't want to go back to those years, but it's still such a cool age. When you're Maggie's age, everything is new and fresh, and so much life happens. You really feel the possibilities of your life ahead of you.

CS: Maggie has a lot of universal adolescent experiences—the loss of someone close, first love, awesome music parents are sure to hate, among other things—but so much has changed since Maggie was growing up in 1993. From the counterculture, to the ease (or lack thereof) of staying in contact with people after moving, how does growing up in the early nineties shape Maggie's development?

JAF: People might think that I set the book in the nineties because that's when I was Maggie's age, with the implication being that she is a prototype of myself, but that's not true at all. Maggie and I were very different teenagers. She was a lot cooler, smarter, and tougher than I was. She also had better taste in music and men. And she learned from her mistakes a lot more quickly than I did.

CS: So no running off to Rome with a boy to see a Nirvana concert during your teen years?

JAF: No, unfortunately. The less exciting truth is, setting the novel in the nineties solved some very important plot problems, the obvious one being the absence of social media. In order for Maggie to grow in the way she did, I felt like she needed to be truly isolated in Bray, truly marooned in this new country. If she's following Selfish Fetus on Facebook, if she's Skyping with Nanny Ei, then she's still got one leg immersed in Chicago, and the need to find her way in Ireland is not as urgent. With the lack of Internet access, it's harder to go back. She's stuck, and she needs to show her mettle.

CS: Kurt Cobain is also such a major background player in the novel. When you were thinking about when to set Maggie's story, was the culture and movement surrounding grunge an important factor?

JAF: I know every generation says this, but I just can't think of any band today that has the capacity for life-alteration as Nirvana had in the early 1990s. And part of that relates back to social media. How mythical would Kurt Cobain be if he'd left behind a trail of Instagram selfies? If he'd Tweeted? And maybe that's why today's teenagers still idolize him as much as the young people of his own time did.

We just *know* too much about today's celebrities—and that makes them far less interesting, far less romantic.

CS: There are two starkly different sexual encounters in the novel—the first when Maggie is emotionally low, and Paul comes onto her in a rough, slithery sort of way. The second coincides with an emotional high for Maggie, and she shares an intimate, fulfilling moment with Eoin. What was the process of writing each of these scenes like?

JAF: Both of these scenes were really difficult for me to write, and both unfolded in very different ways. I felt that the first scene needed to be somewhat graphic, so that the reader could experience the pain and discomfort along with Maggie. What I wanted to come across was not that Paul tacitly forced Maggie to do anything, but that it never occurred to her that she could have said no. She felt like she'd already gone to a certain place with him, and she had no choice but to keep going. Sadly, too many teenage girls feel this way, which is why for many of us, our first sexual encounter is excruciating. I think it's true to life that many young people have to suffer through a Paul experience—sometimes several Paul experiences—before they find their Eoin and realize, oh, *this* is what it's supposed to be like.

As far as the second scene, that time Maggie was ready, and she'd found someone who loved and respected her. Partly because of that, she had a lot more respect for herself. That key difference is what made losing her virginity such a positive thing.

CS: What was your revision process for this novel?

JAF: As I'm sure most writers have experienced, I started off thinking I knew where the novel was headed and then, somewhere around the middle, it turned into a great big mess. Fixing that mess required a lot of returning to the beginning and rewriting, rethinking. All in all, it took me about a year to write the book, and when it was finished, I was so deeply entrenched in it that it was hard to know whether it was actually finished or not. Luckily, my editor was a wonderful guiding force in helping me nail down the final draft. We did about three months of intensive rewrites, focusing mostly on voice and pacing. Those three months just so happened to fall during one of the worst winters in Chicago history, which was great for me. The revision process kept me plenty busy while I was holed up in the house avoiding the polar vortex.

CS: Was there a moment you knew the book was done?

JAF: I wouldn't say there was a particular moment when I knew it was done. I'm hypercritical of my own writing. I never really go back and read any of my published work because of the compulsion I feel to change everything. But I guess I felt like the book was done when I went back and reread it and I only wanted to change small words and phrases, not rip apart whole scenes.

QUESTIONS AND TOPICS FOR DISCUSSION

1) *The Carnival at Bray* is written in third person, rather than the sardonic first person that's common in young adult now. What access does the third-person point of view allow readers that they wouldn't have known in first person? Why do you think the author made this decision?

2) Ronnie asks Maggie a lot of age-inappropriate questions, to which Maggie responds, "I'll tell you when you're my age." How does Uncle Kevin's way of handling this compare to Maggie's? How does Maggie learn about what it means to be an adult?

3) Many of the characters in *The Carnival at Bray* are outsiders in some way. How does being an outsider in Ireland shape Maggie's identity? In what ways are the other characters in the novel outsiders?

4) How does Maggie's relationship with her mother, Laura, mature over the course of the book? What does Maggie understand about Laura at the end of the book that she didn't understand at the beginning?

5) How do the song lyrics and poems quoted throughout the novel shape your understanding of Maggie or the time in which she's living?

6) Mental illness is explored through Eoin's mother, Mary, Uncle Kevin, and Kurt Cobain. Discuss the way the author deals with mental illness in this novel.

7) How does Dan Sean mark the passage of time and the history of Bray in the novel?

8) When Maggie and Eoin run away to Rome, they essentially play house. Laura is often described as doing much of the same with Colm. What do you think Maggie learns about love and relationships from her mother, and where do you think she makes an effort to do something different?

9) How are images of the natural world (e.g., the water surrounding Bray or the Italian countryside) used to set the tone of certain scenes?

10) When Maggie decides to travel to Rome to see Nirvana as per Uncle Kevin's instructions, Dan Sean dubs it a pilgrimage. Throughout the novel, she prays to Uncle Kevin for guidance. Discuss Maggie's faith, whether it be in religion, Cobain, love, or Kevin.

ALSO BY ELEPHANT ROCK BOOKS

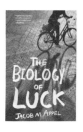

The Biology of Luck
by Jacob M. Appel

"Clever, vigorously written, intently observed, and richly emotional."
–Booklist

Briefly Knocked Unconscious by a Low-Flying Duck: Stories from 2nd Story

"This collection will demand, and receive, return trips from its readers."
–Publishers Weekly, Starred Review

A Vacation on the Island of Ex-Boyfriends
by Stacy Bierlein

"Stellar collection of heady and affecting stories."
–Booklist

The Temple of Air
by Patricia Ann McNair

"This is a beautiful book, intense and original."
–Audrey Niffenegger

 # Uncle Kevin's
Reading Recommendations to Keep Young Nieces Off the Streets

Just Because Your Teacher Assigned It Doesn't Mean It Sucks*

Slaughterhouse-Five - Kurt Vonnegut

The Great Gatsby — F. Scott Fitzgerald

The Odyssey — Homer

Shakespeare - anything

A Streetcar Named Desire — Tennessee Williams

* Warning: Try to pay as little attention as possible in class when studying these works. Otherwise, there is a good chance that your teacher will ruin them for you by systemically strangling them of all life + beauty with one-hundred-question multiple choice tests + worksheets on identifying symbolism. The greatest enemy of literature is the high school English teacher, especially if that English teacher is also the offensive coordinator of the varsity football team. Take this from someone who knows.

Excellent Books with Excellent Sex Scenes

For Whom the Bell Tolls — Ernest Hemingway

Ragtime — E. L. Doctorow

Lady Chatterley's Lover — D. H. Lawrence

Love in the Time of Cholera — Gabriel Garcia Márquez

The Handmaid's Tale — Margaret Atwood

Tropic of Cancer — Henry Miller

Books that if You Read on the El,
You Will Get Get Strange Looks —
In a Good Way

Clean Asshole Poems and Smiling
Vegetable Songs — Peter Orlovsky

White Man, Listen! — Richard Wright

American Psycho — Bret Easton Ellis

The Communist Manifesto — Karl Marx +
Friedrich Engels

Naked Lunch — William S. Burroughs

Lolita — Vladimir Nabokov

Pricksongs and Descants — Robert Coover

Essential Reads

On The Road — Jack Kerouac

The Grapes of Wrath — John Steinbeck

The Man with the Golden Arm — Nelson Algren

Leaves of Grass — Walt Whitman

A Confederacy of Dunces — John Kennedy Toole

A Farewell to Arms — Ernest Hemingway

Borstal Boy — Brendan Behan

Collected Poems of Emily Dickinson (shut up Don't look so surprised)